—SWORDPLAY—

A Novel

Ray Rao

Book Cover Design by Anna Fong

Interior Layout by Derek Vasconi

Printed in the United States of America

ISBN: 9780578674759

Acknowledgment

Bloodbath gave me an opportunity to thank all the people who supported me and gave me the confidence to take the plunge and get published. And here we are again, with my second novel giving me another opportunity to express my heartfelt thanks to all the same people for standing by me, yet again.

To my amazing wife, Kanchan, my muse, and inspiration. Your encouragement and understanding are the reason my parallel career as a writer continues. I couldn't have written my first novel, Bloodbath, without your boundless love, support, and understanding, and the second is no exception. With you by my side, I expect to keep going for as long as we can keep going together.

To my two daughters, Divya and Anjali, my biggest cheerleaders, and my most insightful critics. You, along with your mother, are the reason I dared to take on the tricky task of not just representing how a woman thinks and reacts, but also understanding the emotions that motivate her thoughts and reactions.

To Girish and Ketaki, without whose encouragement and intervention I would never have published Bloodbath, let alone this sequel. Your knowledge and understanding of prevailing norms in current Indian society has helped me avoid betraying how outdated are my recollections of life in India.

To those friends, both Muslim and non-Muslim, whose intimate knowledge of the Holy Quran I relied on to verify that the words quoted from that great scripture are accurate. Thank you for reminding me that those excerpts do not reflect the compassion, tolerance, and inclusivity of that scripture (and religion). The irony—and sad truth!—is that those excerpted words, taken out of context, are used by both fanatical adherents (like some in this story) and ignorant Islamophobes alike to justify their incomprehensible hatreds.

And last, but certainly not least, to Derek Vasconi, for being such an outstanding editorial partner, and to Anna Fong, for her incredible skill in graphic design. Derek's insights into my writing, both negative and positive, are directly responsible for making my writing in Swordplay just as taut and precise as it was in Bloodbath. And Anna's cover design could not be more perfect as a pictorial tease of the story of Swordplay.

—SWORDPLAY—

A Novel

Ray Rao

Prologue

En Garde!

Dr. Ramesh Batra saw only one patient on his last night on call before leaving the tiny Gulf principality of Qumraan. It was the last patient he would ever see. In Qumraan or anywhere else.

A young palace servant named Mohammed Wasim was found unconscious in the desert by nomads and brought to the Casualty Department of the Asad al-Qumraan Medical Center shortly after 1AM. The ER physician ordered a head CT scan after a cursory examination found a swelling over his left temple.

Dr. Batra, the Chief of Radiology, performed the scans. He was scheduled to leave for India the next morning, having completed his four-year tenure. He was on call only because his replacement's flight was delayed, and both the other radiologists were devout Muslims who never took call on *jumu'ah*, the Islamic Friday sabbath.

Dr. Batra was on a flight to Mumbai when the patient died the next afternoon during surgery. A large blood clot from a torn artery under his fractured temple had crushed his brain beyond any hope of salvage. The operative note specifically mentioned that surgery was delayed "because the radiologic diagnosis was missed".

Hakim Elahi, the Chief Supervisor of Palace Personnel, testified at the inquest that Wasim, Prince Khalil's personal attendant, was a known alcoholic who had been caught trying to leave the palace to indulge his alcoholism on three prior occasions. All three times, His Highness's benevolence spared him from being beheaded, but he had been warned there would be no reprieve the next time.

The presiding magistrate rendered a verdict of accidental death caused by head trauma from falling off the palace wall, compounded by medical negligence. Ruling that the operative findings made an autopsy redundant, he ended with a dismissive statement that Wasim's head injury just saved the state executioner from having to cut his head off!

The verdict ignored the glaring inconsistencies in Elahi's testimony. Like how Wasim could break out of a fortified palace with electronic surveillance without setting off alarms, cross the grounds without being seen by patrolling guards, scale an eight-foot wall topped by electrified barbed wire without being electrocuted or shredding his hands and feet, and get half-way to the town of Qumraan, fifteen miles away, after sustaining such a devastating head injury.

Since Wasim was an orphan, his employer, the Indo-Arab Services Corporation, headquartered in Abu Dhabi, paid for his burial in an unmarked grave.

The mystery of his death was buried with him in the desert.

Dr. Batra died in his home in a Mumbai suburb in India on Wednesday, four days after returning from Qumraan.

The cleaning woman, alarmed by the smell of decay, called the police when Dr. Batra failed to answer the doorbell the next morning. The police broke down the door and found Dr. Batra's putrefying body with its wrists slashed, and a bloody surgical scalpel with only Dr. Batra's fingerprints near his right hand. A suicide note left on his laptop read, "I am ashamed to call myself a doctor. I missed a patient's life-threatening injuries because I was drunk, celebrating the end of my tenure in Qumraan. I must pay for his death with my life. I hope God forgives me."

The clincher was a letter from the Qumraani Government, stating that Dr. Batra's extradition was being sought to stand trial for medical negligence causing a patient's death.

Sworn testimony from the Radiology technician established he was drunk, so he was also charged with breaking the strict Sharia code of Qumraan that forbade the consumption of alcohol—a capital offense on jumu'ah, punishable by beheading.

There were no signs of a struggle, the automatic spring lock on the door hadn't been forced, and the autopsy showed no defensive wounds on the body, so the coroner rendered a verdict of 'Suicide by Exsanguination'. The police closed the case and released the body and laptop to his brother, Suresh Batra. He arranged for the body to be cremated, but he kept the laptop. It was a welcome upgrade over his own seven-year-old laptop.

With such overwhelming evidence of suicide, three curious findings were overlooked.

First, there was no envelope with Qumraani postage. The police never looked for one. Second, although Dr. Batra's were the only fingerprints on the laptop, most were smudged. Not all, though. Those on the keys that *didn't* figure in the "suicide" note were pristine. The fingerprint examiner never picked up on that fact, so he never tested for traces of latex from the gloves used to type the note.

The third was a post-office receipt Suresh Batra found tucked in a radiology textbook on the nightstand. It showed that Ramesh mailed a package to his brother on Tuesday afternoon, two days before his death. It wasn't a gift because there was a gift-wrapped package with designer jeans and high-end trekking boots bearing his name in Ramesh's half-packed suitcase.

Anything he sent two days before committing suicide couldn't be good. A confession would be bad enough. But what if it was a *guilt-tripping* confession from beyond the grave? That would beyond bad.

Suresh Batra was a journalist with no medical background, so he paid no attention to the book in which he found the receipt, let alone the bookmarked page. It showed CT images of a "live-donor partial-liver transplant".

Suresh Batra was the only mourner at his brother's cremation. He threw the switch when instructed by the priest and left immediately. He returned the next morning to collect the ashes, scattered them in the Arabian Sea, and took the afternoon flight back to Delhi, feeling depressed.

He wasn't close to Ramesh. A nine-year age difference meant no shared childhood, so no bond from growing up together. His only memories of Ramesh were his sporadic visits during college and medical school. Even those stopped after he graduated. Still, their desultory e-mail exchanges and occasional calls maintained some semblance of family, not counting distant relatives who cared as little for him as he did them.

Now, all he had left was guilt.

He should have known Ramesh might be suicidal when he got his email saying, "I'm sending you a parcel, in case something happens to me before I see you next weekend."

It sounded weird at the time, but he never thought it might be a red flag. If only he had asked why he was being paranoid, Ramesh might've confided in him, and that letter from Qumraan may not have pushed him over the edge.

Ramesh's parcel was waiting for him when he got home. Inside were five DVDs and a letter. He dreaded reading it, but he knew his guilt would skyrocket if he didn't.

Seven lines in, he read the word "Pulitzer", and his hands started trembling with excitement. As he read on, any last vestiges of guilt were obliterated.

This was no 'guilt-tripping *confession*'.

It was Ramesh's eye-witness *testimony* from beyond the grave. To a tale of evil so horrifying it was beyond comprehension.

Day 1

LIVE BY THE SWORD...

Chapter 1

The bomb exploded ninety minutes late.

The delay was caused by its jerry-rigged timer—an ancient wind-up clock with a rusted spring that became increasingly balky as it lost tension.

It was a minor detail, of no consequence to the fifty-three passengers or the driver, conductor, and armed guard it blew to bits on a bus traveling on a rural road in northern India.

Packed in a steel trunk in the luggage rack on the roof, the bomb sent a barrage of nails, bolts, and ball-bearings mushrooming outwards, recruiting shards of glass and sheet metal along the way. It shredded everything within two hundred feet of the bus, leaving a grisly puree of flesh, blood, and pulverized bone in its wake.

That puree, by all rights, should have included Jason Wolf.

It didn't because he was relieving himself behind a banyan tree when the bomb exploded. A curtain of aerial roots several feet deep absorbed the lethal impact of the shrapnel but the shock wave was still powerful enough to knock him unconscious.

Fifteen minutes later, fuzzy awareness dawned. It took a little longer for conscious thought to return. When it finally did, he tried standing up but his equilibrium was still disrupted, and he would've fallen if he hadn't grabbed onto an aerial root as thick as his thigh. He hung on with his eyes closed, swaying like a rag doll, as nausea overtook him.

The swaying and nausea receded, and he became conscious of agonizing pain boring into his ears, and a roaring in his head, like a train speeding through a tunnel. It faded gradually into preternatural silence, and he knew that concussive shock had left his ears temporarily deaf.

Letting go of the aerial root, he adjusted the strap of the duffel bag slung across his back and emerged from behind the banyan tree...to a scene of utter devastation.

The charred remnants of the U.P. State Transport Corporation Bus stood a hundred feet from him, the jagged edges of its roof protruding like a badly cut sardine can. What remained of the sheet metal was pockmarked with gaping rents.

The smell of burnt flesh was so strong that Jason felt his stomach heave. Then a reflexive survival skill, acquired as a former commando in the elite Alpha-Tau Antiterrorist Brigade of the South African Defence Forces kicked in and his visceral reaction subsided.

He trudged wearily back to the smoking shell of the bus, knowing there was no point in looking for survivors. The bomb was extraordinarily powerful, judging from the carnage around the bus. All the vegetation had been blasted away in a two hundred-foot zone, which was strewn with remnants of human existence.

A fragment of a plastic comb. The shredded pages of a magazine. Brightly colored shards of plastic from a child's toy. A can of baby milk, still intact. A few dismembered body parts: a disarticulated leg here, an infant's headless torso there. And chunks of flesh mangled beyond recognition, too many to count.

Why use a bomb of such force to kill fifty passengers on a bus traveling a sparsely traveled rural route? It made no sense. Unless, of course, the real target was Haldwani, a bustling town where the bus made its last stop. The carnage would have been horrific in the midday crowds thronging the bazaar around the bus station. And it would have blown Jason to bits, too. He was sitting in a tea shanty not thirty feet from the bus.

The inexplicable delay might have spared the citizens of Haldwani, but it only postponed the inevitable for the passengers on the bus. Except for him, thanks to an almost impossible confluence of coincidence, karma, and luck.

The coincidence was the ancient bus being forced by a dysfunctional radiator to stop in the middle of nowhere before its overheated engine seized in the midday heat.

The karma was drinking four cups of tea in Haldwani, forcing an insistent bladder to demand release during the unscheduled stop.

And choosing the banyan tree to relieve himself was pure dumb luck.

Half its magnificent canopy was blown off, and the aerial roots on the side facing the bus had been shredded by shrapnel. But it was the only tree still standing within two hundred feet of the bus. All the others in that zone were sheared through, leaving jagged white stumps shimmering in the sun. Further away, the trees were broken and bent over, as if in supplication.

Jason would be dead had he chosen any of those to do his business. Like the owner of the hiking boots sticking out of a clump of shattered eucalypti at the edge of the blast zone, their boles folded over in a tangled mess that covered his body like a bower.

Suddenly, he saw one of the boots twitch!

With hope surging, Jason sprinted to the eucalyptus stand and heaved aside the transected boles of three saplings to expose the body of a man lying on his back, twisted over his backpack. Jason recognized him as the passenger in designer jeans and trekking boots who defied every norm of travel in rural India by working continuously on his laptop without exchanging a word with his fellow passengers. Not that it mattered now. There was a large piece of jagged metal embedded in his abdomen and lower chest, and the ground around him was soaked with blood.

Jason saw the man's chest flicker and put his ear to it. He heard a faint heartbeat but that meant nothing. The end was seconds away.

Jason eased the backpack out from under the man to lay him flat and zipped up his fly. He was about to toss the backpack aside when the man's eyelids fluttered open.

Jason froze, stunned by the awakening of a man he presumed dead. The man's glazed eyes saw the backpack dangling above him, and he reached up to grab it. "This is what they want," he gasped. "I won't let them…"

Those were his last words. The sudden movement dislodged the shrapnel, and he died in a last gush of blood.

Taking a deep breath to settle his shaken nerve, Jason tossed the backpack aside. After confirming the man was dead, he covered the body with the tangled mess of broken trees to keep scavenging animals away until help arrived.

Which brought him to his predicament. He was a *firangi*—foreigner— stranded in the middle of nowhere in rural India with no way to summon help.

He wasn't carrying a cell phone on this trip, reliving memories from his travels six years ago, with only his wits and ingenuity to rely on. That romantic idea now seemed like romantic stupidity!

The man's cell phone was shattered. And forget looking for any others. They would've been incinerated with their owners. That left him with a choice. Make a ten-kilometer trek down the road to Teesrigaon, the village where Alexis and he stayed six years ago. Or wait for some Good Samaritan to come by.

For how long, though? It was now 4:30PM. Forty minutes since the bomb exploded. Surely, someone should've come by—

As if on cue, Jason heard a motorcycle in the distance, approaching from the main Nainital Road. In his haste to get back to the bus, his foot snagged on the backpack and he almost tripped. He was about to kick it aside when he recalled the dying man's last words. Why would whoever "they" were kill fifty people for a backpack? That surely *had* to be a death-bed hallucination. Didn't it…?

The sound grew louder but now there were two motorcycles, running close together.

Two bikers, riding together in rural India? Might be a coincidence, but not likely. Better to lie low until he was sure they were Good Samaritans, not the dead man's "they".

His decision made, Jason headed up a rocky outcrop set back from the road, backpack in hand. At the summit, he crouched down behind a row of scraggly bushes and shrubs, his beige-brown *kudtha pajama*—the traditional Indian garb of knee-length shirt and baggy trousers—blending into the dusty background. From his duffel, he extracted a Dragunov sniper-scope—a memento from a past brush with death—and leaned into the scrub to prevent a glint of sunlight from betraying his presence.

Then he became totally still.

Chapter 2

Three riders dismounted from the motorcycles, showing no surprise at the devastation on view, and sauntered forward as if on a casual stroll.

They split up, with two making a circuit around what was left of the bus, while the third took a quick peek into its burnt shell. He turned around, his swarthy visage jumping out at Jason through the scope, and laughed loudly, saying in Hindi, "The bomb did its job. No way anyone survived. But make sure he didn't."

He began taking pictures of the carnage with a digital camera, while the other two quartered the area, examining the ground with painstaking care. As they got further from the bus, however, the less meticulous they became. They turned back well short of the tangled mess of eucalypti and rejoined their comrade, saying "No journalist, no backpack".

Jason felt a chill go through him. *The man wasn't hallucinating! The bomb really was meant to get rid of him and his backpack.*

The third man, who seemed to be the leader, rubbed his hands with satisfaction, saying briskly, "And no sign of that firangi show-off who everyone was talking about in Haldwani, either. We can use him to deflect attention from the journalist. We'll issue a statement to the papers that this is a warning from *Talwar-e-Rasool* to firangis to stay away from India." He laughed. "I can even give them a great head-line. '*Terror* to Foreigners: Stay Away or Die'!"

The headline was delivered in heavily accented English, with an inexplicable emphasis on 'Terror'.

One of his compatriots responded enthusiastically, "What a great idea! We can reinforce the firangi angle by saying the bomb was deliberately timed to spare the people of Haldwani. That might get us a second headline, '*Terror* Strikes, Spares Haldwani'."

There it was, again—that strange emphasis on 'Terror'.

The leader laughed uproariously, but the third man wasn't amused. "If we say the firangi was the target, the CBI will be called in, and they will go all out to lick the Americans' asses."

Jason recognized the acronym for the Criminal Bureau of Investigation, the Indian equivalent of the FBI.

"You sound like an old woman, Rizwan" the leader replied with a sneer. "It doesn't matter how hard the CBI tries to lick ass, Superintendent Bakshi will make sure they find shit."

Seeing his clever wordplay elicit a reluctant laugh from his less enthusiastic comrade, he said forcefully. "Stop whining and get on board with my decision. It's final."

He made a call on his cell phone. "Lift the roadblocks," he said. After a pause, he added, "Let them be mad. Bakshi will ignore their complaints." He hung up and led his compatriots away. They got back on their motorcycles and rode away.

Jason waited until they were out of sight before standing up.

Roadblocks! That's why no one's come by. And the local Superintendent of Police is in their pocket.

He knew that 'Talwar-e-Rasool' translated to 'Sword of the Prophet'. It was clearly a homegrown jihadi terrorist outfit, and it intended to use Jason's assumed death to hide the fact that the journalist was the target. If a firangi matching the description of the 'show-off' was spotted in their backyard, his life wouldn't be worth a dime. So, if he wanted to stay alive, he had to disappear.

Going to Teesrigaon was out of the question now. So were the heavily populated farmlands south and east, where it would be impossible to remain unseen. To the west was Corbett National Park with its tigers. The problem there was staying alive, not unseen!

It left him with only one option: to go north into the sparsely populated hills and forests of Garhwal until he was clear off Corbett, then head northwest for the holy city of Rishikesh, about 200km away. A firangi catching a train to Delhi would be invisible there among the scores living in the surrounding ashrams.

He transferred the laptop and DVDs from the backpack to his duffel bag and returned to the eucalyptus stand. He uncovered the body of the backpack owner and searched it, finding a wallet with ID for a freelance journalist named Suresh Batra. He added it to his duffel bag, along with Batra's damaged mobile phone and a lighter that would come in handy on his trek.

He was about to swing the trees back when the man's boots caught his attention. They appeared to be his size, and would be infinitely preferable to the sneakers in his duffel for the trek that lay ahead, so he exchanged them for his slippers. They fit perfectly.

He covered the body again and walked away, carrying the empty backpack with him to bury somewhere far away. As he crossed the road, he saw a case of plastic water bottles that had been blown off the roof of the bus. He salvaged three bottles that somehow survived intact and hurried away.

Right then, he felt Alexis's presence, like a hammer blow to his chest.

Chapter 3

A lexis Wolff came awake with her heart pounding with dread.

It was 6:15AM—3:45PM Indian Standard Time—and somewhere in North India, Jason was in deadly trouble.

A single shattering 'pulse' in the psychic bond she shared with her twin—the closest she could come to describing it—had struck like a sledgehammer. After that... nothing. Not the "peaceful silence" when everything was okay. The kind of silence she refused to even *think* about.

Dread morphed into panic, as old terrors, long buried and forgotten, threatened to resurface. For just a moment, she thought of going to Jonathan, sleeping next door in the guest bedroom, but rejected it. This was a battle she had to win on her own.

She sat up, letting the covers fall away, and assumed the lotus pose. Focusing on the pinpoint of blue light behind her closed eyes, she slowed her breathing and sank into a trance.

A thread of consciousness remained connected to her psychic bond with Jason, so she would know the instant the bond came back "online".

She remained motionless, deep in her trance for twenty minutes.

Then her back arched in a violent spasm as if she was doused with a bucket of ice water.

The psychic bond had come alive! Jason wasn't yet 'responding' to her, but he was okay. That was all that mattered. He would respond when he could.

She headed for the kitchen to brew coffee. Ten minutes later, she was on the balcony, coffee in hand, looking out over the East River to Queens and the breaking of dawn. From fifty floors below, she heard the throb of traffic, the heartbeat of the city that never sleeps.

New York!

Rude, smelly, and dirty. But alive. Pulsating with energy.

It was where she learned to *live* again, after four years of hiding from life in a ninja monastery. Where she learned you could fall in love with a place and put down roots after years of rootless living.

Because New York was where Jonathan spent most of his time. He was the biological father she never knew existed until a couple of years ago, and he was directly responsible for her rebirth. Not once, but twice over!

One was psychological. Jonathan's entry into her life allowed her to finally put the horrors in her past behind her, freeing her from the emotional straitjacket that held her captive most of her adult life.

The second was her professional rebirth.

When she returned to the world after four years of monastic seclusion, she was searching for something—anything—to give her life purpose and focus. But finding either purpose or focus for a skill set as eclectic as hers—physician, helicopter pilot, and *ninja*—was an exercise in futility.

Enter Jonathan, to give her life both purpose and focus, in one incredible master stroke.

It was during a meandering conversation with Jason and Jonathan, in the early days after their rapprochement, that she wistfully mentioned her dream of working in something like Australia's Bush Doctor Program. She acknowledged it was a pipedream, because nothing even remotely like it existed anywhere else in the world.

Jason, being Jason, teased her that her dream wasn't to work as a Bush Doctor but to give him nightmares by moving to Australia! Jonathan simply sat stone-faced through it all, saying nothing.

And that was that, as far as she was concerned.

Six months later, on her first birthday after Jonathan came into her life, a card arrived in the mail. It was from Jonathan, and what he wrote made her cry. "Not being there at your birth is my eternal regret. Your rebirth is my joyous penance."

Her "rebirth" was a one-page contract from the Canadian Provincial Governments of British Columbia, Nunavut, the Yukon, and Northern Territories, appointing her as Physician-Director of a Flying Doctor program for delivering primary care to isolated Native Indian communities. It was nothing short of a miracle. And Jonathan, the miracle worker, had used all his legendary negotiating skills, leveraged every contact and connection he had in Canada, and called in several IOUs to make it happen. With an irresistible incentive. A half-*billion*-dollar seed grant from his philanthropic foundation, two helicopters, and funding in perpetuity!

The words he wrote in the card spoke to his deep longing to make up for what *he* had lost. And those same words spoke to a relationship that gave her everything *she* had lost and had been longing for. It was a relationship built on unshakeable trust, giving both of them the confidence to say or ask for anything without being misunderstood.

That trust was front and center last night, when he called, asking to stay with her for a couple of nights to "talk some things over", without telling her why. Just as she told him to stay for as long as he wanted, without asking him why. She couldn't care less that, a day later, he still hadn't mentioned those "things". It was enough that he wanted to spend time with her before he left for India to give the final ok to a deal Jason negotiated before leaving on his trip down memory lane.

She felt an involuntary shudder go through her, remembering those twenty terrifying minutes when her psychic bond with Jason went 'dead', only to come back as if nothing happened. Except something *did* happen in India an hour ago.

A concussion from a traffic accident, maybe? Indian roads were notorious death traps, and buses, Jason's favored mode of travel, were frequent culprits in highway accidents. The police could be undependable but there was no dearth of nosey bystanders willing to help in rural India.

Right then she felt Jason reach out to her through the bond.

Chapter 4

Jason made camp in a cave-like recess under a rocky overhang in the bank of a small river. After making sure there were no scorpions or snakes in the sandy floor, he built a fire to boil eggs purloined from a pheasant's nest. The fire would burn all night to deter nocturnal predators like the jackal, legendarily sneaky and a rabies carrier. Not the tiger, though. The arid scrub terrain afforded little forage for deer, its main prey.

Before bedding down for the night, he reviewed the route he would take tomorrow. Spread out in front of him was an Indian Army ordnance map, showing topographic detail not found in any commercially available map. It was a gift from a good friend, Ravi Iyer, the foremost expert on counterterror intel in India.

He pinpointed the location of his camp, some twenty kilometers from the site of the bus bombing. His route north for the next day and a half would take him through mostly uninhabited open forest terrain, east of Corbett National Park. Once he was well clear of Corbett's northern tip, he would turn west to reach Lansdowne a day later, where it would be safe to call Ravi from a cybercafé. Another three days of trekking to get to Rishikesh, catch an overnight train to Delhi, and dump the whole damn riddle of Talwar-e-Rasool, the bus bombing, the journalist, and the backpack with the DVDs in Ravi's lap.

A fast-flowing tributary of the River Rāmgangā was the only obstacle on his route. Confined in a narrow, rock-walled gorge about fifty feet wide and thirty feet deep, it was impassable, except where the gorge opened into a shallow ravine with a mile-long stretch of rapids. Downstream of the rapids, the river reverted to a raging torrent between walls of sheer rock, accelerating along a five-mile downgrade to plunge over a hundred-foot-high waterfall. After that, it became a wide, slow-moving river that meandered through heavily populated farmlands for several miles, before merging with the River Rāmgangā.

He should reach the rapids around 4PM tomorrow. The water level would be low enough in the summer to expose the rocks, which would serve as steppingstones to cross over.

It would be plain sailing after that. His map showed a dirt track marked "Forest Service Use Only" that dead-ended about a quarter mile from the riverbank. It connected to a rural road a dozen miles away, but he wouldn't need to go that far. Just two miles from the river, the dirt track intersected with a hiking trail that was part of a network crisscrossing the Garhwal wilderness, with Lansdowne as a focal point.

He put away the map and lay down just as a pack of jackals began to howl. In two minutes, he was fast asleep.

Chapter 5

At another campsite forty miles away, a man named Shahid heard a different pack of jackals take up the chorus of howls heard by Jason.

He was preparing for bed and, like Jason, paid them no heed. His focus was on the culmination of his mission tomorrow, when two weeks of careful preparation would reach a climax.

His orders were to go to Nainital, posing as a student on a solo hiking trip in Garhwal, and befriend three young hikers identified as 'the Saluja trio'. It turned out to be almost too easy. A manufactured "chance encounter" led to him tagging along with them "for the day". By the evening, he had been invited to join them as a "plus one" of their trio. After that, it was simply a matter of biding his time until the moment came to dangle the bait and lure them into the trap prepared for them.

That moment arrived last night when the campfire conversation turned to memorable adventures. When it was his turn, he described a whitewater rafting trip down a nearby stretch of river in such glowing terms that the gullible idiots were hooked. They insisted so forcefully on experiencing it themselves that he agreed to call the 'Upper

Ganges River Tour Company' and arrange for a 'guide' to meet them at the jump-off point at noon tomorrow. The trap would be sprung on a desolate riverbank in the middle of nowhere.

"Insha'Allah!" thought Shahid Khan, casting a sidelong glance at his three companions.

They were filthy infidels—two Hindu idolaters and a so-called Christian who had forsaken his religion. The Saluja girl was the worst, with her tight jeans and T-shirt that left nothing to the imagination. Tomorrow, when he tore those off, he wouldn't imagine anymore! He would give her the ultimate adventure an infidel whore deserved: Being fucked to death!

And her brother and boyfriend would get the ultimate adventure *they* deserved: Death!

Shahid felt no pity for them—there was no room for it in his heart. Not when his life's singular purpose was to fulfill the destiny predicted by his name, *Shahid,* which meant 'martyr'. And not when his journey to martyrdom was driven by vengeance against the Hindu infidel for the deaths of his parents' in one of hundreds of local out-breaks of anti-Muslim violence that went unreported across India.

He took the first step of that journey by enrolling in the Aligarh Muslim University. There, a shadowy niche in the student body opened the door to Talwar-e-Rasool and the training he needed to become a jihadi.

The first leg of that journey would be completed with his promo-tion from *Shagird* (apprentice) to full-fledged *Talwari* (swordsman), which rested on the success of this mission. And that was all but guaranteed.

A ransom of six million dollars was peanuts for one of the richest men in India.

Chapter 6

In a high-rise office building in New Delhi's toney business district, Raman Saluja was poring over legal documents pertaining to his biggest ever venture.

The press labeled it "The Largest Outsourcing Deal in History", because it would consolidate Lone Wolf Corporation's worldwide personnel and payroll operations under Saluja Technology Services (Saltech for short, in a whimsical tribute to Caltech, his old stomping grounds). The Bombay stock market was holding its collective breath, anticipating Saltech's shares to triple, even quadruple, after he and Jonathan Wolff inked the deal.

Money was never the point, though. He had more than anyone could spend over several lifetimes. Anyway, money had lost all meaning since the loss of his beloved wife, Mala. Nine years later, the shattering grief of her loss was still with him, like a wound that never heals.

Saluja had made his fortune as a software engineer in Silicon Valley, through brains, hard work, and business savvy. His uncanny sense of timing allowed him to cash in when the dotcoms were at their peak, just before the bubble burst.

He had heaven on earth and everything to live for, with visions of retiring at the tender age of 40, a millionaire many times over!

Then Fate snatched his beloved Mala from him.

It seemed incomprehensible at first. The dreaded words "lump in the breast" were mentioned at her annual gynecologic visit, like a minor inconvenience. After that, everything happened so fast he had no chance to come to grips with it, let alone say a proper goodbye.

The cancer had spread to her lungs and brain, and the last attempts to contain it with experimental chemotherapy achieved nothing. She was gone in a year, leaving him a widower at the age of 38, with two small children, an enormous fortune, and a dead soul.

A year-long battle with near-suicidal depression followed, during which he withdrew from the world. When he finally beat it, he sold everything he owned to escape from his memories and returned to a life of luxury in India, with nothing to live for, except death.

There were times when he thought of ending it all. He never acted on the thought, fortunately. In time, he learned to live again. His children, who were just as devastated by the loss of their beloved mother, were *why*.

Just as important, though, was *how*. By getting back in the game, he discovered he had lost none of his entrepreneurial genius, or impeccable timing.

At the time, India was becoming the Mecca for outsourcing, and joint ventures in software technology were springing up at an unprecedented rate. His name recognition, reputation, and Silicon Valley connections gave him an unparalleled advantage. In five years, Saltech became one of the biggest outsourced service providers in India. And he became one of the richest men in India. After he closed the Lone Wolf deal, the 'one of' prefix would disappear, and his rich-man club membership would go from 'India' to 'the world'.

He came to his senses as if someone kicked him in the head. *If Malini ever hears…*

His mind jumped tracks to his daughter, Malini.

When did his darling daughter turn into a hellcat? He knew she was headstrong and manipulative, but he indulged her, dismissing it as much-needed compensation for a motherless childhood.

Three weeks ago, everything came crashing down when she announced she was going on a trekking expedition in the Himalayas with her boyfriend. Saluja put his foot down for the first time ever, only to provoke a tantrum of epic proportions that started with a screaming harangue of "I hate you! You are a tyrant worse than Hitler, Mussolini, and Stalin put together!" and ended with sneering contempt. "So, all-powerful dictator who thinks he controls my life, I dare you to try to stop me!"

She had called his bluff, knowing he was powerless to enforce it. So, he changed tactics, telling her she had to take a security escort.

She remained defiant. "If you think I'm stupid enough to let your goons come along, think again."

Before things could get worse, Chetan, her brother, defused the situation by offering to go along, as an "escort, not a chaperone", with a promise not to restrict her in any way.

She left three days later without saying goodbye.

His only contact was with Chetan. He called at 8PM every day like clockwork. By all accounts, they were having fun. Malini's boyfriend, Bobby D'Souza, was a capable outdoorsman, and Chetan was an outstanding athlete himself and an Olympic-class archer to boot!

And this new friend, Shahid, who they met two weeks ago, seemed to know the area very well. He was taking them on what he called "a once-in-a-lifetime whitewater rafting trip" down a small river somewhere between Lansdowne and Nainital. It wasn't listed on any tourism website, but if it was really that good he might check it out himself.

Realizing that his mind had wandered way off track, he got back to reading the contract. He couldn't risk looking stupid in front of Jonathan Wolff.

A friend from Silicon Valley had forewarned him that "Wolff is smarter than anyone you care to name. Gates, Zuckerberg, and Jobs? He'd run circles around any of them. But even that isn't the worst of it. That bastard is so ruthless, he'd eat his own grandmother and spit her bones in your face if he thought it would intimidate you!"

Chapter 7

Jonathan Alexander Wolff had been called many things over the years. Most were prefaced by profanities. He embraced them all as badges of honor for the Alpha Wolf in a pack of notoriously predatory Captains of Industry.

Two things he had never been called were timid or diffident. 'Reclusive' was the adjective most frequently associated with his name in media reports before Alexis entered his life. 'Ruthless' came a close second.

His response? "A tiger is reclusive. That doesn't make it a pussycat."

The feline reference was deliberate. Those who felt his bite were known to mutter that his nickname, 'Ole Jaws', was actually a reference to the tiger, not his initials, J.A.W.! His reputation was well-earned. Even the Wall Street Journal, a publication not given to hyperbole, opined that, if Lone Wolf Corporation was indeed named for North America's apex predator, it was missing the second 'f' in its founder's name.

His savvy was the reason Lone Wolf, a multinational conglomerate with subsidiaries in over 100 countries, was the perennial darling of every major stock market in the world, defying the odds and market conditions.

That might be about to change. Alexis's entry into his life had led him to discover something he never knew he possessed until now: A business conscience! When his upcoming decision became public no one would be calling him 'ruthless'. They would assume he had lost his touch, or (less charitably) his marbles.

Headlines like "The Wolff is an Endangered Species" might be the least derisive. More likely, "The Alpha has no Balls". Or "Neutered Wolff"!

Let them have their headlines. He only cared what Alexis thought.

She, of course, would be shocked to hear that. She had no interest in Lone Wolf and would furiously reject any implication that she could influence his business decisions.

It wasn't her rejection he feared, though. It was indifference— that she'd shrug it off as no concern of hers. It was why he couldn't bring himself to tell her yesterday that it was *for* her, not *because* of her.

He couldn't delay any longer, though. He was leaving early tomorrow morning for Delhi, so tonight at dinner was his last chance.

For the first time in his life, Jonathan Wolff knew what it meant to be timid and diffident.

Chapter 8

A rchery had become Alexis's passion in the past year.

Kyudo—the 'way of the bow'—was the one ninja skill that transferred to a competitive sport. Not martial arts, strangely enough. For one thing, her combat skills were drawn from so many different disciplines that restricting her attack sequences to any one form was like expecting a tiger to use only one claw! But, even if she managed to somehow override her instincts, her status as *menkyo kaiden*—the highest level of ninja achievement, conferred on her by her sensei—forbade her from competitive sparring. Nor could she reveal her status to *anyone*, not even Jason. She could practice with him, however, because their sessions, although no-holds-barred, weren't competitive, in the sense of trying to best each other.

Kyudo posed no such problems. But adapting to the modern sport of archery proved far trickier than she anticipated. The ritualistic *bushakei* style of kyudo was as different from competitive archery as the *yumi*—the asymmetric Japanese longbow—was from the compound fiberglass bow. Adapting involved a steep learning curve and, with practice, her skill at archery was now excellent. But not flawless, like it was with the yumi.

She even knew the reason for it.

With the compound bow, she had never been able to attain the Zen-like state of oneness she had with the yumi, when the arrow seemed predestined to strike its target. Maybe the more traditional 'recurve' bow would be different, but it wasn't popular in the U.S., except for Olympic competition, and she wasn't interested in that! Maybe that mystical skill was lost to her, now that ninjutsu was no longer her life.

It was frustrating to think that some of those hard-earned ninja skills might be waning.

Chapter 9

Alexis was happy to let Jonathan linger after dinner. He seemed in no hurry to leave, even though it was getting late and he had a very early start in the morning.

He seemed preoccupied all evening, fidgeting nervously like he was now, spinning a spoon back and forth on the table. He still hadn't mentioned the "few things" he wanted to talk over, which only proved to Alexis that it wasn't something she did or said. There was no room for unspoken misunderstandings in a relationship built on mutual trust and a shared understanding that they viewed the world through different prisms.

His worldview reflected his evolution from loner to apex predator in the shark tank of business. Hers was formed in a loving home and the peaceful confines of a Buddhist monastery. So, it wasn't surprising that their views would clash. What was surprising, though, was their willingness to see things through the other's prism. So much so that he even called her "keeper of my conscience" on one occasion. And "my ethical and moral lodestar" on another.

Those two phrases showed how much he had changed from the days when he was a recluse driven by ruthless, single-minded ambition—what he wryly called "the ritual practice of fiscal amorality in the worship of Mammon". Now, according to Jason, he fretted over the impact of his decisions on the planet and humanity. Not that the predatory tiger known as "Ole Jaws" had turned into a pussycat. But the 'compassion-be-damned' ruthlessness he wore as an armor had gone MIA—as Jason put it, "The tiger has grown a conscience!"

She wasn't surprised to hear that. With the blossoming of their mutual trust, Jonathan became increasingly willing to let his guard down in her presence, so she had witnessed his struggles with a newly-assertive conscience. But his nervous fidgeting betrayed an endearing vulnerability she had never seen before. Nor had anyone else, she was sure. This might be a 'privilege' reserved exclusively for her.

Noticing his coffee cup was empty, she reached over to refill it, saying casually, "I expect you'll see Jason in India, right?"

Jonathan's response was so unexpected that she almost spilled the coffee. "Alexis, will you join me on my trip? Take-off's at 4AM, so I'll understand if you can't at such short notice."

She set down the carafe with exaggerated care and stared at him, stunned.

He misinterpreted her silence. "Please don't think I'm getting you involved in Lone Wolf. I know there's nothing you'd like less. But I'm going from India to the Gulf, and I'm going to need my moral compass there."

So that's what's bothering him!

A quick mental check of her calendar showed two upcoming archery tournaments. Easily skipped. And her next Flying Doctor trip to Nunavut wasn't for four weeks.

She laughed. "I'm very flattered that you'd ask me to come along. Jason never tires of reminding me that my tastes run more to a sleeping bag in a hut in some remote Inuit village than a private bedroom on an airplane."

He stammered, "I...I...I'm so sorry. I didn't realize you'd never flown on my plane!"

She squeezed his hand. "Don't be silly! I find a trip to a remote Inuit village in a chopper more rewarding than all the trips Jason makes on your private jet, and I never miss a chance to tell him that. My rebirth, remember? Your gift to me!"

Seeing him flush with pleasure, she continued. "So don't go all guilty on me because I don't do what Jason does. It's my choice to stay out of your business life, not yours or his. Except, of course, when you need me as... Hmmm. Let me see. How did you describe it this time? Oh yes, your moral compass! That's a new one!"

His eyes came alive and the laugh lines reappeared, so she went on, pretending to scold him. "I see where this is going. I start as keeper of your conscience, then your lodestar, and now I'm your compass! I see a downward trend here, and I don't like it! I guess I should be thankful I'm no longer a deadly weapon. The Sword of Retribution, isn't that what you called me?"

He laughed. "I did, didn't I? But you haven't said you'll come."

"Of course, I will! But where are you going in the Gulf?" She was almost sure she knew the answer.

"A tiny little principality that you probably haven't heard of called Qumraan."

"Where you built a pipeline to bring desalinated water from the sea and an oil pipeline to go the other way?"

"You knew?" he said, surprised.

"I keep up with some of what Lone Wolf is up to. Particularly if I sense my moral compass might be needed for a change of direction!"

She was only teasing him, but it still made him squirm uncomfortably. "You knew that, too?"

"Not 'knew'. 'Felt' is more like it. The Jonathan I know wouldn't build an ultra-modern hospital and airport in the desert to satisfy a despot with delusions of grandeur."

He winced. "You have a way of cutting right to the heart of the matter. So yes, I've decided to change direction, as you put it! I need my compass for that."

"No compass can show you the right direction if you can't find it within yourself. And it looks like you have."

"Better late than never."

She smiled. "It's never too late for that, Jonathan. All that counts is finding the right direction. But why go to Qumraan? In today's electronic age, couldn't you do it without going there?"

"There's a reason I must. The Emir, who died two weeks ago, issued a Royal Proclamation from his deathbed, gifting me a priceless artifact from the tenth century called the Lion of Qumraan. He made his brother, the Crown Prince and heir to the throne, cosign it in the name of Allah, so it can't be revoked. They want to present it to me. It's a big deal for them. And the Metropolitan Museum of Art, just a few blocks from here, is literally salivating at the prospect of adding it to the Lone Wolf permanent collection."

"Why is it such a big deal?"

"History. And iron. Before the discovery of oil, Qumraan was a small oasis town in the Rub al Khali, the Empty Quarter of the Arabian Desert. The economy, if you could even call it that, revolved around metal artisans of exceptional skill and a small iron mine with some of the highest quality iron ore in the world. Their iron sculptures are highly sought after, and the Asad al Qumraan, to give it its correct name, is a one-of-a-kind example of a fast-vanishing art. A rampaging lion, standing on its hind legs, front paws in the air, weighing over 350 pounds."

"Okay. I get that it's a big deal for them and the Met. But how does that relate to your change in direction?"

"The Emir's death came as I was considering your aptly named 'change of direction'. He was, by Middle East standards, a benign despot, who was cultured and intelligent, and enjoyed a good laugh. And, although a devout Muslim, he didn't wear his religion on his sleeve.

"The late Emir has no living heirs. Both his sons died of a hereditary liver disease before transplants became routine, so his brother, Sayf al-Qumraan, will take the throne after the mourning period ends. He is a dour and humorless fanatic, as different from his brother as chalk from cheese. He imposed Sharia law two years ago, when the Emir's declining health forced him to cede administrative authority to his brother. He makes my change of direction easy."

"I see. But if you've already changed direction, why do you need a compass? That doesn't mean I don't want to come along. I just want to know what you want from me."

He replied with uncharacteristic diffidence, "Well…LWOQ, Lone Wolf Oil of Qumraan, was my first international venture. Also my most profitable ever, thanks to an unusual arrangement as a Sole Proprietorship, at the Emir's insistence. So, all its assets are owned and controlled by me personally, including the Qumraani oil concessions, refinery, and desalination plant. I'll be signing the deed of sale for the refinery during this visit. I want you there for that. You, after all, are why I've seen the light."

She didn't know what to say.

He continued. "Why should I spare you from watching me kill off the greatest cash cow in my history?"

She came right back at him. "So, before killing a cow, you're going to the one country where killing a cow is a sin? Makes perfect sense!"

He laughed. "Maybe it's because I need to do some penance to appease the Hindu gods! If I can get their forgiveness, the cow might be reincarnated and find its way to my temple to Mammon!"

She jabbed back. "Seeing how much Lone Wolf shares rose after the Omani buyout, that cow has already made it back to your temple. Don't expect sympathies from me!"

"I'm not asking for any. I'm making out quite handsomely, thank you. The Qumraani buyout is more than twice the Omani buyout of three hundred million dollars for the desalination plant. Nearly seven hundred million, a five hundred percent return on my original investment."

"Wow!"

"Wow, indeed. But there's a difference between the two. Wall Street cheered the Omani buyout as 'cashing in on value'. The refinery and oil concessions, on the other hand, are huge moneymakers. Selling them now, even at a profit, would be interpreted on Wall Street as 'retrenchment'. Lone Wolf shares could take a major hit because the knee-jerk reaction will be that there's another, bigger shoe waiting to drop. Whispers of my retirement have been heard since the Omani buyout. They'll reach a crescendo after this."

"I take it you're not worried?"

"We'll bounce back when that other shoe doesn't drop. And even if we don't, it's too late to change course, now that my compass has taken the helm, so to speak."

"Does that mean I'm in charge and get to boss the boss?"

She saw a strange light in his eyes as he replied. "Boss or not, my dear, you're in charge of more than you can imagine."

She was so taken aback she didn't know what to say.

Jonathan looked at his watch. "Limo pick-up is at 2AM. Need any help getting ready?"

"Thanks, but I always have a bag packed and ready for an emergency trip to the Canadian interior. It just needs an outfit reset from a high temperature of 75°F to 115°F!"

He drained his cup and pushed his wheelchair back from the table, all business again. "I'll call the crew to tell them we'll have an extra passenger."

"And I'll call Ravi to tell him we're arriving in Delhi on Monday." She saw his face go blank and quickly clarified, "Don't worry, I won't be staying with him."

Seeing him relax, she added, "Did you really think the compass would abandon ship?"

He laughed heartily and said, "There goes my last chance to correct course."

She picked up her phone to call Ravi, wondering how Jason would react when he heard she was sticking her nose in Jonathan's business.

On second thought, she knew how he'd react. He wouldn't believe it!

Chapter 10

avi Iyer, the head of the oddly named Division of Information Exchange in the Indian Ministry of Home Affairs, had no family and was a self-confessed workaholic. So, it wasn't unusual for him be at work at 7AM on a Sunday when there was a threat that needed cold and reasoned analysis.

Talwar-e-Rasool, his current focus, wasn't a new threat. In the early days, it was known as TeR, following the 'tradition' of calling jihadi organizations by their initials, like LeT for *Lashkar-e-Toiba* (Army of the Pure) and HuM for *Harkat-ul-Mujahideen* (Movement of Holy Warriors). Then an enterprising reporter saw what escaped everyone else. He appended the word 'Organization', and a clever acronym was born: TeROR.

Like all other Indian jihadi outfits, TeROR's purpose was urban terrorism. Unlike the others, however, TeROR bore no allegiance to the Kashmiri cause. In fact, it had no discernable "philosophy of terror", making it impossible to profile. And it had no regional preference, striking with equal capriciousness across the country, so it left no traceable 'terror footprint'.

The Uttarakhand bus bombing fit that pattern, except for the baffling claim that the bomb's purpose was to scare foreigners away.

They had never claimed specific intent before. Why now, for the first time ever? It made no sense even at face value. Why kill one firangi on a bus when they could make their point with far greater savagery by killing hundreds in Haridwar? As for that ludicrous assertion that the bomb was deliberately timed to go off in a secluded area to spare the citizens of Haldwani? They had no compunction about killing over two thousand pilgrims at a Hindu religious festival just a year ago, so did they really think anyone would buy such a blatantly false claim?

So what game were they playing? More importantly, what were they trying to hide under all those red herrings? And the biggest unsolved mystery of all: Who were 'they'?

Even Kalidas, the most trusted arms supplier in terrorist circles, hadn't solved the riddle of who ran TeROR. His files, an otherwise priceless treasure trove of information on terrorist groups in India, were stunningly silent on the subject, except for one cryptic note. *"Talwar-e-Rasool's decision makers unidentified. Standing invitation to Bloodbath summit forwarded through operatives in Uttarakhand, Mumbai, and Hyderabad. No response. Mukherjee follow-up through Kolkata operatives rebuffed. Invitation withdrawn."*

If Kalidas couldn't get near TeROR's top echelon, their security must be impregnable.

The phone rang, breaking Ravi's train of thought. It was his direct line, known only to senior cabinet members and a handful of friends. He picked it up, feeling a surge of excitement when he saw the caller ID.

"Alexis!" he exclaimed. "What a wonderful surprise!"

"Get ready for another surprise, Ravi."

"What's that?"

"I'm coming to India with Jonathan. We arrive in Delhi Monday morning."

"Why not stay with me? Jonathan will be busy with Saluja, so you'll have time to kill."

She gently declined. "It has to be a 'No' this time, Ravi. I'm staying with Jonathan at the Taj. But I promise to spend as much time with you as possible."

He heard the finality in her voice and knew not to ask why. Her relationship with Jonathan was indecipherable to anyone but Jason. He hid his disappointment. "I understand."

"Do you think you can get word to Jason that I'm coming with Jonathan on his plane? I'd like to know how he reacts."

"The bounder hasn't called and I can't reach him. He was too pig-headed to take a cell phone, because—I'm paraphrasing— 'I didn't need one six years ago, I don't need one now'."

"Typical Jason. Pig-headed doesn't even begin to describe him."

"I guess you'll just have to beam it to him over whatever link you two share," he said jokingly.

"It doesn't work like that, Ravi," she replied in all seriousness. "But it does have some uses. I sensed he ran into some trouble. He seems okay now. Just don't tell him I told you he was 'in trouble'. He can get touchy about such things."

"Thanks for warning me! If he calls I'll just tell him you're coming."

Ravi said goodbye and hung up, thinking about the 'connection' between Alexis and Jason. With a jolt of fear, he remembered that Jason was in Uttarakhand right now. Could the "trouble" Alexis sensed be the bus bombing? Was Jason the firangi who was obliterated with everyone else on the bus?

Then he remembered that Alexis said Jason was all right now and realized he let an overwrought imagination get to him. That weird connection between the two of them had its uses, just like she said.

Jason was in the vicinity, though. He'd be ok if he didn't tangle with Talwar-e-Rasool. Even his exceptional skills might not be enough against those murderous bastards.

Day 2

...DIE BY THE SWORD

Chapter 1

Jason had made excellent time in the nine hours since breaking camp at 6AM.

It helped that the terrain wasn't particularly challenging. Mostly open forest, interspersed with grassland, brush, and patches of dense forest. Not tiger country but vigilance was still warranted. Leopards were ubiquitous in India and, although secretive and fearful of man, they were known to become man-eaters when habitat encroachment forced them into contact with humans and cattle. Thankfully, he saw no signs of either. Deer, though, were plentiful, which was a reassuring sign there were no big cats around. They watched him warily, and he gave them a wide berth to avoid spooking them.

The rumble from the rapids, which had been growing steadily louder for the past hour, became a muted roar when he crested a ridge. Ahead of him was a wide expanse of grassland that sloped down to the shallow ravine in which the river coursed. At the bottom of the slope was a stretch of woodland stretching as far as he could see on both sides. Behind that line of trees lay the rapids.

The sounds from the icy river beckoned to him in the mid-day heat, adding a spring to his stride as he started down the slope with the bracing scent of fresh water filling his nostrils.

Swordplay

At that moment, the silence of the wilderness was shattered by a scream. Not any ordinary scream, but a screech of sobbing agony that hung in the air for an eternity.

Jason froze in mid-stride, the hairs on the nape of his neck rising. The scream abruptly cut off, and he exploded into action.

He raced down the slope in full combat mode, juking through the trees at the bottom without breaking stride, until he reached a small clearing twenty feet from the river's edge. He halted there and, taking care to stay out of sight behind the line of thick bushes bordering the river, he peered out over the river.

He was forewarned by the hair-rising scream to expect something terrible, even satanic. But nothing could have prepared him for the tableau of murder and rape playing out on the opposite bank.

There were three men and one woman. And two bodies sprawled in the unmistakable pose of death.

The woman was naked. One man was kneeling between her thighs, rutting in and out of her. A second crouched dog-like, back towards Jason, pinning her spread-eagled legs with his knees and hands, as he peered around the other man's hip to watch the action. The third was squatting above her head, with her outstretched arms pinned under his haunches, one hand fondling her breast, the other clamped on her mouth.

And an AK-47 semi-automatic on the ground within his reach!

Jason turned sick with rage, knowing he was powerless to intervene. He would die before he got fifty feet from the opposite bank.

Right then, the rapist reared his head back and let out an animal cry of release. He stayed like that, face upturned to the sky, until the crouching man prodded him impatiently in the rear, forcing him to get to his feet. He stepped aside and, without taking his eyes off the naked woman, reached down to pull up his pajamas.

42

Simultaneously, the impatient one jumped up, eager to take his place between her spread-eagled thighs. For one split second, Jason felt his stomach churn before ice-cold detachment descended. His combat computer went into overdrive and his awareness expanded to absorb every detail in the periphery without his eyes leaving the centerpiece of the scene.

The beach extending half a mile on either side the centerpiece. The impassable rock channel downstream where the river turned into a raging torrent. A sharp bend in the river upstream.

The pieces came together, and a plan fell into place.

Two rapists to follow. Time enough to cross the river upstream of the bend without being seen and wait in the trees behind the centerpiece for them to come to him. To their deaths.

The odds of pulling it off—outnumbered three to one and outgunned semiautomatic to Bowie knife—never entered his calculations. It was what he had to do and the odds didn't count.

As it turned out, the odds had no impact on the outcome. Before he could take a step, matters were taken out of his hands.

With no one holding down her legs, the woman lashed out with both feet. That she found the courage to fight back was a miracle. What she achieved beggared belief.

As her erstwhile rapist was bending down to reach for his pajamas, one flailing foot struck him squarely in the forehead. The other smashed into the genitals of the man at her feet.

The effect on both men was catastrophic.

The man she kicked in the groin staggered backwards with a strangled scream. He sank to his knees, clutching his genitals, and folded over. With his forehead resting on the ground, he keeled sideways and curled up in a fetal position.

The effect on her erstwhile rapist was even more devastating.

Her heel slammed into his forehead like a sledgehammer, catapulting him into a backwards somersault. The back of his head smashed into the ground, and his legs, hobbled by the pajamas, cartwheeled over his torso, his bare ass 'mooning' the sky. The instant his legs flopped back, his back went into a violent spasm, lifting his torso and hips off the ground. He stayed in that reverse bow pose for a full second, before the spasm subsided. After a few violent twitches, he became still.

While that was unfolding, the man who was pinning her outstretched arms under his haunches suddenly tore his hand from her mouth and bounced back in a half-squat, blood spurting from his hand where the woman had clearly bitten him.

Her arms now free, she lashed out blindly with clenched fists. One struck her captor flush on the nose, and he recoiled with a howl of pain to sprawl on his back, clutching his nose.

With no one holding her down, the woman leapt to her feet and ran headlong for the river, seeking the illusory sanctuary of the opposite bank. Jumping from rock to exposed rock, she somehow managed to keep her footing on the wet stones, worn smooth over time.

The man she punched in the nose gave chase, his sneakers providing the traction he needed to gain on her with each leap. The man she kicked in the groin followed, clutching his genitals.

She reached the opposite bank just thirty feet ahead of her nearest pursuer. Seeing him closing fast gave her the jolt of adrenaline she needed to scramble up the embankment on all fours. It drove her halfway across the beach before that too was spent. With her breath now coming in great sobbing gulps, she began to reel and stagger, drawn as if by an invisible magnet to where Jason stood, hidden from view.

Seeing that she would reach the trees ahead of her pursuers, Jason ghosted backwards across the clearing and dropped his duffel bag in the undergrowth behind a tree. He was about to reach for his Bowie knife, when his combat computer sounded an alarm, telling him it couldn't figure in the upcoming combat. He reached down, instead, to pick up a heavy rock the size and shape of a softball and stepped out of sight, hefting it in his palm to get a feel for it.

The girl burst into the clearing seconds later, whimpering with terror. Half-way across, her foot caught on a partly buried root and she fell headlong. She made a half-hearted attempt to get up, only to fall back without making it even to her knees. Realizing she was finished, she wrapped her arms around her head and curled into a fetal position, her will shattered.

Her lead pursuer entered the clearing and halted when he saw her lying on the ground. Then he sauntered forwards, his lips peeling back in a predatory grin as he reached down to unzip his fly.

At that moment, Jason stepped out from behind the tree and uncoiled an overarm throw, hurling the rock straight into that grin.

The gliding throw and follow-through were a perfect combination of strength, coordination, and weight transference—the product of hours of practice on the cricket fields of his native South Africa. The rock smashed into the man's face with the force of a pile-driver.

Jason had a nebulous flash of recognition as he made the throw, but the stone hit before it could take shape. A soggy thump merged with the crumpling sound of bone being pulverized, and there was a gush of blood. He was dead before he hit the ground.

The second pursuer had made it across the river, and was now approaching the tree line. He appeared even younger than the girl, but the hatred on his face and the vitriol spewing from his mouth were as old as man himself. "I'm going to send that she-devil to Hell for kicking me in the balls! I'll fuck her so hard and so long that she'll split from her cunt to her ass!"

The obscenities rolled off Jason like water off a duck's back. He watched the youth enter the clearing, oblivious of Jason standing an arm's length away. He stopped dead in his tracks at the sight of his compatriot lying face-down on the ground.

In that moment of utter stupefaction, Jason came up from behind, silent as a ghost, and whispered in Hindi, "Say hello to your friend in Hell!"

Before the youth could react, Jason grabbed his jaw from behind with one hand, clamped the other to the back of his head, and broke his neck with one violent twist.

Jason confirmed both men were dead before checking on the girl. She looked quite young—probably no more than twenty. Her limbs were ice-cold and her pulse was thready and racing, suggesting impending shock. There was little he could do about that, except keep her warm. So, he stripped the shirt off her first pursuer, and put it on her, not only for warmth but also to stop her from freaking out if she woke up naked. Then he zipped her into his sleeping bag to delay the onset of hypothermia, which was inevitable if she remained unconscious for any length of time.

Next, he searched the dead bodies. The youth was carrying a student ID from Aligarh Muslim University identifying him as Shahid Khan. The older man had no photo ID, only a business card in the name of 'Ehsan Mohammad, Tour Guide, Upper Ganges River Tour Company. His face was unrecognizable pulp, so that nebulous flash of recognition would just have to remain…nebulous!

The fact that both rapists were Muslims was of no consequence. Nor did it matter that the AMU student body was known to harbor pockets of Islamic fanaticism. He knew, in his gut, that this had nothing to do with jihad. Gang rape was more in line with the lawless op-

46

portunism now so frighteningly common in India. And sickeningly familiar in its broad outlines: Trusting victims (the rafters) lured by an opportunistic co-conspirator (the student) into a trap set by a feral predator (the guide) at a desolate location.

The perfect crime, with no witnesses, no survivors, and no comebacks!

And it would have worked, too, but for the girl's incredible courage to fight back against hopeless odds. And the caprice of Fate that brought Jason to the right spot at the right moment.

The third man hadn't moved. But was he dead or just out cold? It could mean the difference between life or death with that AK-47 near him. Jason knew he had to check on him before he woke up, but that had to wait. The girl was his first priority. He couldn't risk leaving her. She would run the instant she woke up.

He sat down at her feet and entered a light trance with his eyes open, ready to come alert the instant she or the third man moved.

Chapter 2

A barely audible whimper snapped Jason to full alertness.

The girl's eyelids fluttered open and she whimpered again, reliving the terror of her last waking moment. Then her eyes fell on Jason and she leapt up with a shriek. Enclosed as she was in the sleeping bag, she tripped, falling backwards into Jason's arms, and started thrashing around like a wild animal.

Burying his face in the back of her neck where her gnashing teeth couldn't reach him, Jason held on, wrapping his arms and legs around her with just enough force to restrain her. Then he started crooning, as if to a child, that she was safe and he wouldn't hurt her, alternating between Hindi and English. Suddenly, her shrieks cut off and she became rigid as a board.

Jason lifted his head cautiously to see her staring open-mouthed at the two bodies. Feeling the pressure on her neck ease, she jerked her head around to look up at him, and he went cold, seeing the abject terror in her face. He smiled reassuringly, repeating that she was safe and didn't have to be afraid, and her fear turned to bafflement.

Jason eased his grip slightly, ready to clamp down if she began to fight him again, but she remained motionless, staring up at him. Encouraged by a tiny flicker of wonderment in her eyes, he let go, continuing his mantra of reassurance, but she just lay against his chest with her face upturned, staring at him for several seconds. Her lips twitched into the briefest of smiles, then reality hit, and she began to sob uncontrollably. All he could do then was cradle her in his arms and rock back and forth, repeating his mantra again and again.

Slowly, the sobs dwindled into sniffs and she wriggled free to sit up, the sleeping bag still around her. Jason leaned forward to unzip it, and she recoiled as if from a striking viper, her face stark with revulsion.

Realizing his mistake, Jason held up his hands in surrender, saying, "I'm so sorry. But don't be afraid. I won't hurt you. Do you believe me?"

He used English without thinking, but she responded with an uncertain nod. Seeing it, he stood up and said carefully, "I have to go and check on the third guy. Do you want come with me or wait here until I get back?"

She jumped to her feet with a gasp of fear, forgetting the sleeping bag. It fell away before her frantic hands could grab it, and she stared in shock at the denim shirt hanging to her knees. Her gaze shifted to the shirtless body, then to Jason, and understanding dawned. With wonderment in her face, and the tiniest smile, she said in English, "Thank you. But don't leave me here with…them! Please?"

Jason was surprised. Her accent was unmistakably American. But there was no hiding the lilting cadences of the sub-continent. He nodded. "Okay."

He stuffed the sleeping bag into the duffel and slung it over his shoulder, then drew his Bowie knife, flipping it over to hold it by the blade in readiness to throw. Before he could nod to the girl, she came up to slip her hand into the crook of his left elbow, and they walked out of the clearing together.

Once they were across the river, Jason gently disengaged her grip and motioned to her to hang back while he approached her rapist warily, alert for any sign of movement. He needn't have bothered. The man lay on his back, his pajamas around the ankles and sightless eyes gazing at the sky. The girl took one look at him, exposed from the waist down, and started retching violently, so Jason quickly pulled up the pajamas and retied the drawstring.

The head shifted as he was doing that, exposing a small boulder underneath, shaped like a pyramid, its point smeared with a telltale mixture of grayish-yellow slime and blood. The back of his skull must have landed on it with the full force of that backward somersault, killing him instantaneously.

The bodies of the girl's companions lay nearby. Both wore life vests and appeared to be in their mid-twenties. One had his head twisted around, indicating a broken neck. The other's face was stove-in from a brutal blow inflicted, in all probability, by the blood-smeared butt of the AK-47 near the rapist.

Jason noticed the rapist's bare feet and flip-flop slippers and knew he couldn't have arrived by raft or walked very far to get here.

Jason allowed himself a moment of jubilation when he found an ignition key in the rapist's pajama pocket. It was so old and worn that its make was indecipherable. He couldn't care less. It meant there was a vehicle of some sort parked on the only navigable trail in the vicinity: the dirt track marked "Forest Service Only" on his map.

It solved the problem of getting away, but what they would leave behind was a much bigger problem. Reporting the girl's rape and her companions' murder to the police was out of the question. He and the girl were in an extremely vulnerable position. She because 'victim-shaming' was the police's go-to strategy in rape cases, and he because a firangi was an irresistible target for a corrupt policeman to pin a trumped-up murder charge. And that was without factoring in a "Superintendent Bakshi" in the pockets of the perpetrators.

Leaving the bodies to be discovered wasn't an option. Questions would be asked when the girl returned to civilization without her companions. Once Jason's role in her captors' deaths came to light, he would be trapped in an Indian jail for years while the case worked its way through the Indian courts. And saying he intervened to save the girl would put a big fat target on her back. She was the only eyewitness to the crimes. Without her testimony, all five deaths could be pinned on him because the blunt-force injuries were very similar...

His mind jumped, without warning, to that moment in the clearing when he was reaching for his knife, only to pick up the stone. And he had an epiphany. His combat instinct had anticipated that the death must appear accidental!

He turned to look downstream, the germ of an idea taking shape in his head.

A quarter mile from where he stood, the riverbanks angled sharply inwards to form a narrow channel in which the river reverted to a turbulent fast-flowing torrent confined between jagged walls of rock. His map showed it accelerated down an incline before plunging over a waterfall several miles downstream.

It all came together then, and he knew how to make it appear as if the five dead men perished in a "tragic" rafting accident, without anyone suspecting the girl survived.

He walked upstream to where the rafts were beached, gathering up girl's clothes scattered on the ground. Three life vests lay near the rafts, two that were grimy and well-worn belonging to the men he killed, and one, the girl's, that was brand new.

Clamped to the walls of the raft were a pair of expensive duffel bags and a matching backpack, along with two fraying canvas bags. He took all five bags and set them down next to the girl who was sitting with her knees drawn under her chin and hands clasped around her ankles. He went to the river and soaked her torn shirt in the icy water and returned to kneel in front of her. He motioned as if to wipe her face and she lifted her chin obediently, letting him swab away the crusted blood and dirt.

When he was done, Jason said very gently, "The sooner you wash yourself clean, the better it will be for you. Safer too—"

She leapt up with a wail before he could finish and ran to the stream. Tying the shirt tails under her breasts, she waded in and sat down, submerged to her hips where the eddying current had formed a pool, and began washing herself.

Satisfied that she would be occupied for a while, Jason walked back upstream to put his plan into action. He put the AK-47 and the two grimy life vests in one of the rafts and pushed it across the river to the opposite bank. He transferred the two dead bodies from the clearing to the raft, putting a life vest on each, and threw the stone he used as a projectile into the river. Then he pushed the raft back across the river, beaching it a hundred yards downstream of the girl.

The next part was going to be trickier. He had to get the girl to buy into his plan.

Jason walked back to the girl, who had donned a fresh shirt, jeans, and boots, and pulled her hair into a ponytail. He crouched down next to her, and stared into the distance, saying nothing. After a couple of minutes, she spat out one word, "Why?"

"I don't know," he replied. "Maybe we can figure it out if you tell me what happened. My name is Jason."

"I'm Malini, and that's my brother Chetan, and that's my boyfriend, Bobby," she said, pointing in quick succession to the body with the smashed face and the one with the broken neck.

Then the floodgates burst open, and the tears and words came rushing out in a torrent. She gestured towards the opposite bank. "Shahid joined us ten days ago, pretending to be our friend. He told us about this whitewater rafting trip and introduced us to Ehsan, the guide, who met us around noon. He brought us here, where this man, Firoze, was waiting with a gun." She pointed at the dead rapist.

"Chetan got mad when he saw the gun, demanding to know why they needed a gun. Then all hell broke loose. Ehsan grabbed the gun and hit Chetan with it, Firoze punched Bobby in the stomach, and Shahid grabbed him from behind and broke his neck. I tried to help them, but Firoze tore off my shirt, saying they would kill me too if I didn't let them…" Her voice broke.

Jason felt cold. This wasn't a random act of lawless opportunism. It had been planned and executed with diabolical efficiency. The 'friend' planted in advance to entice them into taking this trip. The 'guide' who met them. The gunman waiting on a beach in the middle of nowhere. And the merciless execution of her companions by breaking one's neck and smashing the other's face while she watched.

The symmetry between the executions and the justice he meted out dawned on him, and he realized it might be just the tonic Malini needed to fight her desolation.

"Do you believe in karma?" he asked softly.

Malini's reply was acerbic. "What do you think? I'm a Hindu. Karma is central to my belief system."

He nodded. "Okay. So, think about this. Ehsan killed Chetan by smashing his face. Guess what? He died from a smashed face. And Shahid, who broke Bobby's neck, died from a broken neck. Whether you call that karma or an eye for an eye, it's justice. Chetan and Bobby are avenged. And you killed Firoze, so you are avenged too.

A flash of vindictive rage crossed her face. "Good!"

"And don't forget *your* karma. If you hadn't fought back, I couldn't have helped you."

Her expression softened, and she said with genuine warmth, "I don't know how to thank you."

"You already have. With your incredible bravery."

Jason meant it. He was truly in awe. It took exceptional courage to fight back under such horrific circumstances.

Her face lit up in a radiant smile. It was the first sign of positive energy from her. She would need that and more to accept what was coming next.

"Did they do or say anything that might give us a clue to why they did this?" Jason asked.

The smile vanished. "They held a gun at my head and took a picture of me, naked. Firoze called on the satellite phone to say he was sending the picture. He then made a second call to say that they were going to have some fun now and not to expect them at the hut before 3AM." Her voice broke with a sob. "Then they made me—"

"Don't think about that!" he cut in sharply. He gave her hand a reassuring squeeze, and she squeezed it back. Encouraged by that, he asked, "Is your father very rich?"

"Yes," she replied, in a flat, emotionless voice, like she didn't care.

"Okay, so it must be for ransom. But we have the advantage now. Whoever's behind this doesn't know you've escaped."

"We must tell the police!"

"We mustn't!" It came out more sharply than he intended.

"Why?" she asked, shocked.

He made a split-second decision to leverage the universal belief in India that *all* police were corrupt, instead of using the snippet he overheard about 'Superintendent Bakshi' to prove that the *local* police were corrupt. "What if the kidnappers have bribed the police?"

She nodded reluctantly. "You're right. But when the police find and ID Chetan and Bobby, it'll come out that I was with them when they were murdered. I'll have to say I killed Firoze and that you rescued me by killing the other two. I can't lie."

"You won't have to lie if we make it look like an accident."

"How?"

Rather than tell her directly what he wanted to do, he answered tangentially. "You know there's a waterfall downstream, right?"

"Yes. So what?"

"So, we make it look like the rafts went over the waterfall, killing everyone."

"Everyone?" She was incredulous. "Chetan and Bobby, too?"

"I'm sorry but their bodies have to go over the waterfall to make it look like everyone died and your body will turn up later."

Malini's eyes filled with tears. "Why?"

"Because whoever's behind the kidnapping must believe you're dead. Otherwise, they'll come after you when you don't show up at that 'hut' at 3AM."

Her shoulders slumped. "If you think that's best…"

Jason sensed she was on the verge of collapse. He couldn't afford that now. He patted her hand. "You've been so strong till now. I just need you to hang in there for a few more minutes while I set things up. Then we'll leave in style. I promise you can rest then."

She perked up immediately. "What do you mean, in style?"

"It's a surprise."

"Okay. But I want to help. Tell me what to do."

Jason pointed to the set of three matching bags at her feet. "Which one's yours?"

She tapped the backpack. "This one. But some of my stuff's in Chetan's duffel, too."

"Put what you need in your backpack. Leave everything else."

While she was doing that, Jason went through the rapists' bags, finding a cell phone and a digital camera. He slipped the phone into his pocket to call Ravi later and put the camera in his duffel, along with the satellite phone used to contact whoever was pulling the strings. Firoze landed on it when he fell, shattering its screen, but Ravi would extract the information it contained. Finally, he pried up the rock on which Firoze smashed his head, kicked loose shale into the depression, and tossed it into the river.

It was time for the last part of his plan.

He carried Firoze's body upstream and placed it kneeling at the prow of the second raft, arms draped over the tube brim. He seated the bodies of Chetan and Bobby on either side of the raft to distribute the weight evenly, and walked back to where Malini was sitting with her backpack packed and ready at her feet.

She smiled at him, saying, "I'm ready to go."

"A few more minutes, and I will be, too."

He stuffed the guide's denim shirt into one of the canvas bags, slung the AK-47 on his shoulder, and carried the duffels and canvas bags to the raft, securing all four to its clamps. Then he dragged the raft into the river and pushed it downstream to where he beached the raft with the bodies from the clearing.

He threw the AK-47 as far as he could into the river, watching it sink without a trace. Taking a firm grip on both rafts, he waded into the river until he felt the current tugging at his thighs Then he pushed the rafts into the river with a twist, watching them accelerate away on the current, spinning faster and faster, until they disappeared into the channel.

Jason waded ashore, satisfied he had set up a convincing "rafting accident". Thanks to his instinctive decision to use the rock instead of the Bowie, the injuries on all five bodies were consistent with the victims being smashed against rocks.

He walked back to Malini and picked up her backpack and his duffel. Slinging one on each shoulder, he said briskly, "Time to go."

"Can't wait," she replied, and they headed into the trees.

A quarter mile from the beach, they came upon a vintage Jeep, its canvas shell faded and frayed but intact. The tires were in good condition, the fuel gauge read three-fourths full, and there was a five-gallon 'jerry-can' of gasoline in the rear rack.

Malini climbed in the back and curled up with his duffel under her head while he got behind the wheel. Before starting the engine, he leaned over to rummage through the glove box for the registration document in case he was stopped by the police. It was brimming with grease-stained service receipts, which spilled out when he opened it. Seeing the document on the floor, he leaned under the passenger-side dash to retrieve it. That was how he spied the yellowing sheet of parchment paper wedged in the metal behind the glove box.

He extracted it carefully and smoothed it out. It was a print copy of a hand-drawn map from British colonial times, titled 'United Provinces, Map No. 85, Royal Indian Forestry Service, 1917'. It showed a tree-covered area with two rivulets merging to form a stream, and a shack-like structure at the confluence, marked 'Forestry Hut'.

It had to be the kidnappers' destination. Without map coordinates or a grid map, though, there was no way to tell where it was in Uttar Pradesh or Uttarakhand, the two Indian states carved out of the old British 'Province'.

Maybe Ravi and Google Maps can put their heads together and figure it out, he thought, as he pulled the starter button. The engine whirred to life. He engaged the floor-mounted gear stick, and released the clutch carefully, anticipating its hard, mechanical feel. The Jeep moved forward without either rabbit-hopping or stalling. It jounced exuberantly on the dirt track, which was baked rock-hard and riddled with ruts and rocks. Handling it without power-assisted steering was a challenge, but he quickly got the hang of it.

Conditions got better after the track joined what passed for a 'road', although its pothole-riddled tarmac made for slow going. It was 8PM by the time he reached Lansdowne, and got on a proper highway. Malini slept through it all.

The next two hundred-plus kilometers to Delhi would be a lot easier, but 50kmph was as fast as he dared go without the vintage Jeep vibrating so violently that Jason feared it might break apart. With all that, he expected to reach the Delhi-UP border checkpoint by 1AM, when it would be safe to call Ravi on Ehsan's phone. Even if it was being tracked by the police or anyone else, it would be too late catch them. The Jeep's trail would vanish in Delhi's night traffic.

At some point, whoever was waiting at the 'Forestry Hut' in 'Map No. 85' would realize something had gone horribly wrong and raise the alarm. By then, Malini would be safe in Ravi's house.

Chapter 3

R izwan Altaf was frustrated and angry.

While his comrades were celebrating the success of the kidnapping with a gang bang, he was stuck in a hut in the middle of the forest, with nothing to do but hang around and wait.

He had nothing to read, because he was done reading the half-a-dozen magazines he brought, twice over. Nothing to listen to, because he didn't bring a short-wave transistor radio to play Hindi film music. And nowhere to go—without the Jeep, the closest village, thirty kilometers away, might as well be on a different planet.

So, nothing to do but stare at blank walls in a damned hut in the middle of nowhere.

He shouldn't curse the hut, though. It was a priceless find, a relic of a bygone era before the advent of motor vehicles, when such huts were needed to shelter Forest Officers making their rounds on foot, with only a gun bearer and cook. Its existence was long forgotten.

Firoze, who worked as a clerk in the Uttarakhand State Forestry Department, stumbled on it when ordered to throw out a century-old set of hand-drawn maps charting the forests of the old United Province in British India. Firoze kept the grid map and the one showing the 'Forestry Hut' deep in the forest and threw out the rest.

The stream was the only landmark that hadn't faded from existence. They followed it upstream to the confluence of its tributaries, to find the hut with its stone walls and tile roof intact—a testament to the sturdy construction of the colonial era—although it was smothered by the jungle, inside and out. It took Ehsan, Firoze, Shahid, and him four weeks to clear the brush, fix the interior, and install a new door and window. With a few basic creature comforts, like a wooden table, canvas chairs, a pair of camp cots, kerosene lamps for light, and a stove for tea, it became the ideal hideaway, unlocatable without the maps. Firoze lost the one showing the location of the hut, and the grid map fell apart, so only the four of them knew it even existed. Here they could do what they wanted with the Saluja girl for as long as they wanted. More correctly, as long as *she* lasted!

He imagined her lying naked, handcuffed to the camp cot, and felt himself getting turned on. She would be his tonight to compensate for missing out on the fun, and he would make sure she "paid" for making him wait.

He had to be careful, though, when extracting his "payment". The warning was menacingly clear in that regard. "Fuck her as many times as you want. Leave any visible marks on her face or body and she'll be the last woman any of you fuck."

Once the ransom was paid, however, they could do whatever they wanted until she died. From being fucked to death!

It would be both a befitting end for an infidel whore and a befitting reward for him and his comrades for their hard work. Setting up the Saluja snatch-and-kill was tough enough. But to have everything thrown into disarray by the order to execute the journalist made it infinitely tougher. Not any garden variety execution, either, but a mass killing, with hundreds of victims to cover the real target. On twenty-four hour notice. Without interrupting or pausing, let alone disrupting, the Saluja snatch-and-kill. And no excuses tolerated: Failure was punishable by death!

Pulling it off took all of the team's abilities. Ehsan's inventive genius to devise the plan. Firoze's bomb-making skill to craft a time-delayed improvised explosive device. And Rizwan's own talents as a conman to get the gullible conductor to swallow a cockamamie story about a trunk left behind by his visiting grandmother, hook, line, and sinker. Handsome bribes to the conductor and driver made it that much easier to swallow!

The only precondition they didn't meet was "hundreds of deaths". Through no fault of their own. Firoze was forced to make do with a jerry-rigged timer, otherwise they would have had five hundred deaths, instead of just fifty. They did catch a lucky break with that grandstanding firangi, though. His death was a useful red herring to deflect attention from the real target.

Best of all, the snatch-and-kill operation had gone off without a hitch. All he had to do now was hold his frustration and anger in check until the girl arrived. Then he could take it all out on her.

Chapter 4

Raman Saluja was trapped in a nightmare.

It began at 4:30PM, when he got a text message with a photograph of Malini naked, an AK-47 at her head. It said, "Look what we found! Call the police and you'll never see your daughter again."

He lost his mind then, trying to imagine what happened before that picture was taken. Or what might be happening even now. And wondering why Chetan wasn't in the picture.

At that point, his mind shut down, only for the cycle of questions to restart after a few seconds, sending his mind spiraling out of control all over again in a terrifying nightmare without end.

At 7PM, his phone rang. And his world collapsed.

The voice on the phone sounded like the personification of evil. Cold, menacing, and utterly terrifying. It said, "Do you want to see your children alive?"

Saluja tried belligerence, saying he wanted proof that Chetan and Malini were alive, or he'd go to the police. It sounded so weak and hollow to even his ears that it was no surprise it failed. Spectacularly.

The caller countered with a dreadful threat. "If you call the police, you will get that proof. *In small pieces.*"

Saluja's will broke. He could only whimper. "Please...please...I beg you..."

"You tried to act tough, you bastard. Now you beg for their lives? Beg all you want but their lives are in your hands, not mine. Do as you're told, or you won't see your kids again. you will first make a good faith payment of ten million rupees right away from your Indian account to keep them alive. To get them back alive, you will transfer six million dollars tomorrow by 2PM from your Swiss bank account to the following bank routing and account number. Ready?"

Saluja made a desperate attempt to buy time. "Wait! The bank in Zurich won't open until 9AM Zurich time—1PM here. It'll take a couple of days for the transfer to go through."

The caller dismissed that contemptuously. "Do you take me for an illiterate fool? You have electronic fund transfer capabilities. If you try tricks like that again, say goodbye to your children. Just make the good faith payment now. Initiate the six million dollar electronic transfer before midnight. Then call your Swiss bank when it opens in Zurich at 1PM tomorrow and confirm it with password authentication. If the money is not transferred by 2PM, they die."

"I will do as you say. Please don't hurt them."

"That's up to you. Ready? I won't repeat this a second time."

The caller recited a string of numbers, starting with the bank routing number then the account number, which he scribbled down and repeated back for confirmation.

"Correct," the caller replied. "Remember, we are watching you. Keep your mouth shut, make the good faith payment and transfer the ransom by 2PM, and you will get your kids back *in one piece*. If you try to call *anyone*, you'll get them back *in pieces*."

Saluja was shaking with terror when he hung up. But he somehow kept it together to make the initial "good faith payment" and initiate the six-million-dollar electronic fund transfer. Tomorrow, he would complete the live password authentication required to transfer such a large sum. It was a secret known to almost no one, so how did this man know it? If he knew that, what else did he know? And who was watching him?

His one last desperate hope was that this was a scam. Even that was erased when, for the first time, he didn't get a call at 8PM from Chetan. He tried calling him but the phone was dead.

All that was left was to pray that money would satisfy the man on the phone. It was his only hope of saving his children.

Chapter 5

Ravi was jolted awake by the ringing of the phone. In his job, a call in the middle of the night was never good news.

His worst fears were realized when he heard Jason say, without preamble, "Ravi? I need your help. I ran into some trouble, then found a young lady in even bigger trouble."

Jason's voice was uncharacteristically taut and clipped. It said more clearly than any words could that the trouble was as bad as it could get. Ravi said simply, "Tell me what you need from me."

"We're headed to your house in a hot vehicle that must vanish until we figure this out. Can you move your car out of your garage?"

Ravi said simply, "Sure. How long before you get here?"

"About an hour. We just passed the Ghaziabad toll booth. And I'm starving!"

"I'll have Indian takeout waiting."

"Thanks. And remember there's two of us."

"I know. And both spare bedrooms are ready."

"Thanks for everything, Ravi. I'll explain when I see you!"

"Wait a minute. I have some news for you. Guess who's coming with Jonathan—"

Jason interrupted. "Alexis! Thank God!"

Ravi asked with good-natured annoyance, "Don't tell me you sensed she was coming?"

"Not sensed. Figured. I don't need ESP to figure out that 'news for me' plus 'who's coming with Jonathan' add up to Alexis!"

Ravi pretended to be exasperated. "Just when I think it's the other thing, you go all cold logic on me. She and Jonathan land at 7AM."

"We'll need her. The girl's in bad shape."

Ravi said goodbye and hung up.

There was no point speculating what the trouble was he or the girl ran into. He'd know soon enough.

He looked forward to having something to take his mind off the riddle of TeROR.

Chapter 6

Rizwan Altaf was startled awake by the howl of a jackal nearby.

The pack joined in, and the unholy chorus rose to an asynchronous crescendo before tapering off. Then there was nothing but the chirping of crickets and rustling of leaves.

He shivered involuntarily—there was something awfully creepy about the silence that followed the howling of jackals at night. And that was when you had company. In the jungle? And alone? Even the chirping of crickets sounded sinister, for God's sake!

He pushed away the thought and sat up to check the time on his satellite phone. The display read 11:40PM. It also showed a blinking light warning of a critically low battery. He had a fully-charged spare with him, but replacing it could wait. He needed a cup of tea first.

He laced up a pair of steel-capped combat boots reaching halfway up his shin. They were a survival essential in the jungle, where some of the deadliest snakes in the world lurked in the undergrowth.

He picked up the kettle and a flashlight and headed down the path to the stream nearby, swinging the flashlight beam from side to side. The moving beam made it easier to spot the shimmering black iridescence of a cobra—coiled death waiting to rear up and strike high in the calf where his boots couldn't protect him.

He breathed more easily when he reached the rock-strewn stream bed. It was dry, except for a foot-wide central channel where the stream was confined in summer. A scattering of scraggly thorn bushes was the only vegetation hardy enough to survive in the arid ground in summer, yet able to maintain a foothold there during the monsoons, when the stream burst out of the channel to fill the entire bed.

He found a gap in the thorn bushes and kicked aside the dead twigs with their two-inch thorns. Then, he knelt down at the edge, bracing his left hand against the lip of the bank, and bent down to dip the kettle in the stream.

With the gurgle of water filling his ears, he never heard the sibilant hiss from a tightly wound ball of dusty brown coils that stirred in a depression near his braced hand. Enraged by the thorny twigs kicked into its place of rest, the krait, notoriously bad-tempered and known for unprovoked aggression, struck with whiplash speed.

The twin fangs of the krait punctured the engorged radial vein coursing across Rizwan Altaf's locked left wrist like a pair of tiny hypodermic needles and squirted its lethal venom directly into his blood stream. A split-second later, the krait's head recoiled and it became an undulating brown rope that slipped away unseen.

All Rizwan felt was a pinprick on his wrist. He twisted it, thinking it was a thorn, and it vanished, so he waited to fill his kettle before standing up. Seeing two tiny droplets of blood on his wrist, he sucked them off, cursing the thorn bushes.

At that moment, he heard the satellite phone ring. Realizing he forgot to turn off the alarm he set for midnight, he hurried back to the hut. If the battery drained completely and the phone was forced

68

to reboot, re-establishing the satellite connection in this remote neck of the woods was no sure thing.

He was almost at the hut's door when his eyelids drooped shut without warning. He tried rearing his head back to see under his eyelids, but his neck seemed to turn into jelly, and it fell forward instead, slamming his suddenly slack jaw against his chest. The kettle and flashlight slipped from his paralyzed grasp, and he staggered like a drunk, his knees buckling under him. He fell backwards, landing awkwardly on his back, his head and shoulders dangling over the edge of the snake trench protecting the hut.

With burgeoning dread, he felt saliva pool in the back of his throat. He tried to swallow, but his tongue and throat refused to respond, and spit began trickling into his lungs. The urge to clear his throat and cough became unbearable, but his chest felt like it was in a vise, making it impossible to even draw a breath, let alone cough.

Dread morphed into supernatural terror, and he tried calling out to Allah to ward off the demon he thought was possessing his soul, but his lips couldn't form the words.

Rizwan Altaf had no idea that the 'demon' was the deadly neurotoxin in the krait's venom. Fifteen times more potent than the venom of the cobra, it coursed through his bloodstream, paralyzing the muscles of his eyes, throat, chest, diaphragm, and limbs in rapid succession as it worked its way down his spinal cord. It spared his mind though, leaving it completely lucid as his life ebbed away inexorably, inch by suffocating inch.

With the yawning pit of eternity reaching up to swallow him, the thought of the virgins he was told would be waiting on the other side never entered his mind. In the final moments of his life, Rizwan Altaf went insane, his mind unhinged by terror.

Day 3

SWORD OF THE PROPHET

Chapter 1

Mir Abdul Qasim was on the balcony of his apartment, looking out over New Delhi's deserted streets.

It was 1AM and an eerie silence blanketed the city—which was extraordinary for a city with 11 million inhabitants, where the honking of horns was a regular feature through the night.

It was almost as if the world was holding its collective breath.

As well it should! The coming dawn would be the start of a new era, heralding the worldwide triumph of Islam.

He hated the city and its residents now. Twenty years ago, when he arrived in Delhi, filled with excitement and boundless expectations, it was so different. He was a newly minted chartered accountant who had landed a coveted job auditing public sector enterprises—large, government-run entities that dominated India's socialist economy at the time and hemorrhaged money to the tune of billions with impunity.

A year later, disillusioned by the mind-numbing futility of 'auditing' bankrupt enterprises propped up by limitless government subsidies, he struck out on his own. He started a company to serve clients in the burgeoning private economic sector. He named it MAQ PLC, not just because those were his initials. Its phonetic name, 'Mack', was a tongue-in-cheek reference to 'Mackie', his schoolyard nickname. It was also a snide dig at the left-leaning Indian intellectual elite, who coined the derisive term, 'McDonaldization', for the rollback of the socialist nanny state's stranglehold on private enterprise.

The Indian economy had the last laugh. When the shackles came off, it skyrocketed. And the demand for corporate accountants skyrocketed with it. Two years later, MAQ PLC became MAQ Associates PLC, with its headquarters in Connaught Place, New Delhi's toney business district, and branches in Mumbai, Chennai, and Kolkata, India's four largest cities.

Those were heady times for Qasim. He was young, personable, and wealthy, with only one goal: to live and enjoy life to the fullest. He attended late-night parties, drank alcohol with abandon, and picked up and discarded women like one of his expensive shirts. He was 'Mackie' to his mostly Hindu friends, and a proudly secular Indian who hadn't read the Holy Quran or attended mosque, let alone recited '*namaaz*', the daily Islamic prayer.

Then came 'Godhra', *the* defining moment in recent times for every Indian Muslim.

It was February 27, 2002, the day he opened a fifth branch office in Bangalore, with plans underway for a sixth in his parents' hometown of Ahmedabad, a city of over 5 million, in the western state of Gujarat, which was becoming an industrial powerhouse.

On that date, a Muslim mob torched a train with Hindu pilgrims outside the small town of Godhra in Gujarat, burning fifty-eight pilgrims alive, including twenty-five women and fifteen children.

'Godhra' exploded onto the national consciousness, as vengeful Hindu mobs rampaged through Gujarat over the next three days, committing acts of unspeakable barbarism on Muslims, while police stood by. The state government strenuously denied it was the prolonged spasm of depravity that, according to press reports, claimed "thousands of deaths". But the government's attempts to downplay it were seriously undercut by the official count of 1044 deaths, 223 missing, and more than 2500 injured.

Qasim was at a bar, celebrating with his buddies, when he saw the rampaging mobs appear on TV. And his world fell apart.

His parents were visiting their hometown, Ahmedabad, the epicenter of the riots. With a dusk-to-dawn curfew in place, all air and rail travel suspended, and no one answering his calls, Qasim hung in agonized limbo for two days, tortured by his worst imaginings. They didn't come close to what really happened.

The spirit of 'Mackie' died that day, collateral damage to the brutal savagery that took the lives of his mother and sister, hacked to death by one of the many mobs rampaging through the streets. His father and two brothers also died that day, mowed down by indiscriminate police gunfire at so-called 'Muslim mobs' that gathered to protest the refusal of police to intervene.

When the curfew was lifted, he went to Ahmedabad, buried what was left of their bodies, and returned to Delhi, consumed by hatred, rage, and an unquenchable thirst for vengeance.

In that time of inconsolable grief, when he was searching for a reason to live, Mir Abdul Qasim discovered his religion. He read the Holy Quran from cover to cover for the first time, and a miracle happened. He found solace.

Not in the hundreds of verses preaching love, tolerance, and compassion, but in the words, "We prescribe for disbelievers: Life for life, eye for eye, nose for nose, ear for ear, tooth for tooth, and for wounds, retaliation."

He found justification for his vitriolic hatred of Hindus in the descriptions of idolaters— *al-mishrikun*—as "unclean," "evil-doers," and "people of hell-fire," who "abide in the fire of hell".

Best of all, he discovered his life's purpose in the *ayat as-sayf*, or 'Sword Verse', which enjoined the faithful to "Slay the idolaters wherever you find them, and take them captive. Besiege them, and prepare for them every ambush."

Finding purpose was one thing. Achieving it was an entirely different kettle of fish. Jihadi websites offered no help, other than recruitment to the Kashmiri cause and meaningless phrases like "weaponize your hatred", "channel your rage into jihad", and "quench your thirst for vengeance with the blood of infidels".

One night, he dreamed of the Prophet riding into battle against the infidels with his sword—*talwar*—upraised, and his destiny was revealed to him.

Thus was born his brainchild, Talwar-e-Rasool. The Sword of the Prophet. His instrument to "besiege, ambush, take captive, and slay" the Hindu al-mishrikun.

He nurtured it like a loving father, watching it go from success to amazing success, before handing it over to a former commando in the Indian Army, Major Mohammed Abbas. He, like Qasim, was an embittered secular idealist who found his faith after his career was blighted by false accusations of pro-Pakistani treachery.

Abbas took over day-to-day management of Talwar-e-Rasool, leaving Qasim to dream of greater things.

Like dreams of global victory for Islamic Jihad.

He had been working to make that dream a reality for the past five years, culminating in the snatch-and-kill. Saluja's six-million-dollar ransom would ensure that the Sword Verse—his destiny!—became the destiny of the world.

Just one intermediary step remained before it came to pass. That was Saluja's initial good-faith payment, which would cement the breaking of his will.

Abbas should be calling soon to confirm it had been received.

Chapter 2

Mohammed Abbas, CEO of Talwar-e-Rasool, and former Major in the Indian Army's elite Black Cat Commando Squadron, was in his study. He was logged into his Bank of Qumraan account on his laptop, counting down the seconds to 1:30AM—midnight Gulf time—when the bank would update his account.

He hit 'Refresh' at precisely 1:30AM and gave a whoop of delight. His account balance had magically increased by $142,687 dollars, the equivalent of Saluja's ten million rupee 'good faith payment'. He had no doubt that Saluja's six-million-dollar ransom would appear just as magically at 2PM tomorrow.

He could finally relax after two harrowing weeks averting one crisis after another. Arranging Ramesh Batra's "suicide" before he could tell his story. Organizing Suresh Batra's execution before he uncovered that twelve-year-old adoption—their one Achilles heel. And pulling off the Saluja snatch-and-kill.

With the grace of Allah, each crisis had been defused. Both Batras were dead. The girl was in the hands of his *talwaris*, meaning swordsmen, which was what members of Talwar-e-Rasool called themselves. And six million dollars was pretty much in the bag. It all added up to a coup that would relegate the fall of the Twin Towers to a minor footnote in the history of jihad.

The seeds of the coup were sown five years earlier, when Saluja's opened his office in the building where MAQ Associates was head-quartered. After a few elevator encounters, Saluja hired MAQ Associates as Saltech's auditors. It was how Qasim discovered Saluja was a multi-billionaire with two kids. The ideal target for a ransom.

The problem was that kidnapping one of his kids was almost impossible. Saluja's security was the best money could buy, so breaching it would take a miracle. Or a Trojan horse!

They got both—a two-for one, with the grace of Allah. Saluja's household manager turned out to be Abbas's former platoon sergeant in the Black Cat Commando Squadron. He, like Abbas, was a survivor of the same jihadi trap that destroyed Abbas's career. Unlike Abbas, he accepted reassignment as a quartermaster in the supply corps until he retired and was hired by Saluja to run his household. A deep grievance over how life treated him left him with no compunction about being their mole-cum-Trojan horse in Saluja's setup. For the most reliable reason of all: Money.

With his Trojan horse in place to disarm security and neutralize the guards, Abbas made plans to lead a team of trained assassins to kidnap Saluja's daughter from her home. A week before launch, however, he got word of the Saluja family spat and aborted the mission. Snatching her in the wilds of Uttarakhand would be a piece of cake compared to assaulting a heavily fortified home.

It couldn't have turned out better!

Saluja's daughter was in the hands of his talwaris, Saluja's will was broken, and six-million dollars were virtually in the bank. Saluja would never see his kids alive, of course. His son was dead, and his daughter would die, too. "From being fucked to death" was how Rizwan put it! Which was no more than she deserved. As Qasim said, "She is al-mishrikun. Shaitan's whore! Her womb is the Devil's breeding ground."

Abbas shut down his laptop, and went to switch off the TV in the living room before calling Qasim. As he reached for the remote, the words "rafting accident in Uttarakhand" exploded in his ears like a thunderclap. He read the caption on the screen, "Uttarakhand Rafting Accident Claims Four Lives" and sank down on the sofa, muscles slack from shock. The camera panned across *two* rafts, and *four* bodies on the riverbank as the voice-over described the victims as "three youths and their guide. Pending autopsy, preliminary indications are that all four died of blunt-force trauma, not drowning".

Abbas struggled to absorb the enormity of the disaster. The photos his talwaris sent showed that the brother and boyfriend were dead, and the girl was helpless. So how could his talwaris bungle it so badly, getting swept away pushing a raft with two dead bodies into the river?

He had no answer, so he switched to damage control.

The brother and boyfriend, and Shahid were the "three youths", and Ehsan was "their guide". Where were the girl and Firoze?

To find out, he had to break his own cardinal rule forbidding communications up the chain of command during an active operation. But he had no choice.

He used an untraceable burn phone to call Firoze's satellite phone, but it was off grid. It wasn't surprising. Satellite service was very unreliable in the remote hinterlands of Uttarakhand. Next, he tried raising Rizwan, who Firoze must have informed of his ETA, but his satellite phone was off grid, too.

He checked the weather in Uttarakhand. It was clear, which made it even more puzzling. He vaguely recalled reading somewhere that 'sunspot activity' could disrupt satellite service. Could it happen at night? He didn't know. But what else could it be? It was laughable to think something had happened to Rizwan in a hut in the middle of nowhere, without a human within thirty miles.

Abbas turned the TV off and dialed Qasim. Instead of the happy news of the good-faith payment, he had to tell him about the rafting disaster. Qasim would panic if he heard it tomorrow on the news.

The TV was off, so Abbas never saw the item with the caption "Update on TeROR Bus Bombing in Uttarakhand." It showed the broken eucalyptus stand in the background with the voice-over saying that the body of an unidentified male had been found there in an advanced state of putrefaction. It had been mutilated beyond hope of recognition by scavenging jackals.

Chapter 3

It was nearing 4AM when Jason ended his narrative.

Ravi sat through it without saying a word. Then he said softly, "If I didn't know Malini was asleep in the guest bedroom and a vintage Jeep was in my garage, I'd say you were delusional!"

Jason smiled. "If I hadn't lived it, I'd think I was delusional too."

Ravi's expression remained grim. "Terror isn't a delusion—!

"Did you just say, 'terror isn't a delusion'? Sounds nonsensical!"

Ravi smiled. "Sorry about that." He scribbled 'TeROR' on his note pad. "Stands for 'Talwar-e-Rasool 'Organization'."

"Very apt. It explains something I overheard. Not important."

Ravi continued, "Okay. The bus bombing fits their modus. And their purpose is urban terror. More correctly *purposeless terror for terror's sake*. So, claiming that the purpose of this attack is to warn foreigners to stay away is out of character."

"I told you it's a red herring. I overheard them say they were using my assumed death to deflect attention from the journalist. That aligns with what Batra said when he died."

"But it makes no sense. Why use a bomb to blowup fifty people just to kill *one* journalist, and why cover it up? Gruesome one-on-one killings are their forte, and they revel in it when they silence moderate Muslim voices. Why be so coy now?"

"His laptop and DVDs might tell us why."

Ravi seemed dubious. "I'm not so sure, but if there is any evidence that Batra was the target my team will find it."

He leaned forward and separated the DVDs, Batra's laptop, and his mobile phone from the other items in Jason's collection.

"Aren't you interested in the stuff from the kidnapping, rape, and murder?" Jason asked.

"Sorry, Jason, but those crimes come under the CBI's jurisdiction, not mine."

Jason's eyes fell on the guide's camera and he felt something niggle at his memory. He picked it up and started scrolling back through the stored images. The three most recent were of a naked Malini at gunpoint and the bodies of Chetan and Bobby. Before those were several pictures of the rafting party. Then came the stunner. A picture of the burnt-out shell of the bus.

He showed it to Ravi without saying a word.

Ravi stared at it, shocked into silence. When he found his voice, he stammered, "But...but...this is the kidnappers' camera."

"Yes, it is."

"But that can't be! Unless..."

Jason completed Ravi's sentence. "...Unless the bus bombers were also the kidnappers." He took a deep breath. "I think I've known it all along. Just before the stone turned the guide's face into unrecognizable pulp, I had this weird feeling I'd seen him. I couldn't pin it down until I saw that image. He was the one taking pictures of the bus bombing."

"If TeROR is behind the kidnap-rape-murder that makes it my responsibility. Their security has been impregnable until now, but we've got our first break, thanks to you. We have the names of two verified talwaris, plus a satellite phone used to pass information up the chain. With those, we can locate and identify people upstream and downstream of these guys."

"Don't forget the laptop and DVDs," Jason replied. "If TeROR killed fifty people to hide the murder of one journalist, he must have found something that threatens their survival."

Ravi smiled. "And we both know the best person to find it."

Chapter 4

The phone rang, yanking Mohan Sinha out of a deep sleep.

Dumb-assed idiot, calling me at 4AM! You think I'm a doctor or something?

He mumbled, "Wrong number" into the phone and was about to slam it back down, when he heard Ravi say, "Mohan?" He shot up, as if doused with ice-water, saying "Sorry, Ravi!"

He listened for several seconds, then said, "I'll be there in half-an-hour." Ten minutes later, he was tiptoeing past his sister's bedroom, laptop in hand, when he was startled to see Seetha emerge, fully dressed.

"Where do you think you're going?" he asked, belligerently.

"I'm coming with you to meet Jason," she replied, unfazed.

"You...you...eavesdropper!" he spluttered.

She rolled her eyes. "Really, Mohan? Is 'eavesdropper' your best comeback? Try again."

Mohan feigned a scowl. "I'll tell Ravi you overheard classified information."

"Do that. If he gets mad, I'll come home."

He gave up. "No chance of that. I know when I'm licked. You've got him wrapped around your little finger. Jason and Alexis, too."

It was true. Seetha could do nothing wrong in their eyes. Or his own, actually. They had all witnessed her incredible courage in the face of unimaginable evil.

As they drove to Ravi's house, he saw the pink fingers of dawn creeping across the horizon, and he remembered a previous dawn, when he and Seetha faced a horrifying death at the hands of that madman, Kalidas. A shiver went through him.

He felt Seetha's hand on his shoulder. "You're remembering Kalidas, right?" she asked.

He nodded without speaking.

She smiled. "Think, instead, of our life before Kalidas, fighting for survival in a Kolkata slum, without hope, let alone a future, and you'll feel better."

"Why would remembering *that* make me feel better?" he asked with surprise. "Our life before Kalidas was terrible. And what does it have to do with that terrible dawn?"

"Everything! That terrible dawn was the dawn of a new life for us. We are now richer than we ever were, and I don't mean the reward. All the riches in the world couldn't buy the gift that dawn gave us: a family. Alexis, Jason, Jonathan, and Ravi are our family. All because of that terrible dawn. Remember the saying, whatever happens, happens for the best?"

Mohan nodded, amazed by Seetha's wisdom. She might be four years younger than him, but she was wise beyond her years.

That saying was the moral of an Indian parable about an old farmer facing ruin because his only son broke his leg at harvest time. When his fellow villagers commiserated with him, he replied, "Whatever happens, happens for the best." They ridiculed him for thinking that a broken leg and lost harvest could ever be "for the best". But he had the last laugh when the king conscripted all able-bodied young men to fight in a war. His son was the only one spared!

Seetha was spot on. Calamitous events could indeed have unexpectedly wonderful consequences. The bonds of trust and friendship forged in Kalidas's crucible of evil proved it. That 'terrible dawn' had given them the most priceless gift of all. A family.

That dawn had also made their lives better in more material ways. The reward money enabled them to put their past in Kolkata behind them. They moved to Delhi where, for the first time in his life, Mohan had no need to work and absolutely nothing to worry about.

Seetha, by contrast, was determined to work even harder than before. It wasn't enough for her to take prep courses for the entrance examination to the All India Institute of Medical Sciences, the most prestigious medical school in India. She also enrolled in pressure-free liberal arts courses at an elite women's college in Delhi. Why? "For fun," she said.

She, of course, aced the entrance exam and would be starting medical studies at AIIMS in a few weeks. Mohan's only regret was that she turned down full scholarships from Harvard and Yale, because the Americans refused Mohan an entry visa, despite the best efforts of Alexis's father, Jonathan.

Who could blame them for that, though? He was an uneducated porter—a *coolie*—with no marketable skills, other than an incredible aptitude for thievery. And that wasn't something you put on a resume, let alone a visa application, no matter how exceptional it was.

His mastery of pickpocketing was developed in the days when he and Seetha were penniless orphans, fighting to survive against unimaginable odds in a Kolkata slum. Over time, he became so skilled at it that he could pick any pocket without his mark realizing it, no matter how alert or on guard. Jason Wolff was Exhibit One in his honor roll of victims!

His pilfering skills didn't end with sleight-of-hand thievery, though. He was just as adept at electronic thievery, which was just a fancy term for hacking. He learned the basics from a gang of identity thieves operating in the slum, but he had long since left them far behind. His expertise was now such that there wasn't a program he couldn't hack, a firewall he couldn't breach, or a security barrier he couldn't break. The two skills differed in one crucial regard, though. He had never used hacking to steal anything.

He kept both skills hidden from Seetha while they were living in Kolkata, fearing she'd disown him if she knew he was a thief. No longer, though. His pickpocketing skills helped save them from Kalidas, and his expertise as a hacker got him a job in Ravi's setup.

His official title was 'Programming Officer'. But the office staff's affectionate nickname for him was a far better descriptor. They called him Chief Cyber '*Chor*'. It meant 'thief'.

To think that Ravi Iyer, the head of all counter-terror intel in India, would call *him*, an uneducated former coolie and thief, to solve a tech problem at 4AM, instead of his high-powered IT team!

All because of *that* dawn.

Chapter 5

While they waited for Mohan to arrive, Jason went over everything again, from start to finish, at Ravi's request. The only missing detail was the name of Malini's father.

That was the priority when she woke up. The other was to arrange an appointment with a gynecologist for the 'morning after' pill. Alexis could handle that after she arrived.

Jason heard a car pull up outside and went with Ravi to the front door to greet Seetha and Mohan. He was about to wave to them when he heard Malini scream.

He whirled around and ran to her bedroom, where he found her sitting up in bed, shaking as if from a seizure, stark terror in her face and tears streaming from her eyes. All he could do was take her in his arms and croon to her like he did in the clearing, telling her he was there and nobody would hurt her.

Slowly, her sobs subsided. The shaking and shivering didn't.

Jason knew Malini was having a full-blown panic attack, and it didn't take great psychological insight to know she had PTSD—Post-

Traumatic Stress Disorder. But he had no clue what to do, other than hold her. And he couldn't do that forever.

Ravi appeared with Mohan and Seetha in the doorway and asked, "What's wrong?"

Malini saw them and screamed "Seetha!" just as Seetha cried out, "Malini!"

Malini squirmed out of Jason's embrace and held her arms out to Seetha, crying and laughing at the same time. Jason gratefully yielded to Seetha. She embraced Malini and gave a quick head tilt towards the door.

Jason got the message and left with Ravi and Mohan. He closed the door and grabbed Mohan by the shoulders, asking, "Mohan! How in hell does Seetha know Malini?"

Mohan stuttered, "She is…uh…was…Seetha's classmate at Lady Shri Ram College. Her name is Malini Saluja. Why is she here?"

Jason was incredulous. "Saluja? Is her father Raman Saluja?"

"Yes. But why is she here?" Mohan asked again.

Jason couldn't believe his ears. Taking a deep breath to gather his scattered wits, he gave Mohan a bare-bones rundown of what had happened, reserving the full story for when Seetha, Jonathan, and Alexis were there to hear it.

He ended by saying, "The unbelievable thing is that I know her father. We negotiated a deal between his company and Lone Wolf, which Jonathan will close today."

Mohan cried out, "That's crazy! That must be pre-destined. Karma."

Jason said forcefully, "That's coincidence, Mohan, not karma. Karma is the metaphysical equivalent of Newton's third law of motion. 'Action begets reaction'. I'm the only survivor among the fifty passengers on the bus when TeROR blows it up, because I pick a banyan tree to do my business. *My* karma. TeROR blows up the bus to destroy that laptop, forcing me to trek through Uttarakhand to escape, so I'm there to foil their plan to kidnap Malini. That's *TeROR's* karma. Malini fights back, giving me a chance to save her. *Her* karma."

He paused before continuing. "Bottom line? Actions have consequences. TeROR has sown the seeds of its own destruction." Jason pointed to the laptop. "You find those seeds, we destroy TeROR."

Mohan sat down with the laptop. "No problem, Jason."

"You surprise me, Jason," Ravi said. "If there's a better description of karma, I haven't heard it."

Jason shrugged. "Just my personal view. Didn't mean to pontificate."

"You didn't. Speaking of actions and consequences," Ravi said, "TeROR doesn't know Malini's escaped, so they'll still be keeping tabs on Saluja, to make sure he pays the ransom. Someone has to tell Saluja that Malini is safe. Can't be you or me. If either of us calls or shows up unannounced, whoever's watching will know something's up and disappear."

Jason thought for a moment. "Jonathan! He's scheduled to meet Saluja later today, so it won't raise a red flag if he shows up."

"Great idea! Can you let Jonathan know he's been volunteered? Mohan and I have to work on the stuff you brought."

"Sure."

Chapter 6

S aluja was slumped over his desk with his head buried in his forearms when the intercom buzzed. He looked up, bleary-eyed, and was shocked to see it was 8:30AM. Sometime during his night of endless torment, he had fallen asleep, overtaken by utter exhaustion.

He spoke into the intercom. "I'm not to be disturbed."

"I'm sorry, Sir,' his secretary replied. "Mr. Jonathan Wolff is here. He says something's come up that can't wait until later. What should I tell him?"

Saluja cursed under his breath. His reflection in the window was unshaven, disheveled, and haggard. Wolff couldn't see him looking like that!

"Please ask Mr. Wolff to give me fifteen minutes," he said and disconnected. After a quick shave and shower, and a change of clothes, he looked more presentable, although his puffy, bloodshot eyes were a dead giveaway that something was horribly wrong. He was in no condition to engage in meaningful negotiation. He needed an excuse to delay until Malini was free. A migraine, perhaps?

He welcomed Jonathan Wolff into his office, only for Wolff to do something very curious when the door closed. He lifted a finger to his lips, pointed to the intercom, then made a cutting motion across his neck.

Saluja was shocked. In India, it was traditional—and legal—to leave the intercom open to record business conversations. Before he could protest, though, Wolff reached over and switched off the intercom.

Saluja was enraged. "Who the hell—"

"I have news of Malini," Wolff interrupted gently.

Saluja was struck speechless. Then he lunged for Wolff's throat.

He never got there.

Wolff grabbed Saluja's wrists with such immense strength that Saluja could only twist impotently. Wolff remained calm. "Malini is safe. She is safe. Do you hear me?"

Saluja fell to his knees, tears welling up in his eyes, and all he could say was, "Malini is safe! Malini is safe! Malini is safe!"

A moment later, his suspicion resurfaced, and he asked furiously, "How do you know she's safe? Are you behind her kidnapping?"

Wolff smiled. "I should've anticipated those questions. I didn't and that's on me. But let me set your mind at rest. I had nothing to do with Malini's kidnapping. I know she is safe because my son, Jason, rescued her and took her to the house of a friend."

Saluja stared at him for a second, goggle-eyed from shock. Then he gasped. "And I thought…How can you ever forgive me?"

"There's nothing to forgive. Your suspicion was justified."

"I will not insult the debt I owe you by saying 'Thank you'. And I have nothing to offer in return, except unconditional friendship, if you will have it."

"There is no greater honor than a hand offered in unconditional friendship." Wolff thrust his hand out towards him. "If you will accept mine in the same spirit, the debt is repaid."

Saluja got up and grabbed Wolff's hand in both of his. "If that is all you want, then you have it, forever. That is my word and my bond, Mr. Wolff—"

Wolff interrupted, "I'm Jonathan to my friends."

"And I'm Raman to mine. You and Jason have my undying gratitude. But where is Malini? Can you take me to her now?"

"I know you are dying to see her, and you will. But first, I need to know about any ransom demand you've received. I hope you haven't paid it?"

"Yes and no. The ransom is in two parts. An initial 'good-faith payment' of a million rupees, equivalent to about $140,000, to keep Malini alive, followed by a six-million-dollar ransom to get her back alive. I paid the first right after they called. I also initiated the transfer of six million dollars from my Swiss bank account to a numbered bank account. I'm supposed to call the bank with live password authentication when it opens in Zurich at 1:30PM ..." He checked his watch. "...In just over four hours."

"Did you initiate it last *night*? When did they contact you?"

"I got a photo of Malini held at gunpoint around 4:30PM, with a text message saying she'd die if I called the police. The call with ransom instructions came around 7:30PM."

Jonathan laughed. "Just as Jason figured. They don't know she escaped!"

"I can't wait to see her."

"You will, Raman, but we have to be careful. You may be under surveillance."

Saluja "They said they were watching me."

"So, they could follow you and find Malini."

It made sense to Saluja. "All right. I'm going to trust your judgment. What should I do?"

"Everyone, including your secretary, must think my visit was for business. So, when we open the door, we fake a heated discussion. You fake like you're pleading with me to postpone our discussions, and I fake like I'm furious because you won't tell my why."

"I never thought you could 'fake it' in business."

"If both parties agree to fake it, it becomes real. Like two minuses make a plus."

Saluja felt his spirits rise. "I'll fake anything to keep my kids safe. Which reminds me. You didn't mention Chetan. Is he with Malini?"

He saw Jonathan's face melt with sorrow. "Raman, I am truly sorry, but Chetan died defending his sister. Her boyfriend, too."

Saluja staggered as if he was struck. Then grief welled up, threatening to tear him apart. He somehow held it together. "We must inform the police!" he said hoarsely.

Jonathan's reply was sharp. "No! Jason thinks the police may be in on this. But we know someone in India's counter-terror set-up with resources vastly superior to the police. Jason and I would trust him with our lives. Malini's life too. She's in his house, right now."

Saluja was persuaded. "That's good enough for me. But I want to see Malini. When can I see her?"

95

"Very soon, Raman. After I leave, lock yourself in your office, with instructions not to be disturbed. In an hour, drive to Humayun's Tomb, buy a ticket for admission, and enter the grounds. There'll be no one around this early in the morning, so it'll be easy for Jason to spot a tail. If no one's tailing you, he'll make contact. If someone is, he'll figure out what to do. Okay?"

Saluja nodded. "My gut tells me it's right to wait. My heart? Not so much."

"Tell your heart to wait an hour. Then it can go ballistic."

Malini's miraculous escape was something to celebrate. It was also his only defense against a corrosive sorrow that was all too familiar. But this wasn't the time to mourn for Chetan. His top priority was Malini. And then to find the bastards who killed Chetan.

I'm still young, he thought sadly, as he escorted Wolff out. *I've got plenty of time to grieve. And plenty of practice, too.*

Chapter 7

Qasim was in his office, still trying to grasp the enormity of the disaster that had befallen them .

Last night, when Abbas called with the news that Ehsan and Shahid were both dead, there was at least some hope that Firoze must be on his way to the hut with the girl. That hope was now dead—Abbas had just called to say that Rizwan and Firoze must also be dead.

It made no sense. Both men had called to confirm that everything was going to plan, Firoze from a beach in the middle of nowhere, and Rizwan from a hut miles from civilization that no one knew even existed. Since then, nothing. Their silence was no longer deafening. It was the silence of death.

There was one silver lining in that very dark cloud, though. Saluja's daughter must also be dead, otherwise Saluja wouldn't have made the good-faith payment, or initiated the transfer of the ransom last night. It was something to hold on to.

The phone rang again, startling him out of his miserable reverie. It was Saluja's secretary.

"Good morning, Sir," she said. "Do you have a moment to talk to Mr. Saluja? It's about postponing the Lone Wolf meeting today."

Qasim's misery evaporated in a blaze of exultation! Saluja was jeopardizing the biggest deal of his life in a desperate attempt to save his daughter. "Please put him through."

"Thank you, Sir! Please hold."

He heard a couple of clicks, then Saluja came on the line. Qasim got his first shock when he heard Saluja's voice. It was strong and vibrant, not quavering like a man on the verge of collapse.

"Mr. Qasim," Saluja said, "I'm forced to postpone today's meeting with Jonathan Wolff. He is obviously upset, but I have no choice. Something personal has come up that needs my urgent attention. And tonight's dinner is also canceled. I hope you understand."

The man sounded decisive and confident. How could this be? With his senses reeling, Qasim somehow managed to say, "No problem, Mr. Saluja. I hope the postponement isn't health-related?"

"Oh, no!" Saluja replied. "I have been dealing with a terrible migraine. The consequence, I'm afraid, of going over the top last night, celebrating the blockbuster deal I'm going to sign today. What can I say? It was as premature as it was immature."

Shock piled on shock! The man was being flippant, even though his daughter faced death or worse. Qasim forced himself to sound concerned, saying, "I am relieved to hear that." Then, with a dreadful suspicion taking shape in his mind, he added, "I hope your kids are well and are enjoying their trip?"

It was a desperate attempt to bait Saluja into revealing what was going on. And it worked. Saluja's conspiratorial whisper exploded in Qasim's ears like a grenade.

"Malini is back and I am on my way to see her. Don't tell anyone, my friend, because it's a secret. I can't say more right now, but I promise to explain later. Okay?"

With his world collapsing around him, Qasim gathered his reeling senses just in time to say, "Of course! Friends are supposed to understand such things! Let me not keep you from your daughter."

He hung up without waiting for a reply and fell back in his chair as darkness closed in.

Chapter 8

Alexis was in Ravi's study, alone for the first time since her arrival.

Seetha was upstairs, watching over Malini while she slept, Jonathan and Jason had gone to pick up Malini's father, and Mohan and Ravi were at the office, working on extracting information from the devices Jason brought back from the two atrocities he witnessed.

His descriptions of those encounters was as bare bones as it could get, but she could fill in almost every meaningful detail from her first-hand knowledge of his extraordinary combat skills and unique ability to improvise. And it left her stunned.

To foil Malini's kidnapping and kill her rapists was impressive enough. However, to have the prescience to override his instinctive reach for the Bowie, so the rapists' deaths were consistent with a rafting accident, was mind-boggling. It spoke of a level of *sakki*—the ability to foresee how combat would unfold—that was the exclusive provenance of the ultimate combat master.

All that after surviving the bus bombing with a concussion, hiding Batra's body, saving the laptop and DVDs from being found, and picking the perfect route to escape from the site undetected.

Thanks to him, they had two keys to unlocking what Ravi called "the enigma of TeROR". The laptop, which Mohan was working on unlocking, and the DVDs, which she was tasked with figuring out.

When she asked, "Why me?" Jason's cryptic reply was "No one else knows how to make sense of them". So, something medically related, she figured.

She inserted the DVD labeled #1 into Ravi's desktop computer. A few seconds later, the words "Asad al-Qumraan Medical Center, Radiology Department" appeared on the screen, and she got goosebumps. What were the odds that she'd be viewing a DVD from Qumraan, a place she barely knew about until two days ago and would be visiting in a week?

It was an abdominal CT scan of a seventeen-year-old Qumraani male named Mohammed Wasim with a ruptured spleen and left kidney. As she scrolled through the images, she became increasingly perplexed. Except for the fact that Wasim was missing half his liver and his right kidney, it was no different from a CT from any of the hundreds of traffic accident victims across America on any given day. Why would an Indian jihadi group want to destroy *that*?

She was even more mystified when she viewed the second DVD. It was a CT brain scan of Mohammed Wasim showing a devastating head injury that was entirely consistent with a bad traffic accident. Although tragic, such injuries were an everyday occurrence—certainly not a reason to massacre fifty people just to destroy the evidence!

By the time Alexis started on the third DVD, she was convinced that the DVDs couldn't be the reason TeROR wanted to kill Batra. It was, if anything, even more innocuous; a textbook-worthy abdominal CT of a six-year-old boy, Ganga Prasad, illustrating a child's normal internal anatomy. Still, the juxtaposition of a child's normal scan with Wasim's brutal injuries was unsettling enough to pique her interest.

It wasn't until she began scrolling through the fourth DVD that she got her first inkling of the terrible secret hidden in the disks. As the secret revealed itself, her mind revolted violently, refusing to accept the incomprehensible. And it triggered such a maelstrom of horror, rage, revulsion, and sorrow that she had to walk away from the computer before it overwhelmed her.

It took several minutes for her to clamp a lid on her emotions and bring herself to view the last of the five DVDs. When she was done and finally sat back, there was no escaping the truth, as unfathomable as it was.

The scans of Mohammed Wasim from ten days ago, and the two on Ganga Prasad performed twelve years ago, bore witness to an evil that beggared belief. Between those two sets of dates was something so monstrous that she felt violated, as if her soul was tainted by the corruption she just touched..

For starters, Ganga Prasad's scans were taken four days apart, *before and after one kidney and half his liver were removed!*

Second, Ganga Prasad and Mohammed Wasim *had the same date of birth!*

Third, Mohammed Wasim's brain MRI showed that he was the victim of devastating blunt-force trauma. There was a large, depressed fracture of the skull, with a huge clot pressing on his brain, which was swollen, contused, and bleeding. Even with emergency surgery to remove the clot and repair his ruptured spleen and kidney, *survival was highly unlikely. Without surgery, death was guaranteed.*

The savagery of the assault that likely killed him paled in comparison with the fourth fact. *Half his liver and his right kidney were missing!*

The boy, Ganga Prasad, *was* the youth, Mohammed Wasim.

Forget the identical dates of birth. The identical number of metal clips in the two scans ('hardware,' in radiologists' jargon) and their placement relative to bony landmarks were as distinctive as fingerprints. And just as damning.

Ganga Prasad/Mohammed Wasim had half his liver and his right kidney harvested *as a little boy of six!*

Finally, the fifth DVD, an abdominal CT performed the day after Ganga Prasad's second CT, proved that *his organs were transplanted into a ten-year old male* identified only as "al-Qumraan", meaning he must be a Qumraani royal.

Her heart broke, and she couldn't hold back her tears. Tears of grief, for a childhood lost. Tears of pain, for a child denied love. Tears of anger, for the brutal act of medical rape—!

She gasped, as if punched in the gut.

She had no idea how or why the term, 'medical rape' came to her, but it evoked an explosion of volcanic rage directed at the modern-day Mengele who betrayed the most basic tenets of humanity to harvest a child's organs. He deprived Ganga Prasad, the child, of meaningful life, just as surely as the brutal murderer who beat the life out of the seventeen-year-old empty shell that was left.

Her upcoming visit to Qumraan with Jonathan was no longer a lark. It was now a mission of vengeance.

She had no idea how she would find the perpetrators of those crimes. Or get justice for Ganga Prasad.

All she had were questions without answers.

Who was the surgeon?

Who was the recipient?

Who was Ganga Prasad?

How did he get to Qumraan?

Who made the disks and why?

How did Batra get the disks?

What was he doing in Uttarakhand?

Why was Talwar-e-Rasool so hell-bent on destroying evidence of crimes committed in Qumraan?

Chapter 9

J ason arrived with Jonathan and Saluja minutes after Ravi and Mohan returned to the house.

In the giddy euphoria of Saluja's reunion with Malini, even the news that Mohan had unlocked Batra's computer seemed unimportant. Alexis couldn't imagine corrupting the joy of that moment with the obscene secret in the DVDs. Not that her reluctance made a difference in the end.

Mohan's shriek of "Oh! My God!" took care of that. He must have slipped away unnoticed in the hubbub, unable to resist the lure of Batra's laptop, to see what there was to find. Ashen faced and his voice quavering with emotion, he started reading from the screen.

My dear brother Suresh,

Please forgive me if I sound like I'm not making sense. I'm really upset, but you will understand why as you read on.

The five enclosed DVDs are the present I told you I was sending. But the story behind them is equally important. Put them together and solve the riddle, and you'll be in line for a Pulitzer!

Without the DVDs, no one will ever believe the story. Why? Because the evil hidden in them is truly beyond belief! No one knows we have them, but if the people behind that evil discover we have them, they will stop at nothing, not even murder, to keep it hidden. That's why I couldn't tell you over the phone. So, tell no one and trust no one.

I will be coming to Delhi this weekend to discuss this with you. As a journalist, you will know the best way to go forward.

Let me tell you what I know. It is so vile that I feel like vomiting as I write it.

The story goes back twelve years, but it began for me with the last case I saw before I left Qumraan. So that's where I'll start.

My last night in Qumraan was a Friday, and I was on call. The reason isn't important, but I was hoping for a quiet night. It wasn't to be.

I was called at 1 AM to perform a brain scan on a young palace servant named Mohammed Wasim who was critically ill and in shock, with a large soggy swelling over his left temple. The clinical justification for a scan said, "Stuporous, muttering incoherently".

He also had bruising over his flanks suggesting he was bleeding into his abdomen—something the Casualty doctor missed—so I decided to also do a CT of his abdomen.

I must add that, as horrible as the injuries sound, we do see them from time to time. Under Qumraani law, desertion from duty is punishable with one hundred lashes of the whip. Few survive it, so it might as well be a death sentence. And the servant's master is always right in what passes for Qumraani justice. That's just the way it is!

So, the situation was 'routine', even though it sounds callous to say it. Still, there were things about the youth that weren't 'routine'.

First, his work permit showed he had been a palace servant for twelve years, meaning that he started work at age five! I had never heard of any palace servants that young, so that was very suspicious. How could anyone 'consent' to work at such a young age?

Second, he looked like a fellow countryman—someone from the subcontinent, not the Middle East. What twist of fate had brought him so far from his homeland at such a young age, only to die so young? And who brought him?

Third, he was very malnourished, compared to most palace servants, who are generally well-fed. Why was this boy starved?

Fourth, the injuries were consistent with blunt force trauma from something like a club. Why was he beaten so brutally, instead of being given a lashing?

These questions worried me even before I examined him, so I did much more than my usual 'radiologist's quick look' exam. And the questions just kept piling up.

I found scars on his abdomen and flank, indicating he underwent major abdominal surgery years earlier. Why?

I shone a light in his eyes and looked inside for signs of swelling in his brain—another thing the Casualty physician neglected to do. For some strange reason I felt compelled to do what we call a retinal exam even though I hadn't used an ophthalmoscope in years. So, I bent down to look inside his eyes, knowing I was fooling myself to think I would see anything.

I was right. I saw nothing—not that I would've known what it meant, even if did see something! But it wasn't what I did or didn't see, it was what I heard.

My ear was almost at his cheek, so I heard him mumbling. And he was anything but incoherent! He was repeating one clear sentence in Hindi again and again, almost like a mantra. "I am Ganga Prasad from Gandhi Orphanage, Bareilly."

Can you imagine my shock? It meant that Mohammed Wasim was really an orphan brought to Qumraan from India and converted to Islam when he was five! I thought it couldn't get any more horrifying than that. I was wrong.

The technician wheeled the patient into the scanner and got busy performing the scans, so I was alone in the viewing booth when the images appeared.

I will show you the images when I come this weekend. Then you will understand why the DVDs are so important. They prove that Wasim's right kidney and half his liver were removed when he was a child. On top of that, his remaining kidney and his spleen were ruptured and bleeding, and he had a life-threatening head injury, with a large clot pressing on his brain.

I immediately alerted the Chief Surgeon that the boy needed emergency surgery to evacuate the clot in his head, remove his spleen, and save his one remaining kidney. He disagreed, saying Wasim's injuries were beyond salvage, but he'd rethink his decision if Wasim made it through the night. I'm not a surgeon, so I have no idea whether surgery could have saved him. I only know that, without surgery, he was sure to die. The delay signed his death warrant.

I have no idea who beat him to death, but I can prove something just as terrible—maybe even worse! The five DVDs I am sending you show that Ganga Prasad was brought to Qumraan for the specific purpose of harvesting his organs for transplantation.

Two of them are the scans I performed on Wasim. Two others are the ones performed on Ganga Prasad before and after he had one kidney and half his liver removed at age six. The matching birthdates and hardware prove Ganga Prasad was Mohammed Wasim.

Lastly, I conducted a blind search of the radiology data for a postoperative CT scan in a recipient of a liver or kidney transplant on the same date as the boy's surgery, and I hit the jackpot. I copied that scan as well. It is the final piece in the puzzle.

I could not access the clinical chart of either the donor or the recipient, because they were tagged as "High Security, Restricted Access Only", which I do not have as a radiologist. But I did find something very interesting in the radiology data base.

Every requisition for a scan or x-ray must have clinical justification. The reason for requesting the recipient's post-operative scan was, "Unexplained postoperative fever. Organ rejection unlikely. Donor a perfect HLA match"!

A perfect match!

Do you know how impossible it would be to get a perfect match between a recipient in Qumraan and a random child from an orphanage in India?

No way it was random! They must have searched among hundreds, maybe thousands of children in orphanages before finding a perfect match at Gandhi Orphanage in Bareilly. One place to start is the lab that performed HLA typing. Fifteen years ago, there were no more than 3 or 4 labs in India that could handle the thousands of tests needed for that! Find the lab and track down who hired them.

A second is the Gandhi Orphanage in Bareilly. Was he adopted or abducted? If he was adopted, his adoption papers will reveal who was responsible for taking him to Qumraan.

The third is the surgeon who perpetrated this despicable crime. It won't be easy to track him down without access to the charts, but it shows they had to keep it secret. For all I know, there could be many more 'Ganga Prasads'. There is scuttlebutt about the OR going into lockdown on some days, when everyone, except for a very small number of staff, gets the day off. And there is a secret wing in the hospital that very few can enter.

Forget looking for the answer in Qumraan. Your best bet is to track down whoever oversaw the transplant program at that time. He'll know who did the surgery.

With all three pieces of the puzzle, the picture will be complete. You will have full credibility when you break this terrible story to the world.

There is one trail, though, that I must warn you not to follow. It's the recipient. The last name, 'al-Qumraan,' indicates a Qumraani royal. They left out the first name to protect the recipient's identity, so it could be any of five hundred-plus royals. But such a crime could only be perpetrated for a "major" royal, not some peripheral member of the family.

That's why I'm being so cautious. There are rumors that the Qumraani royals have close links to jihadi groups in India. If they discover we are on their trail, they will order our execution. So, stay away from tracking down the recipient.

There is nothing left for me to say, except that this could put your name on the list of the greatest scoops in the history of Indian journalism.

I feel proud to be a part of this. I know you will make both of us proud.

Your loving brother,

Ramesh.

Chapter 10

S hock. Horror. Revulsion. Rage.

Alexis saw those writ large in every face after Mohan's voice trailed off into pin-drop silence—which was exactly how she felt earlier. And how she felt now, too.

The narrative detail in Ramesh Batra's letter provided the answers to many, but not all the questions raised by the scan images. She said as much, making no effort to hide the anger simmering inside her.

"The letter fills in the gaps left after I viewed the scan images in the DVDs. What I saw proved that a six-year-old boy named Ganga Prasad had his organs harvested for transplantation. I thought that was obscene enough. Dr. Batra's letter proves something even more heinous. That Ganga Prasad was an orphan who was abducted from India just to harvest his organs."

"The bastards!" Mohan spat out. "I don't care if I have to tear open every database to do it, but I'm going to find who kidnapped this boy and consigned him to such a horrific fate."

Ravi said softly, "I know something that ties all this together. Ramesh Batra, the letter writer, was found dead in Mumbai ten days ago. His wrists were slashed with a scalpel bearing only his prints, and a suicide note was found on his laptop."

"Oh my god!" Mohan cried out. "Someone deleted everything on this laptop exactly ten days ago. But the idiot didn't wipe it clean, so I was able to recover the files. The laptop belongs to Ramesh, not Suresh Batra. It has the suicide note he supposedly wrote the day he died and the letter I read out earlier. The man who wrote that letter wasn't suicidal. This was murder. TeROR was hired by the Qumraani royals to murder him and his brother to keep their 'kidnapping-organ harvesting' scheme quiet."

"You've hit it on the head, Mohan." Ravi said. "Only it wasn't for hire. It's far more diabolical. TeROR had to be in on the plot from the outset."

"How come?" Mohan asked.

"Look at the timeline. Ramesh, the doctor, dies on Wednesday, four days after returning from Qumraan. Suresh, his brother, flies back to Delhi on Sunday, finds the letter and DVD's waiting for him, and takes Monday's train to Bareilly. He visits the Gandhi Orphanage on Tuesday and dies four days later on Saturday."

"So?" Alexis asked with a frown.

"The Qumraanis couldn't have known Suresh was following Ganga Prasad's trail. How did they manage in just four days to select TeROR out of all the Indian jihadi outfits, negotiate and finalize a deal to eliminate him, and still leave enough time for TeROR to plan and pull off the bus bombing? All in just four days."

Jason added, "Impossible, unless TeROR was monitoring the orphanage. So, as Ravi said, TeROR had to be up to its neck in the plot."

112

Alexis was mystified. "Why on earth would TeROR monitor some random orphanage?"

"Because it wasn't random. They had installed an early warning system to alert them if someone came looking for the paper trail!"

"Exactly," Ravi added. "They had to kill Batra before he found that paper trail."

"Can you two please stop talking in riddles?" Alexis snapped. "What paper trail?"

"Adoption records!" Ravi and Jason said simultaneously.

Alexis was stunned, like everyone else.

Mohan was the first to find his voice. "The Uttar Pradesh state government database will have the adoption record, cross-referenced by name, location, and date. I will find it."

Ravi shook his head. "You won't find a twelve-year-old adoption in any electronic database. And requisitioning the paper records from the state government could take weeks. It's a lot quicker to get passport records. They'll have the name of his adoptive father, who must be connected in some way to someone at the top of TeROR's hierarchy. We find him, and we find the heart of TeROR."

Saluja spoke for the first time. "Amen to that."

Ravi looked at him. "Mr. Saluja—"

Saluja interrupted. "I'm Raman to everyone. Seetha and Mohan, too, age be damned!"

"Okay, Raman," Ravi said. "I expect you'll be going to Uttarakhand to claim your son's body, right?"

"Yes, but I'm worried that reporters will badger Malini, the lone survivor of the so-called accident, until she breaks, just to find out what happened. She will not survive their harassment."

113

Jason spoke very gently. "I get that you're worried, Raman. But there is a way to protect her. Stick to a simple script that keeps the spotlight off Malini. Say that she showed up with a bump on her head, suffering from amnesia. When you heard your son died in a rafting accident, you put two and two together. Your daughter remembers nothing, and your son is dead. She needs time to heal and you need time to mourn, so neither of you will be available to the press."

"My God, Jason!" Saluja cried out. "That's sheer genius. Especially the 'amnesia' part. It'll buy me time to get Malini to California, hopefully by the weekend."

Ravi chimed in, "Jason's script has another benefit. Talwar-e-Rasool will think no one knows they tried to kidnap Malini. If they try again, we'll have them!"

Alexis saw Saluja almost explode with anger. "Wait a minute! Are you suggesting we use Malini as bait, hoping they'll come after her again?"

Ravi looked uncomfortable. "Not bait, Raman. There's no way TeROR can trace her here. I was speaking hypothetically."

"It's not hypothetical," Saluja snapped back. "All those bastards have to do is connect three firangi dots. The firangi they think died in the bus bombing. The firangi spotted by toll booth attendants, heading for Delhi in the kidnappers' Jeep. And the firangi son of Jonathan Wolff who has been negotiating with me, the father of the girl they tried to kidnap. If you think they won't connect those dots, you're crazy."

"He's right, Ravi," Alexis agreed.

Saluja continued. "I won't take that chance. She'll be much safer at my estate home in Haryana, just outside Delhi. It sits in one hundred acres of private orchards and woods patrolled by guard dogs at night and enclosed by a wall topped by an electric fence. There is only one gate, manned twenty-four hours a day by armed guards, all ex-commandos."

Malini wailed, "I won't go there! I want to stay with Seetha!"

"I'll go with you, Malini," Seetha said.

"I'll come, too," Alexis added.

"It's decided then," Saluja said. "The three ladies will fly there today in my helicopter, while Jason, Ravi and Mohan work on finding these murderers, and Jonathan and I finish our pending business."

"Raman, if you like the deal as it stands, I'm happy to sign off on it," Jonathan said. "We might have to strong-arm the legal worrywarts, but they'll come around if both of us agree."

"Agreed," Saluja said. He checked his watch. "It's 1PM. How about 6PM for the signing? Enough time to get the lawyers in line."

"Works for me," Jonathan replied.

"After that, the five us, Mohan included, can get together for dinner and join the ladies tomorrow."

Alexis patted Malini on the shoulder. "Let them have their Boys Club dinner, Malini. We'll have fun."

Chapter 11

Saluja's estate home was a veritable fortress

Surrounded by a ten-foot wall of concrete, topped by a three-foot metal trellis with high-voltage signs. Concrete pylons guarding the approach to the only point of entry. An electrified gate that could only be opened from inside. Video surveillance cameras peering over the wall from twelve-foot poles placed around the perimeter.

It was a sad commentary on the siege mentality of the rich in India, in response to a burgeoning kidnap-ransom industry fostered by the economic boom.

An E-series Mercedes, corporate India's ultimate status symbol, was waiting to take them to the house when they landed at the helipad. As they passed through the gate, Alexis glimpsed a hi-tech guard house with banks of video monitors; then the road was swallowed by lush orchard groves. Five minutes later, they burst onto a driveway encircling a lawn ringed by flower beds.

Alexis gasped at her first sight of the house.

Made of hand-quarried stone, it harkened back to the feudal era, when landed gentry called *zamindars*—literally, 'lords of the land'—were accorded the status of local royalty by the indentured peasants living on their holdings. Its two floors matched the height of any modern five-story building. Built in an era without air-conditioning, its height allowed warm air to escape through draft vents in vaulted ceilings, pulling cool air from below through windows shaded by a deep verandah.

The car pulled into the porch, where a crowd of servants was waiting. They surrounded Malini when she alighted, chanting salutations of "Namaste, Baby."

Alexis slipped away from the hubbub and went into the house…only to be stopped dead by the breathtaking grandeur of the cavernous atrium she had entered.

The view was dominated by a magnificent staircase at the far end of the atrium. Made of white marble veined with dull maroon, it rose to a landing halfway up, where it split into two limbs that swept gracefully upwards on either side to a balcony skirting the inner perimeter of the upper floor.

A ten-foot square skylight was placed eccentrically above the staircase landing—not the formal sitting area at the center of the atrium. The placement struck Alexis as odd, but it provided enough light to make the crystal chandeliers under the cantilevered balcony redundant during the day.

A sharp intake of breath made her turn around to see Seetha enter, looking equally stunned. Behind her was Malini, leaning on the arm of an older man she introduced as "our Household Manager, Hira Lal-*ji*," the suffix indicating a station of respect.

Hira Lal bowed. "I hope the *Memsahibs* find their stay comfortable."

Alexis found the man's demeanor unsettling. The female honorific, "Memsahib", was supposed to show respect, but something didn't seem quite right. Did she sense a hint of...disdain? Maybe she was doing him an injustice, but there was an undeniable lack of warmth very much at odds with Malini's clingy affection.

As for Malini, it was amazing she was even functional, given what she had endured. Alexis addressed her with gentle concern. "Why don't you rest, Malini? You look like you need it, and Seetha and I don't need babysitting."

Malini responded with surprising vigor. "This is my home, Alexis. As your hostess, I must be the one to show you the house."

She had clearly tapped into a reserve of strength because she let go of Hira Lal's arm and walked briskly to the right side of the atrium. The first door led into what she called the 'study'. It turned out to be a self-contained suite where Jonathan would stay, since the upper floor wasn't wheelchair accessible.

The rest of that side of the atrium was occupied by a huge gym with exercise equipment of almost every description, which Malini began describing in excruciating detail. Alexis tuned her out, letting her eyes wander around the gym.

Her gaze was arrested by a display on the back wall of the gym, where six unstrung recurve bows, the kind used in international archery competitions, were mounted.

Two were junior-sized, but the other four were 70-inch bows for a right-handed archer who held the bow in the left and drew with the right. All were premium models by the two major brands, Hoyt and PSE, with increasing draw weights for a dedicated archer of growing skill, strength, and maturity. The mounted bows were flanked by photographs of Chetan holding a variety of trophies, flanked by Malini and Saluja. The most recent showed Chetan was as tall as his father: five-ten. Her height.

On a table under the display was a bow-case with a 70-inch Samick Master Recurve, with a rack next to it stacked with arrows made of aluminum-carbon composite.

It was Alexis's first encounter with a top-notch recurve bow. Realizing that its 44-pound draw weight, the arrows' 28-inch draw, and Chetan's height matched her own, she reached to pick it up.

Before her hand touched it, though, she heard Malini say with a catch in her voice, "That...was Chetan's competition bow. He was trying to make the Indian Olympic team. He is...uh...was...very good. The fourth highest-ranked archer in India."

Alexis snatched her hand back, saying, "I'm so sorry, Malini, I—"

Malini interrupted her with surprising firmness, "No! Don't apologize. I'm being silly. Do you know how to shoot a bow?"

Caught by surprise, Alexis stammered, "Well...uh...yes...I mean, no! Not this kind of bow. But I do know archery."

"Do you want to try it? Chetan's practice range is in the back."

Alexis didn't know how to respond, but she saw Seetha give a small nod, as if to say, 'Humor her', and took heart. "I will be honored to use one of your brother's bows."

She was relieved when Malini clapped her hands, saying excitedly to Hira Lal, "Tell the guards to set things up for Memsahib to practice tomorrow morning."

"I don't want to trouble Hira Lal-ji," Alexis replied carefully.

Malini's response was swift and decisive. "Nonsense. No one will object. Anything that honors Chetan isn't trouble." She looked at Hira Lal "Tell the guards to string whichever bow Memsahib picks."

"I'll do it myself, if you don't mind, Malini," Alexis said gently, pointing to the bow stringer on the table.

Malini laughed. "Just like Chetan! He didn't let anyone else do it, either."

The exchange seemed to add an extra bounce to Malini's step as they left the gym, erasing any hope for a quick end to the 'tour'. Alexis resigned herself to hearing every excruciating detail of the house and its layout. Little did she know that, in a few hours, those details would be the difference between life and death.

As they crossed the atrium, Alexis saw a digital security panel on the side of the staircase, displaying zone alarms for the gate and every breach point in the house. They made a brief stop at an enormous banquet-style dining room on the other side before heading upstairs.

There were seven bedrooms on the upper floor, arranged in a rectangle around the balcony overlooking the atrium. The master suite occupied most of the front of the house. There were two "front corner" bedrooms extending halfway down both sides of the rectangle, with a "side bedroom" occupying the rest. She saw her suitcase in one corner bedroom and Jason's duffel, which he sent ahead, in the other, with Seetha in the side bedroom next to Jason. The rear of the rectangle had two large bedrooms for Malini and Chetan.

Alexis was puzzled by the arrangement, leaving a vacant bedroom (Chetan's) between Seetha and Malini and another (a side bedroom) between Malini and Alexis. It made no sense for Seetha to be in the opposite side bedroom instead of the one between Alexis and Malini, but who was she to question Hira Lal's household arrangements?

Malini's energy ran out at that point. But that didn't end the tour. Before going to lie down, she ordered Hira Lal to show them the outside of the house. He didn't protest, although he appeared none too pleased as he escorted them down and around the staircase to the kitchen at the back of the house. They exited to a rectangular yard half the size of a soccer field, bounded by a long one-story building at the back that Hira Lal called "servants' quarters". On either side of the yard was a row of garages served by gravel roads.

The yard had four dog runs, each with a tethered "Alsatian," the Indian breed-equivalent of the German Shepherd. Alexis made to go to them, but Hira Lal stopped her, saying sharply, "They are guard dogs, not pets. They run free at night and are trained to attack and kill strangers. It isn't safe to get close to them."

Their last stop was the archery range behind the servants' quarters. It was as impressive as any 'professional' range she had used in the US—and wholly worthy of an aspiring Olympian.

As they returned to the house, Alexis couldn't help thinking, *Killer dogs, armed sentries, fortified gate, impossible-to-climb wall, electrified fence, video cameras, and hi-tech security system. No wonder Saluja wanted Malini here!*

Day 4

SHIELD AGAINST SWORD

Chapter 1

A jackal howled and Alexis came awake, every faculty alert.

It was half past three—she knew that instinctively, without having to look at the LED clock, glowing red on the nightstand.

She ignored the jackal's howl and the plaintive chorus of yips that followed. Her subconscious had 'heard' those twice without awakening her from sleep. Something was very different this time.

Something so nebulous that she couldn't put her finger on it…

In that instant, she knew it wasn't something she *heard* that awakened her. It was something she *didn't* hear.

The dogs! They were silent.

A ninja sense, deeply ingrained but never far from the surface, awoke to a deadly menace stalking the night in that unnatural silence. With every nerve stretched taut, Alexis went to the window overlooking the front lawn and parted the curtains, knowing anyone outside would be blinded by the floodlights on the roof.

She saw nothing. But that was irrelevant. The dogs had been silenced. Which meant the intruders had inside help. *Intruders*, not burglars. No burglar would break in on the one day the house was occupied! These intruders were coming *because* it was occupied.

And they were coming for Malini.

At that moment, the floodlights went out, plunging the grounds into darkness.

She felt a ripple of fear and closed her eyes, letting it wash over her without taking hold. She cradled the spurt of adrenaline that came with it and fed it to her combat instinct.

So!

The intruders would have numbers on their side. All she had was surprise, and that did her no good unless she saw them before—!

She knew what to do before she finished the thought.

Donning an all-black outfit and rubber-soled moccasins, she headed for the other corner bedroom. On the way there, she glanced down at the security panel in the atrium. It showed all sensors still armed. For now…

She found a black shoe-cream dispenser among Jason's toiletries, which she took, but what she was really after was a Dragunov sniperscope that now accompanied him on all his travels. It came from the Dragunov rifle that played such a key role in helping her face down a menace just as lethal as this in Myanmar. She kept the rifle as a memento, but Jason claimed the nightscope was rightfully his because "it was dead like I almost was, and it didn't figure in our escape, just like me!" She only gave it to him after he took back those words. Repaired and restored to full functionality, the scope could well be the difference between life and death for her.

She crouched down at the front window and slipped the sniperscope between the drapes to look out on a ghostly, green-black landscape.

Seeing nothing on the front lawn, she moved to the side window...and there it was. A patch of bright green in the undergrowth shaped like a dog. Still warm, from the brightness of the image, but no way to tell whether dead or alive. So, the dogs were neutralized, just as she thought. And the guards must be too. It wouldn't be long before the alarm system was disabled and breached.

Before that happened, she had to get the girls out of the house, leaving the killers no choice but to split up to search for them. Then, with her face blackened by shoe cream and the nightscope to see in the dark, she would become the hunter.

She hurried to Seetha's bedroom and shook the sleeping girl gently by the shoulder, one hand ready to clamp down on her mouth. It wasn't needed. Seetha opened her eyes, saw Alexis, and sat up without a sound, fully alert.

Alexis whispered, "Someone's coming for Malini. Go wake her up without spooking her and tell her we must get out of the house."

Alarm flared in Seetha's eyes, but all she said was "Okay, Alexis."

"I'm not sure how much time we have, but we've got to move fast. Put on a black or dark blue outfit, get Malini to do the same, and wait for me outside her room. Whatever you do, don't turn on any lights!"

Alexis ran back to her own bedroom and examined the surroundings on that side. She found two more bright green patches of dogs lying unmoving in the undergrowth. She was about to head for Malini's room when she heard footsteps on the gravel road in front of the house. She ran to the master suite just in time to see a blob of green heading towards the gate.

A servant on his way to the gate to let in the intruders!

She thought of going after him, only to think better of it almost immediately. He seemed in no hurry, but he'd be too far away to catch by the time she woke Malini to disable the alarm. At his pace, though, it should take him ten-to-twelve minutes to get there, two-to-three to let in the intruders, and another ten-to-twelve to return. It meant she had about twenty-five minutes to get the girls to safety.

She returned to Malini's bedroom at a dead run.

Chapter 2

Alexis's heart sank when she entered Malini's bedroom.
Seetha was crouched at the bedside, shaking Malini and whispering her name urgently, without response. A bottle of sleeping pills on the nightstand showed why.

Fear knifed through Alexis's gut. Forget getting out of the house into the relative safety of the orchard. She was defenseless, trapped inside the house, with nowhere to hide.

Her fear escalated, threatening to overwhelm her. Just for a moment. That was all it took for the ninja in her to take over. Her fear dissipated, and her combat instinct took over.

So!

If Talwar-e-Rasool was coming to kidnap Malini, she must either fight or die. Not that it was really a choice. With nothing but her bare hands to fight an unknown number of armed assassins, it was fight *until* she died. If only she had a weapon—!

Suddenly, it was so obvious that she smacked her forehead with a sibilant "Idiot!"

"What?" Seetha exclaimed with alarm.

Alexis didn't answer. She was too busy calculating and discarding options as she stared through the door of Malini's bedroom into the atrium, her eyes flicking from the staircase landing to the master bedroom suite and back. Then everything fell into place.

Three minutes since she saw the man walking away. Maybe twenty minutes before the killers arrived.

She handed Seetha the night vision scope. "Go to the master bedroom, slip this between the window drapes, making sure you stay hidden, and look through it with your eye against the rubber eyepiece. When you see them, I need you to confirm three things. How many? Are they wearing helmets and goggles? And are they carrying automatic rifles like—"

Alexis saw Seetha nod vigorously, and knew she didn't have to lay it out. That terrible time in Myanmar was still quite raw in Seetha's memory. "Once you've confirmed those three things, go to the balcony and whisper my name. I'll hear you. And remember, no lights."

Without waiting for a reply, Alexis ran down the stairs to the gym. She had tested each of the full-size bows after dinner in advance of her practice session in the morning, finding the Samick Recurve, Chetan's competition bow, most to her liking. She had then spent an hour making two adjustments that were essential for accuracy.

One was the distance between the bowstring and the riser, or brace height. She set that to 9 inches using Chetan's bow square. The other was the tiller, which she fine-tuned to distribute the force required to pull the bowstring evenly between the shorter upper and longer lower limb of the bow, relative to the arrow rest.

Those two settings could be the difference between the inevitability of death and a sliver of hope.

She picked up the bow and removed the bow sight, which was useless because her targets wouldn't be stationary, or at a fixed distance. It meant relying on her eye and instinct in the hope that her years of training with the unsophisticated Japanese yumi transferred to the recurve bow.

She made several experimental half-draws on the bowstring to get the feel of the bow. Then she made a full draw.

She locked her left elbow in full extension and pulled the bowstring back with her eyes shut. The heel of her right hand brushed her cheek and tucked into the angle of her jaw at her right ear, the bow flexing in perfect symmetry around the brace.

Holding the draw with her right elbow slightly above and behind her right shoulder, she let her mind "travel" through her neck, shoulders, and back, and down her arms to her hands, one gripping the brace, the other pulling the bowstring.

All of a sudden, the power of her locked muscles and the resistance of the bow crystallized into a single continuum of vibrant energy, and she found herself in a mystical domain in which the bow became a "living force" that merged with her own.

She reveled in that sensation for half a second, then drew down. She repeated the draw, achieving the same state of oneness with the bow, but this time she released the bowstring. It snapped back with a soft thrum that would be inaudible beyond fifty feet.

She repeated her draw and release twice more before her internal metronome flashed a warning: Eight minutes elapsed.

She thrust a dozen arrows from the rack into Chetan's belt quiver, then snapped a billiard cue over her knee, keeping only the thicker half, and sprinted out of the gym.

131

As she crossed the atrium, a series of soft beeps drew her attention to the security panel. All the red lights winked out, and the zone-intrusion light at the gate started flashing.

Ten minutes, twelve at most, before they're here.

She ran up the stairs to the master suite to find Seetha crouched at the window, peering through the night scope. Seetha heard her come in and said without turning around, "Nothing yet."

"Okay. Keep looking."

Alexis lined up the arrows on the dresser within reach of her right hand. Then she uncapped the cylindrical shoe cream dispenser she found in Jason's toiletries and twisted its base to expel a liberal amount of black cream onto the sponge at the top. Taking care not to let the cream overflow onto her fingers, she smeared the cream across her face and neck, covering every inch of exposed skin.

Her preparations complete, she took up position inside the doorway, from where she commanded a clear sightline to the staircase landing. The marble was radiating a crystalline brilliance in the silvery-bright moonlight streaming from the overhead skylight, but the ethereal beauty on display didn't even register. All she saw was the edge Fate had gifted her.

It was as if a spotlight was shining on the landing. Anyone looking up at the balcony from there would be virtually night blind, unable to spot her blackened face in the darkness of the doorway.

Her mental clock ticked off four minutes since the security system was disarmed…six more before the assassins arrived. She used the time to practice the draw several more times.

A sharp intake of breath from Seetha made her turn around. She felt calm and relaxed, her hands rock steady.

Seetha got to her feet and said, "Four. No headgear. No automatic rifles."

Everything she needed, not a single wasted word! She could almost kiss Seetha! No time for that, though. Not when she faced four assassins who were so confident that they couldn't be bothered with night-vision goggles or automatic weapons. Why shouldn't they be, with their overwhelming superiority in numbers and weaponry against three presumably drugged and defenseless women.

That overconfidence might be just enough for her to turn the tables. With surprise on her side, she could strike without the killers realizing they were under attack. The trick was to finish it before they realized they faced just one woman with a bow.

Alexis told Seetha, "Go to Malini's room and bolt the door. Then stand behind it with the cue on your shoulder, like this…" She gripped the broken cue like a baseball bat, the intact end resting on her right shoulder. "If anyone breaks down the door, wait until he's inside, swing the cue at his head, and grab his gun. What you do after that is up to you."

Seetha nodded and took off at a run with the makeshift cudgel. Alexis heard the soft whisper of a bolt sliding home seconds later and forgot about Seetha.

Standing motionless in the shadows of the doorway, bow in her left hand, she let her awareness expand to everything around her, so she could "see" without having to look. She picked up an arrow and instinctively commenced the *hassetsu,* the eight-stage kyudo ritual whose mystical spirit she could never capture in competition.

Ashibumi. With the bow held at her left hip and the arrow in her right hand, she set her stance sideways to the door, her weight distributed evenly between her feet.

Dozukuri. She pulled her back erect, and braced her shoulders in alignment with her hips.

Yugamae. She readied the bow, holding it upright at waist level, arrow nocked at the draw point with the first three fingers of her right hand flexed around the bowstring…and halted.

This was the inflection point of the hassetsu—the last chance to pause the ritual. The second half of yugamae, *monomi,* involved the acquisition of the target. Once initiated, the five remaining stages would flow instinctively and the hassetsu would be irrevocable.

To her, though, monomi was much more than just *acquiring* a target. It meant *becoming one with it*—a mystic concept understood by only the supreme ninja.

That was what she had reverted to now. She was no longer Alexis Wolff.

She was Lexi-san, *menkyo kaiden.* Ninja without peer.

Chapter 3

The silence was broken by a beep from the security panel, followed by a barely audible 'thunk' of the door being closed.

Three black-clad forms wearing stocking masks appeared at the bottom of the stairs, and Alexis instantly registered the absence of the fourth man. He was now a rogue factor—not in the upcoming combat but very much in play later.

The three figures paused at the bottom of the staircase and performed 360° scans of the upper level without once overlapping their fields. An unseen signal seemed to pass between them, and the man in the middle ascended the staircase to the landing, where he made another scan of the upper floor. Although much slower and deliberate than the first, his eyes passed right over Alexis in the doorway of the master bedroom, as if she was invisible.

It was the perfect illustration of "ninja invisibility". Despite its frequent portrayal in ninja lore as something supernatural, there was nothing magical or other-worldly about the skillful blending of movement and stillness, darkness and light, and camouflage and color, with subtlety and subterfuge.

So it was that the assassin, night blind in the moonlight and expecting movement to betray human presence, didn't see Alexis, standing motionless in the enveloping darkness of the balcony, with her face blackened.

He raised a hand and one of the others came up to join him. The instant he arrived on the landing, they separated to ascend the limbs of the staircase, and the third started a backward ascent to the landing. It was executed in such perfect unison that the third man arrived on the landing just as his two comrades reached the upper floor on opposite sides.

After a brief halt for their eyes to adjust, the first two moved in unison, one heading for Malini's room on the left, and the other towards Seetha's on the right. Now the reason for the unusual sleeping arrangements was clear. A vacant bedroom on either side isolated Malini, the abductee, from the two women slated for execution.

These men weren't jihadi terrorists. They were professional assassins, operating like a team of commandos on a seek-and-destroy mission against enemy combatants. And all she had to fight them was a bow and arrows.

Fear rippled through her gut. Before it could subvert her will, though, her ninja instinct reasserted control, and the ripple sank without trace into the stillness of her mind. Then time slowed to a crawl, and her focus shrank to the bow and the three targets.

In that state of hyper-clarity, her sakki—the ability to anticipate the flow of combat before intent is revealed—knew exactly how it would play out. She resumed the hassetsu from where she paused, midway through yugamae. What followed seemed almost preordained.

Yugamae. Monomi. Her sakki identified the man outside Malini's room as the first to take out, and her focus narrowed to him.

136

Uchiokoshi. She raised the bow forty-five degrees above horizontal, with the arrow nocked and bowstring relaxed, her arms slightly flexed at the elbows.

Hikiwake. She brought the bow down and began the draw, locking her left arm in full extension and pulling back on the bowstring to align the shaft of the arrow with her line of sight…and time came to a standstill.

Kai. She was now in that mystical domain in which the bow was one with her, and the arrow an extension of her right eye, locked on the chest of her target, instinctively adjusting for flight drop.

Hanare. She released the bowstring. The arrow sprang forward with a soft thrum.

Zanshin. Her hand went behind her shoulder in a continuation of the release as her eye followed the flight of the arrow. It drove through her target's chest and pinned him to the door with a thud.

A split-second later, she had another arrow nocked and drawn, zeroing in on the man on the landing, and re-launched the hassetsu.

He presented a much more challenging target, standing side-on fifteen feet below her, his attention fixed on the third man who was entering Seetha's bedroom. Difficulty was immaterial in her state of perfect oneness with the bow. It was as if she could reach out and touch him with the arrow.

As she released the bowstring, the arrow pinning her first target snapped under his weight, and there was a sound like a pistol shot. Before the sound could register in the assassin's ears, her second arrow transfixed him through his neck, driving him to his knees.

Even before he keeled over, Alexis had a third arrow nocked and ready, shifting her focus to the third assassin. He emerged from Seetha's bedroom to see his comrade on the landing struck down.

A half-second of stunned incomprehension followed.

That half-second was all Alexis needed to draw, acquire her target, and release the arrow. As the bowstring sprang back, brushing her cheek, she saw the assassin whirl around and lunge for the doorway behind him.

The arrow should have impaled him in the chest, but Fate, firmly on Alexis's side until now, decided to balance the scales. The assassin's flailing right hand deflected the arrow and he disappeared into Seetha's bedroom with a sharp cry. The gun in his hand flew over the balcony rail to land on the floor below with a clatter.

Alexis dropped the bow and raced to Seetha's bedroom, skidding to a halt in the doorway. The third assassin stood ten feet from her, poised in a defensive fighting stance, his face slack from disbelief. A bloodied right hand was his only visible injury.

Disbelief changed to shock when he saw her appear. Then it dawned on him that he held every advantage in hand-to-hand combat with an unarmed woman. He came at her fast and hard, telegraphing the typical hip-torque of *Tang-su-do*, the Korean martial art featuring attack moves with the feet.

Everything slowed down again, and she reacted instinctively, her sakki divining his intent. She stumbled backwards and went down awkwardly, legs flailing in the air, landing on her back with a thump that coincided with the slap of her breakfall hitting the floor.

It was an opening her opponent couldn't resist. He swerved around her flailing legs to plant his left foot near her hip and swept his right leg back to launch a kick to shatter her ribcage…and the trap sprang shut.

Ashi-gatana. Foot sword.

She rolled left and brought her left shin scything down in a paralyzing strike on the Achilles tendon of his plant foot.

Ashi-barai. Foot sweep.

She hooked her foot around his heel as his leg buckled and swept his plant foot out from under him, upending him backwards.

Hasami-ashi. Scissor legs.

As he fell back, her right leg arced over his torso in a scissor-leg maneuver.

Kakato-geri. Axe kick.

Her right heel smashed into his throat as the back of his head hit the ground, shattering his larynx. She knew he was dead without having to check. She did it, anyway

As she got to her feet, she heard someone running on the balcony. She spun around to face the door, furious at herself for letting down her guard. Then Seetha appeared in the doorway, jaw set in fierce determination and cue held ready to swing.

It was so anticlimactic that Alexis couldn't suppress a hysterical laugh. Then Seetha began to laugh as well, and suddenly they were in each other's arms, words tumbling out in unison.

"You looked as if you were—"

"Who did you think I was—"

They were both overcome by another fit of laughter. When it subsided, Alexis said severely, "I told you not to leave the room before I came to get you!"

"I know, but I heard a cry and thought you needed help."

Alexis was taken aback. For Seetha to leave the sanctuary of a locked room and run towards potentially lethal danger was an act of unimaginable bravery. "They're lucky they didn't have you to deal with," she said lightly.

Seetha started to giggle, but cut it off, saying urgently, "Alexis! There's something I must tell you. When I reached Malini's room, I heard footsteps on the gravel path outside, so I looked out with the nightscope and saw someone walking to the servants' quarters. His outline was loose and baggy, like he was wearing a kudtha pajama, not a body suit like this man." She pointed to the body on the ground. "And he went into the first servants' quarter, the one Hira Lal said was his."

Alexis was stunned. The fuzzy green world of the image-enhancer was totally alien to Seetha, and yet she had observed a level of detail worthy of a trained observer, not a novice.

"You amaze me!" Alexis said with wonder.

She saw Seetha flush with pleasure, then she became business-like. "It makes sense. Who better than Hira Lal to put the guards, servants, and the dogs out of commission? And the *masaala chai* served to us at dinner, which you and I didn't drink, I because caffeine worsens my jet lag, and you because tea after 5PM gives you insomnia. Otherwise, TeROR's assassins would have waltzed in, killed us, and abducted Malini."

"Malini drank all three cups. That's why we couldn't wake her!"

"Good thing, too. That left three empty cups and Hira Lal none the wiser!" Alexis gave a sigh. "I need to stop drinking masaala chai in India. This is the second time it's been used on me. I was lucky this time. Not so much the last time."

Her allusion to her capture by Kalidas's henchmen evoked a grimace from Seetha. It spoke more loudly than any words.

As they walked to Malini's room, Alexis mulled her next move. She had to get to Hira Lal before he made a run for it. He was their best hope of breaking into TeROR.

When they reached Malini's room, Alexis was surprised to see the time. 4:05AM. Was it only forty minutes since she was jolted awake by her first premonition of danger? It felt more like forty lifetimes, with death stalking each moment! But the worst was over.

She relaxed, feeling the tightly wound knot in her gut dissolve... and gasped as if she was punched in the gut *and* body slammed by the frenzied pulsation in the psychic bond!

She realized that Jason had lived through every frantic second of those "forty lifetimes" without getting a 'response' from her.

She reached out to him and the pulsation eased.

"You know," she said to Seetha with a smile, "Those brothers of ours will act like it's our fault that TeROR came for us. Better call Mohan and tell him what happened."

Seetha giggled a little hysterically. "Jason knows, right?"

Alexis nodded. "Yes. But that doesn't mean he won't be expecting a call from me. Or won't be upset. Like Mohan will be. So, brace yourself."

Chapter 4

J ason leapt out of the chopper the instant it touched down on the front lawn—its proximity to the house wasn't why they didn't use the helipad. It was to keep the pilots from seeing the carnage at the gatehouse until Ravi figured out how to handle the fallout.

Jason lifted Jonathan out of the chopper and settled him in his wheelchair before racing to the verandah, where Alexis and Seetha were waiting. He crushed them in a bear hug that released all the fear and tension he felt when Alexis's life was in mortal danger.

Mohan came up to join in the group hug. He was still visibly distraught, almost losing his mind when he heard what happened. It showed in the fierceness of his embrace and the tears in his eyes when he thanked Alexis for saving Seetha's life yet again.

Seeing Jonathan approaching with Saluja, Alexis ran to him with a cry of joy. She knelt down to hug him, saying in one breathless rush how sorry she was for worrying him, but it turned out fine so there was nothing to worry about.

Jonathan held her tight, not saying a word. His ashen face said it all. When it came to Alexis, he was anything but "tough as old leather and hard as nails", as Jason once described him. He still blamed himself for Alexis almost ending up as collateral in Kalidas's vendetta against him. To almost lose her, yet again, to TeROR's vendetta against Saluja must be devastating.

Saluja appeared to be in even worse shape than Jonathan. Jason couldn't begin to understand what he must be going through. One day after learning about Malini's rape and his son's murder, here comes a second attempt to kidnap Malini. No wonder he looked ready to fall apart!

Ravi joined them just as the chopper's rotor began turning. They hurried inside before it reached the brain-scrambling crescendo of takeoff and the downwash upended Jonathan in his wheelchair.

Seetha escorted Saluja up the stairs to Malini's room, with Mohan tagging along, but Jason stopped on the landing to reconstruct Alexis's shot…and he was stunned.

To shoot a man dead even with a rifle, shooting downward from the balcony in moonlight without a telescopic sight, required marksmanship of a high order. Striking the neck first shot with an unfamiliar bow, adjusting for distance and arrow drop, without any prior practice? That was the definition of 'beyond belief'!

He acknowledged it by inclining his head fractionally at Alexis, his eyes alight with admiration. She nodded without smiling.

"There's something very strange about this," she said. "No one knew Malini would be here until yesterday. It took weeks of advance planning to plant the mole and assemble a team of professional assassins capable of pulling it off on twelve-hours' notice. Why use rank amateurs for the snatch-and-kill in Uttarakhand when you have a pro team on stand-by? It doesn't make sense."

"It does if this was Plan A. It got shelved in favor of the wilderness snatch-and-kill. Far less dicey, easy for amateurs to execute, and simple enough to fake as a rafting accident. When it failed, they went back to Plan A."

"Easier to bungle, too, when you use rank amateurs!"

Ravi joined them in time to hear their last exchange. "They didn't bungle it, Alexis. They came within a hair of pulling it off, were it not for that meddlesome firangi who refused to die on the bus."

Alexis persisted, "It still doesn't explain why they didn't use their pro team in the first place."

"The only ones that know aren't talking," Jason said grimly.

"Let's see who this one is," Ravi bent down to remove the dead man's mask...and gasped. "Good God! This man is Major Mohammed Abbas, a former commando in India's crack counter-terror Black Cat Commando squad."

"Did you say former?"

"Yes. Fourteen years ago, he led a strike against a militant Muslim stronghold in Kashmir that turned out to be a trap. Only Abbas, his second in command, and his platoon sergeant survived. They were also the only ones who knew all the operational details, making them prime suspects. After a year of investigation, there wasn't a shred of evidence of treachery. So, instead of being court martialed, they were reassigned to desk jobs. Abbas preferred premature retirement."

"Seems like an injustice if there was no incriminating evidence," Jason murmured.

Ravi shrugged. "There wasn't any exculpatory evidence, either. And religion had nothing to do with what happened to Abbas. Both the other survivors were Hindus. Unlike Abbas, they accepted reassignment, and stayed in service until they retired with full pension benefits. Not that Abbas did too badly. Last I heard, he was CEO of a Gulf outfit with no known jihadi ties."

"So, what is he?" Jason asked. "A member of Talwar-e-Rasool, or a killer for hire?"

"Makes no difference, either way," Ravi replied. "Such a high-value asset must either be in TeROR's highest echelon, or in direct contact with it. There must be an electronic trail connecting Abbas to Malini's kidnappers and whoever runs TeROR."

"If TeROR, Abbas, and Saluja are involved, the publicity will be sky-high." Alexis said. "I want my name kept out of this."

Ravi shook his head "I'm sorry, Alexis, but I can't hide the facts. The guards were disabled—"

Alexis interrupted him. "The guards aren't disabled," she said, her voice taut with anger. "They're dead. The vicious bastards killed them even though they were drugged and helpless."

"Makes it even more difficult to hide the facts. You were in the house when the assassins came. They died from arrow wounds. And you've made no secret of your passion for archery on social media. Anyone can connect those dots to come up with the truth."

Jason said carefully, "We could reconfigure the dots…"

"Reconfigure the dots all you want, but you can't hide the truth. Alexis killed the assassins and saying anything else would be a lie."

"I'm not suggesting we lie. Reconfiguring the dots means we make their connections less obvious. To *bend* the truth, not hide it, and not just to help Alexis, but to get an edge against TeROR."

"I'm all for getting an edge against TeROR, but how?"

"If TeROR believe Abbas was betrayed, they'll start looking for traitors in their ranks. It could unsettle them into making a mistake. For it to work, though, the mole must be kept under wraps."

Alexis grimaced. "Two moles, Jay. Hira Lal and the cook. And both are under wraps—under a shroud, actually. Seetha saw the servant who let in the killers go back to Hira Lal's quarters. I couldn't go after him until I made sure there wasn't a fourth assassin outside, which took a while."

"Smart," Ravi said.

"Not so smart. By the time I got there, they knew the jig was up and were ready to make a run for it. Hira Lal started shooting when he saw me."

She flicked at a rent in her shirt. "He came pretty close too! I was a little on edge and got both with one of the assassins' gun. So, there's no one left to talk."

Ravi jumped in before Jason could. "Are you crazy? Do you know how lucky you are to be alive? Hira Lal was a trained commando—Abbas's platoon sergeant who survived the massacre that ended both their careers. You're damn lucky he missed and you didn't."

Jason said thoughtfully, "If you killed them with an assassin's gun, it fits right in with my plan to reconfigure those dots."

"How's that?"

"We make it look like the guards and TeROR's assassins killed each other."

"But the assassins were killed by arrows!"

"I know," Jason replied. "So, we cut off the vanes, extract the arrows through the wound track, shoot a bullet down that same track with the guards' guns, and arrange the bodies to simulate a shootout at the gate. It shifts the crime scene from the house, so your clean-up team won't have to nose around the house. But it won't work unless Saluja agrees to call it that way."

"I'm sure he will," Alexis said firmly. "He can deflect attention from Malini by announcing rewards to the families of the guards for their 'heroic sacrifice'. If he also includes Hira Lal and the cook, it will cement the betrayal narrative that the assassins killed the moles."

Ravi nodded thoughtfully. "I like it. TeROR will be on its heels, hunting for traitors in its ranks, giving us time to find Abbas's connections to TeROR's hierarchy and hunt them down."

Saluja came down from Malini's room and seized Alexis by the shoulders, saying intensely, "Seetha told me what you did. First Jason, now you. Saving Malini must run in the family. Nothing I say or do can show you how grateful I am."

"You don't have to thank me, Raman. It was self-interest. I wanted to stay alive."

"Joke all you want. I owe your family a debt I can't repay if I live to be a hundred."

"Thanks, Raman," Jason said. "We won't hold you to it."

Saluja stared at him, puzzled, then the joke dawned on him and he laughed. "I deserve that for being an idiot! But I'm glad it's over."

Jason was happy that Raman took comfort in that thought. But it wasn't over. Not by a long shot. There was one unanswered question that loomed over everything.

Why did TeROR need six million dollars so desperately that they would try to kidnap Malini twice in two days?

Day 5

SWORD OF GOD

Chapter 1

*Q*asim was dreaming.

He was striding across a battlefield strewn with the hacked and mutilated bodies of infidels, holding the Sword of the Prophet, dripping with blood.

Suddenly, a hill appeared in the distance. On it was another sword, so effulgent with power that it blazed brighter than the sun. Khuda ki Talwar! The Sword of God.

Between him and the hill was a kneeling figure, head bent to expose the back of his neck.

Saluja!

Qasim had only to behead him and the Sword of God would be his!

He ran to Saluja, Sword of the Prophet upraised in readiness to strike, when Saluja leapt up and the Sword slipped from his grasp and shattered.

Then he saw a body at Saluja's feet, a dagger buried in its chest.

Abbas!

Swordplay

Qasim screamed, "Khuda ki Talwar!" and lunged for the Sword of God. But it exploded. Searing blue fire erupted, engulfing him, and he felt mortal agony...

---〗〙〗〘---

Qasim's eyes snapped open, his mind still in the grip of his nightmare. He had lost everything. Abbas. Talwar-e-Rasool. Khuda ki Talwar.

Then reality hit. It took a few minutes before he could gather his wits and make sense of the terrifying imagery in his dream.

The bloodied Sword of the Prophet and battlefield strewn with dead bodies represented his life's mission. That was clear enough.

A subjugated Saluja, awaiting his metaphoric decapitation, should have been his greatest triumph.

And Khuda ki Talwar, waiting to be claimed after he beheaded Saluja, was the destiny he saw in his dreams.

That dream became a nightmare with the intrusion of two events reported in last night's news. Saluja's 'survival' and Abbas's death.

He could live with that nightmare if it ended there. It didn't. The ending sequence was what turned the nightmare into bowel-loosening night terror: Talwar-e-Rasool shattering and Khuda ki Talwar going up in flames, engulfing him.

A premonition? *Surely not!* He would be twelve thousand miles away when Khuda ki Talwar exploded. It *had* to be his subconscious dread of hellfire—his fear that he would burn in Hell for eternity unless he wiped away the sins of his earlier hedonistic life by dedicating his life to jihad.

He knew that escaping the Devil's clutches wouldn't be easy. But he never imagined that Shaitan himself would take a hand to stop

152

him. How else to explain the terrible setbacks that snatched success from his grasp, just when it seemed assured?

First, the kidnapping fails. Three skilled Talwaris abduct the Saluja girl on a remote beach. Just when it seemed nothing could go wrong they are swept to their deaths. With *no human* within miles.

Their hostage somehow survives, somehow covering two hundred kilometers of wilderness terrain on foot in a single day to return to Delhi. With *no human* help.

Then Rizwan disappears from a hut in the middle of nowhere, with *no human* within miles.

And now the final straw. With Saluja's guards and servants disabled, and their targets drugged and defenseless, three skilled commandos, led by the incomparable Abbas, are killed, despite *no human* opposition.

There was one common thread connecting all the setbacks: 'No *human*'. So, something *in*human. And there was only one inhuman force with that kind of power: The Devil. *Shaitan!* He knew he had to destroy the Sword of God before it destroyed him in all three of his earthly incarnations identified by the late, great Osama bin Laden.

The United States—the Great Shaitan—would be paralyzed by panic and chaos when Khuda ki Talwar struck its heart.

Then there was Israel, the Little Shaitan. Its existence would end without the Great Shaitan to prop it up.

Finally, there was India. Hindustan. Osama's 'Hindu Shaitan' would disappear when an Islamic Caliphate rose, Khuda ki Talwar in hand, to girdle the world from Indonesia in the East to Morocco in the West.

That Manifest Destiny was now in grave jeopardy. In one stroke, Shaitan had bankrupted the Sword of the Prophet, cut off its sword arm, Abbas, and made sure the Hindu Shaitan got its hands on Abbas's laptop, giving them a virtual road map for destroying TeROR.

Qasim himself was not in jeopardy, because he didn't figure in TeROR's operational record. But what use was his survival if he couldn't carry the fight to Shaitan? Without Talwar-e-Rasool, he had no weapon to fight back, and with Talwar-e-Rasool's coffers empty he couldn't even wage a proxy fight, let alone deploy Khuda ki Talwar.

Saluja's ransom was supposed to replenish those coffers and repay his childhood friend, Mirza Mullick, who had kept TeROR solvent during lean times.

Mirza would have to be told the ransom had gone up in smoke, so he could wave goodbye to the money he invested in TeROR over the years. Not only that, Qasim would have to beg Mirza to cough up another million to save Khuda ki Talwar, with no hope of recouping that. Not with Abbas dead and TeROR on the verge of extinction.

Qasim couldn't do that over the phone—that would be dishonorable. He had to do it face to face.

Chapter 2

B y all rights, Mirza Mullick and Mir Abdul Qasim—Mackie to his schoolmates—should never have become friends.

Although both were Muslim, Mackie's parents were affluent, well-educated professionals with firmly secular beliefs, whereas Mirza came from a deeply religious, blue-collar family who attended mosque every day and believed every word in the Quran.

Their lives should never have intersected. Except they did. On the cricket field.

Cricket brought them together as schoolboys, bridging a social, religious, and cultural chasm so vast that their parents would have vehemently opposed their friendship, so they kept it secret.

It remained steadfast until adolescence when Mirza discovered he was gay and, in a moment of madness, tried to kiss his best friend when they embraced. Mackie was so enraged and disgusted that their relationship never recovered. They drifted apart, until their friendship was essentially moribund by the time they left school.

Mackie went on to study Chartered Accounting at Mumbai University, whereas Mirza joined a small local college where hoodlums ruled and education was non-existent. With their lives following such widely divergent arcs, 'moribund' turned into 'dead'. So, Mirza didn't know when Mackie left Mumbai to take a job as an accountant in Delhi. He was working as a busboy in a five-star hotel, when a rich Arab took a real fancy to him, inviting Mirza to accompany him to Abu Dhabi as his 'personal companion'. Mirza accepted instantly.

His family promptly disowned him, but family and religion were nothing compared to being the pampered love companion of a member of the Gulf aristocracy. He manipulated his besotted lover into adopting him and, with the legitimacy of UAE citizenship, parlayed his 'father's' wealth, position and contacts into a lucrative business opportunity.

With millions of desperate Indians and Pakistanis looking for any way out of blinding poverty, and thousands of newly rich Arabs clamoring for domestic help, it was a classic case of matching supply to demand. He started an Abu Dhabi-based company called the Indo-Arab Services Company (IASC), hiring Indians, Pakistanis, and Bangladeshis to work in the Gulf. Within two years, the enterprise became the number one provider of domestic labor in the Gulf.

The secret to its success was that, as a Gulf-based company, it was immune from Indian domestic labor laws. Gulf laws, on the other hand, were so lax that even cases of violent abuse went nowhere. That, coupled with the desperation of job applicants, was the reason abuse of domestics was so rampant in the Gulf. Indian employers were obliged to take abuse seriously, or else be held liable for damages. With no such legal constraints, Mirza's willingness to ignore abuse became a priceless 'benefit' in the eyes of his rich clientele.

With success came grander visions. First, Mirza rid himself of his lover by giving him a double dose of his prescribed sleeping pill, followed by ten times his usual dose of insulin. The old fool was found dead the next morning. He was known to have diabetes and a bad heart, so the doctors assured the grieving heir that his 'father' died from a heart attack while asleep.

Mirza had done his research well. With no reason to suspect foul play, no autopsy was performed. Nor were post-mortem blood sugar or insulin levels checked. So, the cause of death wasn't discovered.

Free now, and rich beyond his wildest dreams, Mirza used his inherited wealth to expand his business empire. He hired a disgruntled ex-Army officer, Major Mohammed Abbas, as CEO of IASC's operations in India, not knowing that Abbas was Talwar-e-Rasool's sword arm.

One day, Mackie called out of the blue to say he was in Dubai for the opening of MAQ Associates first branch office outside India. That first meeting was strained. Over time, the uncomfortable memory of their breakup faded and their friendship reawakened. IASC became MAQ Associates' first Gulf client.

Mirza found Mackie changed beyond recognition. In a strange role reversal, Mirza was now the hedonistic pleasure seeker, and Mackie the orthodox, observant Muslim who forsook all pleasures. When Mirza learned of Mackie's devastating loss in the Godhra riots, he realized that "the plight of Muslims in India" wasn't a fabrication of the Pakistani media. Nothing validated that narrative better than Mackie's rejection of the secular beliefs he held so dear in the past.

Mackie's transformation reawakened Mirza's long-dormant faith. He confessed to Mackie that he lost his way and thanked him tearfully for showing him the light. That was when Mackie revealed that he was Talwar-e-Rasool's philosopher-guide and Abbas was its operational leader. Mirza became its patron, embracing jihad against the Hindu oppressors with the fanatical fervor of a repentant sinner.

Their business tie-up became a legitimate conduit for transferring millions through the Bank of Qumraan to keep TeROR solvent.

It was also a pragmatic cover for regular meetings and phone calls without raising red flags. So, there was nothing unusual about getting a call from Mackie in Delhi, requesting a meeting to discuss one of two things: "finances", which was their code for TeROR, or "accounts", which referred to a legitimate auditing concern with IASC.

This latest call from Mackie was anything but 'usual', calling at 3AM—1:30AM in India—sounding so agitated, and being so cryptic. All he said was he was landing in Abu Dhabi at 7AM and would come straight to his office to discuss an "urgent problem". Then he hung up.

Mirza didn't dare ask on an open line, but he assumed the 'problem' had something to do with TeROR or IASC, given how agitated Mackie sounded. Could it be something else? No point speculating. He would know soon enough.

Chapter 3

Qasim finished describing the awful setbacks of the past week. Two Batra crises. Two failed Saluja kidnap attempts. And two devastating losses, one irrevocable (Abbas), and one impending (Talwar-e-Rasool). And their dreams dead.

He was weeping by the time he ended his narrative. "Without Saluja's ransom, we are bankrupt and your investment in Khuda ki Talwar is gone. I can't ask for forgiveness. I don't deserve it."

"Mackie, my brother," Mirza said. "There is nothing to forgive! All the money in the world can't equal what your friendship means to me. Anyway, you have repaid my investment ten times over through your help with my organ procurement business. Forget the past. Our future is at hand!"

"You mean...?" Qasim didn't dare finish the sentence.

"Yes. Khuda ki Talwar is ready to strike the heart of the Great Shaitan!"

"*Allah-u-Akbar!*" Qasim cried. "Tell me when and where."

"The plan came together after the Emir died three weeks ago. On his deathbed, the fool willed a priceless Qumraani artifact called the Asad al-Qumraan to an American, Jonathan Wolff. It will be presented to him in five days. He will take it back to New York City."

He paused for dramatic effect and added, "...With Khuda ki Talwar inside!" He slapped the table. "Our destiny will be fulfilled."

Qasim's spirits soared. Khuda ki Talwar would add the names of Mirza Mullick and Mir Abdul Qasim to the pantheon of the greatest Defenders of Islam.

Names like Saladin, Liberator of Jerusalem. And Osama bin Laden, Destroyer of the Twin Towers.

Chapter 4

Mirza Mullick dropped Mackie at the airport and drove back to his office, feeling good about life. All because of Mackie.

It was Mackie who opened his eyes to the emptiness of a life focused on accumulating wealth. It was Mackie's singular focus on jihad that gave his life purpose. And it was Mackie who showed him how to use his wealth as a weapon in the cause. It was the foundation of the marriage between IASC and TeROR, which gave the birth to their brainchild, Khuda ki Talwar.

The Sword of God. A nuclear device that harnessed the power of Allah, the Creator.

It was the culmination of a journey that began shortly after he set up IASC nearly twenty years ago.

He received a phone call from the Chief of Transplant Surgery at the Asad al-Qumraan Hospital, an ambitious, young Pakistani surgeon named Saleem Kureishi. He said an employee Mirza placed in Qumraan had suffered a serious accident, and His Royal Highness,

Swordplay

Crown Prince Sayf al-Qumraan, wanted a life-saving liver transplant to be performed. Since the servant had no family in India, and Mirza was listed as 'next-of-kin', his written approval was needed.

Stunned that any employer in the Gulf should show such kindness to a lowly servant, Mirza flew to Qumraan, little knowing his life would be changed forever.

The so-called 'accident' was nothing but murder. The servant was brain dead and on life support after being beaten by the Crown Prince. And Mirza's approval was needed to harvest his liver to save the life of the Crown Prince's oldest son, who was dying of liver failure.

Mullick signed the authorization to harvest the victim's organs without hesitation, earning the undying gratitude of the Crown Prince, one hundred thousand dollars, and a Qumraani death certificate stating death was caused by a fall from a second-floor balcony.

That first involuntary 'organ donation' ended badly. The transplant was rejected, and the Crown Prince's son died. But it opened Mirza's eyes to a world of new opportunities. He read up all he could about 'graft rejection' and 'HLA matching', and the germ of an idea was born. Over the next several weeks, he fleshed out the details, concluding that, with sufficient advance notice, it was possible to find a 'perfect match', if three conditions were satisfied.

A large pool of desperate individuals who could be bribed or coerced to sell their organs.

A surgeon without ethical qualms.

And a group of filthy-rich recipients willing to pay an exorbitant fee for a donor organ without asking where or who it came from.

Getting the first would be easy. IASC had a pool of impoverished applicants who would fall over themselves to donate a kidney for the right price. All Mirza had to do was include an HLA screen in every

162

IASC job applicant's health screening to create a huge pool of potential donors to match to a recipient needing an organ.

He knew he had the second. Kureishi wouldn't be deterred by ethics if he was willing to overlook murder.

And Kureishi's royal clients would meet the third. Mirza knew only too well that Gulf aristocrats had neither mercy nor compassion for the wretched menials who worked for them. They would have no compunction about taking advantage of their poverty.

When Mirza presented his idea of 'Purchased Procurement' to Kureishi, he got an enthusiastic thumbs-up. That was how he started his organ procurement business, focusing on kidneys, the most sought-after organ (and the easiest to coerce a 'donor' to sell). Some might call purchasing organs for transplantation unethical and immoral, but it wasn't illegal.

Best of all, the profits dwarfed his 25% return on investment from IASC's legitimate enterprise. The $100,000 "procurement fee" he charged for a kidney was ten times the $10,000 pittance he paid his live organ 'donors'. That was more than six times the going price for a kidney in India of 100,000 rupees ("one lakh rupees" in Indian parlance, equivalent to about $1600). It wasn't surprising that every kidney 'donor' jumped at it.

The scheme worked smoothly for three years. Then Kureishi threw him a curve ball. He requisitioned a liver. And not for any ordinary 'royal', but the only surviving heir to the Qumraani throne.

Khalil, the ten-year old son of Crown Prince Sayf al-Qumraan, had inherited the same hereditary liver disease that claimed the lives of the Emir's sons and his older brother. He was developing progressive liver failure and would die in two years without a liver transplant. Kureishi said jokingly that it was too much to ask the Crown Prince to provide a random 'donor' on demand, like he did for his older son. An "elective perfect match" would be far more preferable.

Mirza wasn't laughing at the joke. Finding a perfect match in IASC's applicant pool was tough enough, he said. Finding one willing to donate a part of their liver? Forget it!

Kureishi responded with a truly daring proposition. Why not abandon ethics and harvest organs without consent?

It was a great idea in concept, but where could you find a pool of 'donors' without any loved ones to raise a stink when their organs were harvested without consent?

Mirza found the answer: Orphans.

IASC began offering free 'health screenings' at orphanages under the guise of a philanthropic scheme, with secret HLA typing.

It took a year to find a perfect match for the prince—a five-year-old boy at an orphanage in Bareilly. Mirza adopted him, exploiting the lax rules in India at the time, and placed him in a boarding school in India to 'continue his education'. During his next winter vacation to visit his adoptive father, an 'abduction' was staged in Qumraan. Mirza played the role of the frantic father to perfection, even offering a large reward for his safe return. After several months, the missing person case faded from memory.

Memories might fade. Not the paper trail leading straight to him and Mackie, who served as a reference on both the adoption and passport application. That was the trail that wretched journalist, Batra, was following when Abbas eliminated him, so the trail was again dormant. Fortunately, it was the only one. He never used 'Adoptive Procurement' again. He found something much better. He called it 'Abducted Procurement'.

Now, whenever Kureishi requisitioned a liver, he simply matched the recipient to one of the thousands of orphans in his database. The orphan was abducted by TeROR with the connivance of orphanage staff, smuggled across the Arabian Sea to Nishtun in war-torn Yemen, and brought overland to Qumraan to wait, like a goat for slaughter, until the organ was needed.

His Qumraani menagerie of 'goats for slaughter' had grown to eight with the arrival two weeks ago of its most recent entrant, a female who was the second 'perfect match' for Khalil, whose first transplant was failing. As the first adult orphan to come willingly to Qumraan as an IASC applicant, she didn't fit neatly into any of his procurement categories. But she got Mirza the status and respect that eluded him for years.

The Crown Prince was so grateful for giving his only surviving heir a third lease on life was off the charts that he gave Mirza the reward he had been craving: a 49% stake in the Royal Qumraan Oil Company, the successor to Lone Wolf Oil Corporation. When Jonathan Wolff signed the deed of sale next week, the Bank of Qumraan would instantly transfer *three hundred and sixty-eight million dollars* of Mirza's money to Wolff. And Mirza's status would rise from small-time domestic service provider to big-time tycoon in the Gulf oil industry.

He owed it all to Ganga Prasad, the boy who opened the door to this reward.

How appropriate! 'Ganga' was the Hindu river of salvation. And 'Prasad' meant gift.

My son, Ganga Prasad. The gift of Mother Ganga. A worthless orphan who singlehandedly fused two swords to gift his father the super-weapon that would be the salvation of the world.

The Sword of the Prophet, which delivered you to me in Qumraan.

The Sword of Qumraan, whose gratitude was earned by your "selfless" organ donation.

History would not remember, let alone care about the penniless nobody, buried in an unmarked grave, who made the Sword of God possible. History would honor the three visionaries responsible for changing the course of history.

Mackie, the Architect, who created the blueprint for building the Sword of God.

Mirza, the Banker, who provided the funds to build it.

And Sayf al-Qumraan, the Patron, under whose protection it was built.

To turn their visionary dream into reality they needed a Builder. Mirza found him in Kazakhstan, of all places!

Chapter 5

Mehmet Suleimanbayev hadn't known happiness or contentment for over twenty-five years.

He was a nuclear scientist, living at the apex of communist society. Then came the so-called 'Dawn of Democracy' (how he hated that phrase). The Soviet Union fell apart. And the Soviet nuclear program fell apart with it.

Like many other state institutions, the prestigious research lab where he worked in Moscow went bankrupt. Not only did he lose his job, he was forcibly 'repatriated' to his native Kazakhstan, a victim of the xenophobia sweeping through Russia at the time.

Things were no better in his homeland. The U.S. obsession with securing the Soviet nuclear arsenal meant that a wholesale nuclear retrenchment was underway, with Kazakhstan's aging nuclear weapons becoming bargaining chips to be traded for more basic needs.

Suleimanbayev was reduced to working as a physics teacher, with a pittance for a salary and none of the perks and luxuries of his old life. The daily struggle to feed and clothe himself was a harbinger of an even more penurious retirement at age sixty.

For twenty-five years nothing changed. Then, one night, a man named Mirza Mullick came calling. Suleimanbayev had no idea how Mullick found him. He was just glad he did.

It was amazing it took that long. A disgruntled Muslim nuclear scientist should have been highly sought-after by jihadi groups lusting for a nuclear device. Not that he had any interest in jihad. He wasn't a practicing Muslim, let alone a fanatic, so he cared nothing of Mullick's purpose. Escaping purgatory was all that mattered to him. And the money Mirza offered—more than he'd earn in several lifetimes in Kazakhstan—would secure him the life of luxury he still craved.

He had no family because his Russian wife preferred divorce to moving to Kazakhstan. The school wouldn't miss his services—there would be dozens of replacements lining up for his job. And the police wouldn't waste their time searching for a missing physics teacher.

It took him two minutes to decide. He left that night, with one suitcase and no regrets.

Over the past year, he had acquired everything he needed to build a nuclear device. Except the weapons-grade plutonium. Mullick got that from Pakistan, courtesy of the infamous Khan Research Laboratories, named after its founder, Abdul Qader Khan, the father of Pakistan's nuclear weapons program. Hailed in Pakistan as a hero, 'AQ' was the renegade nuclear scientist who gave North Korea the bomb but got caught trying to do the same for Gaddafi. When the Americans discovered his role in the clandestine nuclear bazaar, they forced the Pakistanis to put him under house arrest.

It was a farce. His work never stopped.

How Mullick acquired the plutonium was a mystery. As with much that happened in Pakistan, the facts were impossible to ascertain, let alone prove. Twenty kilograms of weapons-grade plutonium couldn't disappear without connivance from someone in authority, any more than Osama could 'disappear' from sight in Abbotabad, a town run by the Pakistan military!

Smuggling the plutonium out of Pakistan wasn't difficult. A pair of fanatical Army officers transported it to Karachi secretly in a convoy, and a smuggler with a ramshackle boat and connections with Karachi Customs brought it across the Arabian Sea to the Yemeni port of Nishtun. From there, it was a two-day trip overland to Qumraan.

Suleimanbayev procured everything else on the Russian black market with Mirza's money. Except the krytron triggers for detonating an implosion device, which were the most critical component other than the fissile material. He stole those years earlier from the Moscow lab. Amidst the chaos of the Soviet Union's break-up, no one knew or even cared they were missing.

With everything in hand, he assembled an implosion device equipped for remote detonation anywhere in the world with an untraceable satellite phone from Kazakhstan.

The Sword of God was now ready to strike its target. Mullick had even found a virtually foolproof way to get it into the U.S. without US Customs or TSA finding it.

The late Emir had gifted a priceless metal statue of a rampaging lion, called the Asad al Qumraan, to a billionaire named Jonathan Wolff, who planned to donate it to the Metropolitan Museum of Art in New York City.

Under Sayf's orders, a highly skilled Qumraani iron artisan had cut open the belly of the Asad and sealed the Sword of God inside, leaving no trace of his work. Wolff would take the Asad with the Sword of God in its belly into the heart of New York City, where it would detonate. The first ever act of nuclear terrorism would turn America's financial and emotional heart into a nuclear wasteland.

Suleimanbayev couldn't be happier. It would be just retribution for the U.S. role in the Soviet Union's collapse, forcing that idiot Gorbachev to accept openness (*glasnost*) and reform (*perestroika*). All that did was fracture the bonds holding the disparate republics together, bringing the drunkard Yeltsin to power in Russia. His policies condemned Russia to bankruptcy and Suleimanbayev to twenty-five years in purgatory. The Sword of God would exact sweet revenge for the misery the US inflicted on him.

The future looked very promising. He had purchased, sight unseen, a villa on a remote South Pacific island he never knew existed. All that mattered was that never again would he have to live through either Qumraan's pitiless desert heat or Kazakhstan's brutal winter cold.

Chapter 6

Mohan's exclamation of "Oh my God!" brought everyone rushing over to see what he was looking at on Abbas's laptop.

Saluja saw the folder on the screen and blurted out, "Khuda ki Talwar! Why is there something named 'Sword of God' on a laptop belonging to the leader of the Sword of the Prophet?"

"I don't know, Raman" Mohan replied. "It's just a hundred kilobytes, but it must be important, seeing how far Abbas went to hide it. He buried it so deep in the operating system that the IT guys never suspected it existed. Abbas's computer skills had to be exceptional to hide something inside the OS without messing it up. And put in a second kill-switch even trickier than the self-destruct command the tech guys disabled. You have to open a specific sequence of files in the Talwar-e-Rasool folder before this one, or the hard drive will be irretrievably erased."

"What is it?" Saluja asked.

"A word document created twelve years ago," Mohan replied. "Accessed many times, most recently the day before yesterday, but never modified since its creation."

"Two similar names," Saluja said with a frown. "Talwar-e-Rasool. Khuda ki Talwar. Could TeROR have been planning a name change?"

Ravi shook his head. "I don't think so. Traditional jihadi names are grandiose. Think *Talwar-e-Khuda*. 'Khuda ki Talwar' sounds almost prosaic. Practical. Like an operation of some sort. Where have we heard that before?"

"*Khoon ka Snaan!*" Seetha whispered, with such unfathomable horror in her voice that Saluja felt the hairs on his neck rise. The phrase meant 'Bloodbath' in Hindi, but Seetha's reaction reflected something far more malevolent than even its literal translation. And Mohan clearly shared the horror she expressed, seeing the way he flinched when he heard her say the phrase out loud.

Mohan took a few seconds to gather his wits and refocus. "Getting back to the Word file. It's a thirty-digit string. Seven groups of four digits, plus a '01' at the end. It must be a code for something, but I have no idea what. Maybe we need a code-breaker." He tapped the screen. "Unless one of you can figure it out."

Saluja leaned forward to follow Mohan's finger…and recoiled with a cry of horror. "It-it can't b-be!" he stammered. "I've seen—I n-n-know…th-those numbers!"

Ravi was incredulous. "Raman, how could you know a string of random numbers in a file created by Abbas over a decade ago?"

Rage made Saluja hoarse. "This is no random string. Those numbers are burned in my memory, like the words of a death warrant. I will carry them to my grave." He jabbed a finger at the screen. "It's the account number where I was ordered to transfer Malini's ransom day before yesterday. When the file was last accessed."

Stunned silence followed. Jonathan broke it after several seconds. "Wait a minute!" he exclaimed, leaning forward to look at the screen. "Those thirty digits are an International Bank Account Number, or IBAN. The last four-digit group, 2627, stands for QR in the IBAN alphanumeric code, and the last pair, 01, is the branch code. Which means this account is at the Royal Bank of Qumraan's head office!"

Saluja could barely control his rage. "The bastards! Khuda ki Talwar must be the codename for Malini's kidnapping."

Ravi demurred. "I don't think so, Raman. This file was created twelve years ago, long before you became a ransom target in India."

"Then what does Khuda ki Talwar refer to if not the kidnapping?"

"I don't know, Raman. But, with Talwar-e-Rasool bankrupt and leaderless, the Sword of God can't be an active threat. No matter what it is, we can make it 'defunct' by slaying the hydra before it grows another head. And Abbas's laptop is just the weapon for killing it. It has a complete list of TeROR cells, organized by region and district across India. TeROR will die soon."

He paused, before adding with finality, "And whatever Khuda ki Talwar is will die with it."

Chapter 7

Jonathan saw the steely glint in Alexis's eye and felt a familiar sense of foreboding. The finality in Ravi's hydra imagery had no effect on whatever crusade she was on.

"It's great," Alexis said softly, her voice dripping with sarcasm. "When the Sword of the Prophet dies, the Sword of God will die with it, and everyone in India will sleep better. Is that justice?"

"It *is* justice, Alexis," Ravi said. "Abbas is dead and TeROR will be soon. Isn't that enough?"

"It *isn't* enough!" Alexis said fiercely. "What about justice for one little boy? For twelve years of unrelenting misery. For his brutal murder. And for the Batras who died trying to expose an evil beyond human comprehension. Do we forget them, just because everyone gets to sleep more peacefully?"

She looked around the room, daring someone to challenge her. When no one did, she continued. "So, Mohan, do you know how Ganga Prasad ended up in Qumraan?"

"Yes, I do, Alexis. He was adopted and abducted, just as Ravi and Jason suspected. I found his name in an obscure Foreign Ministry database listing expatriate adoptions. We've requisitioned the paperwork from his adoption, but it could be a while before we get them.

"I've also requisitioned the paperwork from his passport application, but I found a copy of his passport in the Foreign Ministry's database. It lists Mirza Mullick, the owner of IASC, as his adoptive father. It was cancelled a year later by the embassy in Abu Dhabi, six months after he went missing while he and his father were visiting—can you guess where? No prizes if you guessed Qumraan!"

Alexis gasped. "The monsters adopted him just to take him to Qumraan and harvest his organs! And they got off scot free. Is that justice, Ravi?"

Ravi stayed silent. Wisely.

Alexis turned to Mohan. "Did you figure out how they found the one boy who was a perfect match in a remote orphanage in Bareilly?"

"Yes, Alexis, thanks to Dr. Batra. He gave us the roadmap to figure it out. I searched the databases of three commercial labs certified for HLA typing at the time, just as he advised. Sriram Path Labs, or SPL for short, has performed over a hundred thousand tissue compatibility tests for IASC to date. Several thousand addresses on the list were orphanages. Sample 11263 was Ganga Prasad's."

"How did they manage to get samples from orphanages?"

"Oh my God!" Seetha cried out. "I know how. IASC came to the Hostel for Destitute Girls in Kolkata, offering free blood tests and health screenings to anyone willing to apply for jobs in the Gulf. All the girls lined up to get the screenings, except me. Mohan said it was too good to be true."

Alexis's voice was sibilant with rage. "Is there no limit to their evil? Offering free health screenings to orphanages to get HLA profiles of orphans to abduct. Any idea how many others they found with their 'free health screenings'?"

"No way to tell without knowing their names," Mohan said.

Ravi spoke up. "There've been several cases of paid live organ donations by IASC's employees. It might be distasteful, but the donors were all consenting adults who had no complaints about their care or compensation. Three participants in an IASC promotional program died while travelling in the Gulf and had their organs harvested, with the consent of their next of kin. There was no evidence of coercion, and the families were handsomely compensated through travel insurance paid for by IASC. So, everything was above board.

"I couldn't care less about adults," Alexis snapped back, "It may be unethical, but it isn't illegal, as long as consent wasn't coerced."

She jumped to her feet and began pacing the room.

"But a six-year old boy? Is there anyone who thinks it should go unpunished? Abbas, who initiated the crime by finding Ganga Prasad in India, might be dead, but the story doesn't end there. It was Mirza Mullick in Abu Dhabi who adopted and abducted him, and the royals in Qumraan who conspired in the crime by requisitioning the perfect match. Do we let them off scot free?"

Jonathan tried to speak, but Alexis silenced him with a peremptory wave. "India, Abu Dhabi, and Qumraan. Three corners of what I call the Triangle of Terror, each contributing to the murder of a little boy for his organs. But even that doesn't complete the story."

She paused to take a deep breath. "There are three others. The psychopath who beat him to death. The royal who happily accepted a child's liver, bartering that child's life for his own. And the sixth. The worst of them all. Without him, the Triangle wouldn't exist."

Then she said softly, each word dripping with hatred, "The surgeon who cut out the liver and kidney of a defenseless child."

The silence dragged on and on, until Jonathan couldn't stand it anymore. He finally spoke. "Alexis, I know you want justice. As does everyone in this room. But let's face facts. Everyone left on your list is out of reach of justice. We don't know who they are, apart from Mullick. All your witnesses are dead. No outside court will accept jurisdiction for crimes committed in Qumraan. And Qumraan certainly won't prosecute if the royals are involved."

If his logic fazed Alexis, she gave no sign of it. "You're right that four of the five are out of reach of justice. Not the transplant surgeon. I don't need a court of law to crucify him. I will expose him to the world as a murderer. Call it professional homicide—"

"You can't be serious!" Jonathan interrupted.

"I've never been more serious. What do you think any editor of a major newspaper in the U.S. or U.K. would do with Batra's letter, the scans, and the surgeon's name? I'm betting they'll see 'Pulitzer' dancing on their desks. Talk about poetic justice for the Batras, too!"

"But how will you find him?" Jonathan asked. "Dr. Batra set off alarms when he tried to access the records. How will you get them?"

"Didn't Lone Wolff install the computer systems in Qumraan?" Alexis asked.

"Yes, but—"

She wouldn't let him finish. "Lone Wolf must have admin access to the hospital's data warehouse. With it, Mohan can find the surgeon's name. And spare me any sanctimonious crap about the ethics of unauthorized access. Someone who abandoned every ethical constraint to eviscerate a small child without consent doesn't deserve ethical protection. Anyway, Mohan will read only one operative note in one specific chart. Ganga Prasad's. Do you think he'd deny us permission to view his chart, if it exposes who destroyed his life?"

She looked around the room, challenging someone to disagree. Jonathan couldn't help asking, plaintively, "Why are you so hell-bent on doing this, Alexis?"

"Because, Jonathan, something about Ganga Prasad got to me in a way that's only happened once before. Remember Pammie Siddhu?"

Jonathan gave a weary nod. "I remember."

"Then you must know why I'm hell-bent on this. I want justice and I don't give a damn about due process. I'm not a court of law."

Jonathan gave a wry smile. "No, my dear, you're not. You're the Sword of Retribution!"

She laughed with delight. "Then you do understand. Are you okay with it?"

"I understand, but don't ask me to be okay with what you're getting yourself into. It was the same with Pammie. I couldn't stop you then, and I can't now. I know when I'm licked. I'll get Mohan the access to find the name of the surgeon for you."

"Not for me, Jonathan. For Ganga Prasad."

Chapter 8

It was late afternoon when a bleary-eyed Mohan emerged from Ravi's study. Everyone was anticipating a bombshell. It wasn't even a damp squib!

His very first words made that very clear.

"I'm so sorry, Alexis, but I couldn't access the records of Ganga Prasad's surgery even with Lone Wolf's admin override. I don't know who the surgeon was.."

"How come?" If Alexis was disappointed, she didn't show it.

"I tried every trick in the hacker's book, hoping the records were hidden behind some high-security file partition. No luck. It was as if the records never existed in the server database. Then I stumbled on something in an obscure corner of the administrative records titled "Special Project to Protect Sensitive Information". It authorized one of the database's six servers to be disconnected from the mainframe and moved offline a week ago. That server contained five years of data spanning the date of Ganga Prasad's surgery. So, I had no way to find the info you need." Then he added drily, "Just in case anyone was worried, I couldn't cross any ethical boundaries even if I tried."

"I wasn't worried," Alexis said with a smile. "But the timing of that so-called 'Special Project' to move the sever offline is very suspicious. Right after the breach by Dr. Batra to make sure no one else accessed the chart. So, it looks like a dead end. I'm sorry I sent you on this wild goose chase."

"Don't be," Mohan replied. "It's not a complete dead end. I did find something in the admin records, although I don't know how useful it is. The transplant program was established and run by a Pakistani surgeon named Saleem Kureishi. He left two years before Ganga Prasad's surgery, after which each of the three remaining surgeons acted as Interim Chief a few months at a time until a new Chief was appointed three years later. It wasn't clear who was Interim Chief at the time of Ganga Prasad's surgery." He shrugged. "It isn't much…"

"It is, Mohan," Alexis said excitedly. "There's an excellent chance Kureishi knows the surgeons on staff when Ganga Prasad had his surgery. Do you know where he is now?"

"I thought you'd ask, so I tracked him down. I have his number in London—"

"Thanks, Mohan, but I can't do this over the phone. He'll never accept anything so ethically damaging without looking at the scans. I have to see him, but I can't tell his secretary why, so I'll have to wait my turn for a regular appointment."

Jonathan spoke up. "No, you won't, Alexis. My foundation is a major donor to the program Saleem Kureishi chairs in London. He can't refuse if I tell him you're coming to London to meet him."

"That would be really great. I'll try to get on a flight to London tonight."

"No again, Alexis. You're taking my plane. And I won't take no for an answer. I'm not giving you an excuse to get out of our trip to Qumraan next week."

Everyone laughed. Even Alexis.

Jonathan continued. "You'll have to arrive by noon if you want to meet Kureishi tomorrow. It means an 11PM departure tonight."

"Looks like I don't have a choice," Alexis said with a rueful smile. "But I'm not complaining." The smile vanished. "The sooner I get there, the quicker I'll find what I need."

Mohan saw the same implacable set of her jaw he remembered from Myanmar, when she faced impossible odds against an unimaginable evil. If she didn't give up then, no way she was going to now. She was coming for whoever operated on Ganga Prasad and, no matter who or where he might be, he didn't stand a chance.

Kureishi had no idea how lucky he was that she wasn't coming for *him*.

Day 6

DEVIL BLADE

Chapter 1

Kureishi saw three skinheads emerge from the shadows and knew the fish were hooked.

He was the bait, a single Asian male walking on a deserted street just after midnight in this East London neighborhood, where several skinhead attacks had occurred in the last two months. He had dangled the bait three times this week. Third time was the charm!

He pretended to cower in terror as the three men split up to surround him, begging them not to hurt him because it would embolden them. Sure enough, they started kicking his shins with their hobnailed jackboots, mouthing filthy abuse. He flinched and cried out, faking pain he didn't feel because he was wearing shin guards under his jeans.

The skinhead in front of him, who seemed to be the leader, asked if his "moolaah beard" was made of "cock 'air," which his side-kicks thought was hilarious. They joined in the fun, calling him "Fuckin' Mozzy Packy", the colloquial insult for Muslim Pakistanis, and "Skinless Piss'ead," mocking his circumcision.

185

'Skinhead Number One' noticed his narrow, pointed shoes and asked with a sneer, "Did the 'moolaah' miss and cut off your piss'ead? Do your dago shoes make up for a short dick?"

Funny that he should notice the shoes. Handmade in Pakistan, with quarter-inch thick titanium plates in the toecaps and soles, they would play a big part in what was to come.

Then Skinhead Number One's saw his gloves. "Are you afraid of touching your skinless piss'ead, Piss'ead?"

For some reason, the double "piss'ead" insult got to him. He started to seethe, biding his time until the moment came to strike.

Number One continued, "If you don't 'ave a dickhead, yer not allowed to 'ave cock 'air in yer crotch or yer faice, Fuckin' Packy. I'm gonna cut off yer moolah beard first, then we'll see about yer crotch."

Kureishi saw him take out a jackknife and reach for the beard …and exploded into action.

His left hand fastened on Number One's wrist and twisted viciously, dislocating Number One's elbow. In the same motion, he pulled the man's arm down, jerking him forward, and delivered an *empi* strike with the point of his right elbow to his face, shattering his nose.

Keeping his grip on Number One's wrist, Kureishi leaned to his left and launched a *yoko geri* side snap kick with his right leg at Skinhead Number Two. The steel edge of his shoe smashed into the man's groin, sending him hurtling backwards. He landed on the ground and curled into a fetal position, clutching his groin.

Still holding Skinhead Number One's wrist, Kureishi pivoted to face the third man. He had taken a step back at the transformation of the supposed victim into lethal predator. Kureishi's left foot scythed upward in a *mae geri* front kick, and the steel-capped toe of his shoe socketed into the hollow under the chin, shattering his jaw and crushing his larynx. Skinhead Number Three fell backwards with a spasmodic gurgle.

Even before the third man hit the ground, Kureishi launched himself over Skinhead Number One without letting go of his wrist. He was still bent over, so his arm twisted up and over his back, wrenching the shoulder right out of its socket. Kureishi landed knees-first on the man's back, smashing his face into the sidewalk, and he went limp.

Kureishi got to his feet and went over to where Skinhead Number Two lay curled up on his side, mouth opening and closing without a sound. He drove his steel-capped shoe deep into the man's chest, feeling the ribs shatter, then delivered another kick to the back of his head, just hard enough for it to crumple without shattering. The man's back arched and his legs jerked into extension, then he flopped back and became still.

Kureishi stepped back, allowing himself a moment of self-congratulation. He had replicated the injuries inflicted in the last skinhead attack. His signature!

Number One would survive, but he would be out of action for the foreseeable future, needing reconstruction of his smashed face and shredded shoulder and elbow. Number Two was still breathing, but even if he somehow survived that crushed skull, he would be little more than a vegetable. Number Three was dead.

All done with barely a sound. Not that anyone was awake to hear it in the row houses lining the deserted street.

But he wasn't done yet.

He turned Number One on his back, unzipped the man's fly, and pulled out his uncircumcised organ. Using the skinhead's jackknife, he cut the skin around the tip, taking care not to let the blood soil his gloves, and left him exposed and bleeding. Then he cut two fistfuls of hair from the false beard that so amused his would-be attackers and stuffed them into the unconscious man's mouth.

As he got to his feet he heard a groan and saw Number One stir. The man's eyelids fluttered, and he gagged, vomiting a bloody mess over his chest.

Using a Cockney accent, Kureishi sneered, "Eat my moolah cock 'air, you fuckin' skin'ead wiv' a skinless piss'ead! Yer dick's bin cut wiv your own fuckin' blyde."

Then he bent down and whispered, "Tell every fucking skinhead dick who likes to go Packy-bashing that the Dagger of Allah will be waiting to make them skinless pisshead dicks, like you."

He straightened up and melted into the darkness as Number One began to shriek in agony. He was long gone by the time the first lights came on in windows up and down the street.

Chapter 2

D etective Chief Inspector Harry Smithers of Scotland Yard sat back after reading the report on the latest skinhead killing in Whitechapel and scratched his chin. All he had was a whole lot of fanciful speculation without a shred of hard evidence. As for the killer or killers? They might as well be phantoms.

He shuddered at the thought of telling that to the Assistant Commissioner of Police, his boss. The ACP's penchant for deadpan sarcasm could be quite tiresome. After the last attack, he asked Smithers whether Scotland Yard's Section on Hate Crimes should be renamed "Investigative Section for Unsolved Crimes and Killings". It wasn't until later that Smithers realized the acronym for the made-up name was "I-S-U-C-K."

There was a kernel of truth to it, though. Four identical hate crimes in the past year, all unsolved. Leicester, Birmingham, Manchester, Bradford. And now, London. All with the same pattern. Skinheads maimed and killed in reprisal for recent attacks in the same localities on Muslims from India, Pakistan, or Bangladesh. *Always* Muslims, never Hindus. *Always* with the pre-meditated savagery of the Quranic and Old Testament dictum of 'an eye for an eye'. And *always* replicating the injuries inflicted by skinheads in that locality with grisly precision. To the extent that the injuries exactly mirrored those suffered by the victims of the original attacks.

Two skinheads in Leicester dead, a third left in a vegetative state, bludgeoned by a war club with a triangular head. Four in Birmingham with major jaw and facial fractures, serious rib injuries and punctured lungs, inflicted by the same 'war club'. Three beaten with the same triangular bludgeon in Manchester, two dead and one quadriplegic from a broken spine. Two stabbed to death in Bradford with a *janbi-yah,* the curved Arab dagger with a ridged blade, and a third left with irreversible brain damage.

The latest attack in London followed the same pattern—one survivor with major trauma to hands, face, and head, and two bludgeoned with that same war club with a triangular head.

But what to make of the macabre 'extras' that weren't in the original skinhead attack? Like the circumcision. The smashed genitals. The mouth stuffed with synthetic hair. And only one dead, instead of two, although the second was technically brain-dead and on life support.

There wasn't much hope of solving the mystery. None of the survivors were talking, although there were whispers on the street of "that Packy bastard," and "the butch bitch in black." And a nurse thought she heard the surviving London skinhead mumble under sedation something like either 'Dagger of Allah', or 'Beard of Mullah'. Maybe both. They sounded similar when slurred.

Was it just the hallucination of a skinhead with a scrambled brain? Or could it be a reference to a sanctified weapon of some sort? Or a mullah performing vengeful circumcisions on skinheads?

The very thought of mentioning "vengeful circumcision" to the ACP made Smithers cringe. The ACPs acid tongue already had a field day with the 'butch bitch in black' rumor, asking if it referred to the police. After all, he said, they might as well be emasculated if they couldn't find a single clue to the perpetrators after four incidents that left six dead.

That number would rise to eight today, after the last night's brain-dead victim had his organs harvested for transplantation. It was small consolation, but at least some good would come from this latest incident.

Right then, Smithers had a strange feeling he was overlooking some little detail, but it was like reaching for a puff of steam that vanished the moment you touched it.

Chapter 3

Euphoria!

There was no better word to describe how Kureishi felt when his eyes opened shortly after dawn. Just like he did after every successful "hunt".

He wondered if this was how a junky felt after a fix. If so, he was a bona fide junky when it came to skinheads. Luckily, his fixes were freely available. And too dumb to know they were being buggered. Five times in a row, and yet those stupid pricks kept coming back for more.

Which brought up an interesting thought. Pavlovian dogma held that any form of life with a brain, no matter how rudimentary, develops an aversion response. Not skinheads, though. Which only proved that skinheads had no brain.

Darwin might also be in play here. Nature's fail-safe to ensure the *un*-fit didn't survive. If so, he was delighted to serve the noble cause of natural selection. But he had to be careful. Five in a row was pushing the limits of even his phenomenal luck.

It wasn't just luck, of course. It took incredible skill to pull it off five times without getting even nicked. Not that he ever doubted he could. As a sixth *dan* black belt in karate—*roku-yudanshu*—and Muay Thai kickboxing master, he never doubted he had what it took in life-or-death, hand-to-hand combat. Although, to be fair, skinheads weren't a real test. They were so sure no 'Packy' would ever hit back that it was over before they knew what hit them!

That first time, in Leicester, he bludgeoned two to death with his steel-capped shoes and reduced the third to drooling imbecility. The triangular impressions left by his shoes created a media fixation with 'a Native American war club with a triangular head', which Kureishi found truly hilarious.

Even more comical was the inevitable ethnic conflation that led to tabloid headlines like "Skinhead Cowboys and Indian Revenge" and "Renegade Indian Vigilante."

More serious journalists focused on the uncanny parallel between his first reprisal in Leicester and the skinhead attack, leaving two dead and a third with irreversible brain damage.

It was pure coincidence, but headlines proclaiming, "Biblical Vengeance" and "Old Testament Retribution" inspired him. He made it his 'signature'. Except, his inspiration was the Quranic injunction of "a life for a life, an eye for an eye, a nose for a nose, an ear for an ear, a tooth for a tooth, and a wound for a wound."

The press called it the work of a "serial skinhead killer," but he found that offensive. He was an executioner, delivering justice with the clinical detachment of a hangman.

Except this time. He lost his cool and made three stupid mistakes. The surgical circumcision. The hair stuffed in Number One's mouth. And the 'Dagger of Allah' taunt. Thanks to his phenomenal luck, though, he should get away with all three.

His "Bearded Mullah" disguise should provide cover for the skill of the circumcision. The beard hair would be too contaminated by Skinhead Number One's blood for any traces of his DNA to be detected. And whatever passed for the skinhead's brain was likely too scrambled to register his taunt.

Best, though, to lie low for a while, and let the media hype die down before venturing out again. This fix would have to last a while.

The thought brought him back to earth, and he snapped out of his reverie.

It was 5:45AM. Time to get up.

His first case was scheduled at 7:30AM.

Chapter 4

The estimable title, 'Mister', bestowed on surgeons in Britain, was a quaint relic of medieval times. It harkened back to an era when an inviolable line separated the two ancient professions of 'barber-surgeon' and 'physician-apothecary', before both were subsumed by modern-day medicine.

Mister Saleem Kureishi, Chief of Transplant Surgery, was unusually elated when he returned to his office after the finishing the latest 'liver' in the world-famous program he chaired. Not the surgery—transplanting a liver was boringly routine, limited only by donor availability. Transplanting a liver that you made available was a unique first, even for him. Not a first he could ever claim, though. Because the 'donor' was the brain-dead skinhead from last night!

It was quite hilarious, hearing the pious anger with which his assistant said, "A liver from a brain-dead victim of a traffic accident is one thing. But a brain-dead victim of murderous vigilantes with a warped sense of justice? That just isn't right."

It was ridiculous. How could someone without a brain be brain-dead? And calling a skinhead a victim was like calling a rabid jackal a victim of rabies.

Keeping a straight face, he responded just as piously, "At least some good's come from it. The donor can rest in peace, knowing his liver is in the best hands."

His assistant just sniffed.

Kureishi knew his colleagues found his arrogance insufferable. He didn't give a damn. He was untouchable. He had singlehandedly made this small private hospital on the outskirts of London the envy of its much larger competitors.

The hospital coffers overflowed with the gratitude of his patients. Many of them came from the richest families in the Middle East. The most generous were the Qumraani royals. Centuries of inbreeding had resulted in an extraordinarily high prevalence of two inherited disorders, one causing premature liver failure, the other uncontrollable hypertension leading to premature kidney failure. Kureishi's skills had saved several of them.

With genetic testing able to predict who would need a transplant well before liver or kidney failure developed, it was possible to identify a perfectly matched donor ahead of time. That was the secret behind a published success rate unmatched in the world.

It began twenty years ago when he applied on impulse for a job as Chief of Transplant Surgery at a state-of-the-art facility in Qumraan, having just completed a grueling two-year fellowship at the acclaimed transplant surgery program in Pittsburgh. He had zero experience, but he got the job anyway. All that mattered to the Crown Prince of Qumraan was that Kureishi was a practicing Muslim.

It was the first step on a journey that had brought him to the pinnacle of his profession. Once he established his reputation as a

surgeon of exceptional skill, demand skyrocketed. The only constraint was the scarcity of organ donors in the Middle East.

His big break came when the Crown Prince beat a servant into an
irreversible coma. With Mirza Mullick's connivance, he harvested the
liver and two kidneys, transplanting the liver into the Crown Prince's
older son, and the kidneys into two other members of the royal family. The liver was rejected, and the recipient died soon after, but the
kidneys saved two royal lives.

It was his first taste of harvesting organs without consent, and he
was hooked. He bought enthusiastically into Mirza's idea of 'Purchased Procurement' of organs from applicants in his pool, and demand went through the roof.

Then, the Crown Prince's younger son, Khalil al-Qumraan, the
only remaining male heir to the throne, developed liver failure. With
no perfect match to be found in IASC's applicant pool, the choice
was between making do with a less-than-perfect match, or abandoning ethics altogether to harvest organs without consent from a perfectly matched living donor.

Mirza's plan to adopt an orphan as a transplant 'donor' was pure
genius. It took a year to set up his 'philanthropic' scheme to provide
free health screenings at orphanages and locate a perfectly matched
orphan donor. By the time one was found, Kureishi had moved to
London. So, he returned to Qumraan to transplant half the boy's liver and one of his kidneys into Khalil.

By all rights, it should have been hailed as the first successful
child-to-child, live-donor transplant ever performed in the world—
yet another 'first' that was denied to him by those sanctimonious
Westerners and their damnable "ethical constraints". It was quite insufferable, because those same hypocrites swore by Darwin's mantra
of 'survival of the fittest'. So, how was it wrong to sacrifice an orphan
who wasn't fit to survive, to save Khalil, a royal whose right to life

was unquestioned, and whose survival was assured by unlimited resources?

And survive he did. For twelve years! Unfortunately, Khalil had grown into an incurable alcoholic and there was only so much alcohol any liver could handle, so the transplant was now failing. A second liver transplant should have been a cinch, if only the orphan whose liver he harvested years ago been alive. He wasn't, because Khalil, who inherited his father's sadistic streak, beat the original 'donor' to death two weeks ago.

Luckily, Mirza found a second perfectly matched donor. She had just entered palace service in Qumraan, like the first 'donor'. Unlike him, though, she wouldn't survive her 'donation'. He no longer needed to keep donors alive because Mirza could find donors at will. To twist that old metaphor about breaking eggs to make omelets, why keep broken shells after the omelet was made? Better to crush the shell and end the misery of their worthless lives.

The best part was that his 'broken shells' were buried under the sands of Qumraan, whereas his fifty-plus 'omelets', members of the richest families in the world, were a living testimonial to his skill. They had brought him international acclaim and wealth beyond his wildest dreams.

There was one transplant he valued more than all his acclaim and wealth; a transplant that no one, not even Mirza, knew about. It involved a 'donor' in Pakistan who was nameless, and a recipient who could never be named.

A transplant that changed the history of the world.

Shortly after he came to Qumraan, an obscure member of the Saudi royal family came seeking Kureishi's opinion about a kidney transplant. He was a tall, bearded man everyone called 'Sheik', but his given name was fated to become synonymous with the fall of the Twin Towers.

Osama bin Laden.

That destiny was still some years in the future, but there was, even then, an aura of messianic zeal and an incandescent charisma that mesmerized Kureishi. He was in the early stages of kidney failure, and a kidney transplant would be needed in a couple of years. Kureishi drew a blood sample for HLA typing and scheduled a return visit in six months. The Sheik never kept it. His name was on the FBI's Most Wanted Terrorist Watch List and he couldn't leave Afghanistan, where he was living under the protection of the Taliban.

A year later, a message arrived that the Sheik was in dire need of a kidney transplant. Under the pretext of a long-overdue trip to see his dying mother, he went to Pakistan, where he quietly disappeared for two weeks with the help of the all-powerful Pakistan Inter-Services Intelligence Agency.

At a secret facility equipped with the best technology, he operated on the Sheik, transplanting a kidney from a living 'donor' whose life was of no consequence. When it came time to leave, the Sheik gave Kureishi an ornate janbiyah dagger with a jewel-encrusted handle as a parting gift and anointed him the 'Dagger of Allah', with a cryptic comment that the most dangerous weapon in the world was a sheathed dagger kept hidden from view, until it was plunged without warning into the heart of an unsuspecting enemy.

Kureishi had no idea what that meant, but he had the words 'Dagger of Allah' etched on the blade in Arabic upon returning to Qumraan. It became his most treasured possession.

A year later, Kureishi was making rounds in the hospital when he saw the images on TV of the planes taking down the World Trade Center. He joined in the exclamations of horror as the Towers fell, all the while exulting at his contribution to the history of the world. Osama bin Laden, the 'Sheik', whose life he saved, had struck a mortal blow to the cultural and economic heart of the Great Shaitan.

And he understood, at last, what Osama meant when he referred to plunging a sheathed dagger without warning into of an unsuspecting enemy!

Exultation turned into euphoria two years later, when Osama bin Laden, the most hated man in the West, escaped certain death in the caves of Tora Bora to become the scourge of the Great Shaitan and a beacon of hope to all true believers. If Kureishi—the Dagger of Allah—hadn't cut his tether to a dialysis machine, Osama would surely have died in the caves.

For the next decade, the beacon burned bright and clear. Then, in the early hours of the morning on May 2, 2011, it was extinguished in a hail of bullets in a bungalow in Abbotabad, Pakistan.

When he heard the news, Kureishi felt a murderous desire to lash out. He knew better than to show it, so he clenched his teeth and joined the 'celebrations'. Left bereft and rudderless, he clung to Osama's parting benediction for solace in the hope it might show him a way to find his destiny.

It took four years—and Brexit—for him to find it. He became Osama's 'Dagger of Allah' to seek retribution for a wave of racial attacks unleashed by a newly energized skinhead movement—

The intercom beeped, drawing a frown of irritation from Kureishi at being interrupted just before he got to the best part: How he became judge, jury, and executioner.

He barked sharply into the intercom, making no attempt to hide his anger, "What?"

His secretary replied calmly, "Jonathan Wolff is asking to speak to you, Mr. Kureishi."

Kureishi cursed under his breath. He hated pandering to donors, but Jonathan Wolf was one donor he didn't dare offend.

"Put him through."

When Wolff came on the line, Kureishi greeted him effusively. "Mr. Wolff! A personal call from you is an unexpected pleasure!"

"Doctor—I mean Mister Kureishi! Please forgive the slip."

Kureishi laughed. "Nothing to forgive. The U.K. is the only country where a surgeon isn't a 'Doctor'. But I'm sure one of the richest men in the world has better things to do than discuss arcane British traditions. What can I do for you?"

"I need a personal favor, Mr. Kureishi. My daughter, Alexis, needs your help in a matter she can only discuss when she meets you in person. All I can tell you is that it doesn't involve her personally."

Kureishi was secretly amused. Subterfuge and denial were dead giveaways that it must be something socially unacceptable. Like AIDS or hepatitis. He said solemnly, "I'm honored to help the daughter of a friend and benefactor, Mr. Wolff. Is she in London?"

"She's arriving there tomorrow. Could you spare some time for her after 2PM?"

"Sure. I'll keep the afternoon open for Ms. Wolff."

"Thank you, Mr. Kureishi. By the way, she is a physician."

"As a colleague, I'm all the more excited to meet her."

After exchanging a few pleasantries, Kureishi hung up and sat back to think.

Why be so coy about the reason for consulting me? There's no shame in needing a liver transplant for hepatitis—needle exposure is an occupational hazard for physicians. Must be something she needs to hide if she's coming to London. Drug addiction? Not unheard of in physicians. And shameful—you lose your license if it becomes public. What if it's something even more intriguing? Like AIDS from sexual promiscuity! Wonder what kind of body...

An image of Wolff's grotesque physique rose unbidden in his mind and his fantasy came to a screeching halt.

201

The laws of genetics dictated there had to be something of the father in her. Even if it was just ten percent, she had to be—what did the Americans say? —a dog!

No! A wolf!

He burst out laughing at his clever pun.

Chapter 5

A lexis felt a ripple of alarm when she laid eyes on Saleem Kureishi.

He was almost devilishly handsome. Tall and rangy...but with the arrogant virility of a man who might have been called a 'blade' in a bygone era. It was vaguely repellant but not enough to trigger alarm.

It was an indefinable aura of danger that set her ninja sense on edge...a lithe fluidity in the way he moved. Almost like...*a ninja?*

Stifling the unsettling thought, she sat down across from Kureishi, saying, "Thank you, Mr. Kureishi, for accommodating me at short notice. I hope I didn't inconvenience you."

"Not at all, Dr. Wolff. Happy to help the daughter of someone to whom I owe so much. I got my start at the hospital your father built in Qumraan. And his philanthropic foundation continues to support my work here, in London. So, it's a pleasure, not an inconvenience. Mr. Wolff said it was something of a delicate nature..."

"Yes, Mr. Kureishi. It has to do with the Transplant Surgery program in Qumraan."

His face froze for just an instant, then melted into a charming grin. "Do I hear the rattling of skeletons in my closet?

"The skeleton isn't in your closet, Mr. Kureishi. But it's as heinous as it gets."

"What on earth are you talking about?" There was that face-freeze again.

"I have unassailable proof that, after you left, somebody in the program used a six-year-old boy from India as a live organ donor to harvest his liver and kidney."

She saw Kureishi's face turn grey and go slack. She wasn't surprised. No physician would accept that any member of the profession, let alone a colleague, could commit such a heinous act. She continued, "I need your help to identify the surgeon who performed that one transplant a year after you left Qumraan. I have the date and name."

His face stiffened into an expressionless mask, and his voice was so mellow he might have been discussing the weather. "If you have unassailable proof, it would be my duty to join your crusade—may I call it that...?"

Wondering what he was driving at, she gave a non-committal shrug.

Then he added, his lips curling into a sneer, "But don't expect me to take the word of someone who knows nothing about transplant surgery. Unless you show me this so-called unassailable proof and tell me how you came by it, our conversation is at an end."

Alexis couldn't believe her ears. Disbelief was one thing. Sneering contempt was beyond the pale. And it was none of his business how she got the proof.

Controlling her anger, she took out the DVDs and proffered them to him. "These five DVDs were obtained by a journalist. They

204

are the proof." The sneer was still there, so she added spiritedly, "And you don't need to be a transplant surgeon to see it. It's staring you in the face."

Kureishi turned around to insert the DVD labeled '#1' into the computer behind him and began scrolling through the images on the monitor.

It took him a while to view all five disks. When he finally turned around, her ninja instinct reacted instantly, sensing deadly danger behind the mask on his face. Then his face became wreathed in a smile of such warmth and charm that she thought she imagined it.

"Dr. Wolff," he said. "These images are really unbelievable." He paused, and the sneer reappeared. "So unbelievable, in fact, that they can only be fake. An out-and-out fraud perpetrated by a sensation-hungry journalist trying to make his name by destroying the reputation of some poor surgeon. *You* might be naïve enough to be taken in by this hoax, *I* am not. If you persist with this ridiculous claim, not only will I refuse to stand with you, I will make it my duty to denounce you as either a gullible fool or a downright charlatan!"

She reeled in her anger, but there was ice in her reply. "Mr. Kureishi, I don't give a damn whether you stand with me or denounce me. Just give me the name of the transplant surgeon."

"I refuse, unless you tell me how you're so sure the disks aren't doctored fakes."

"The disks have a date of creation that is critical to the backstory, which involves people, places and circumstances that are real and verifiable. Any IT expert could establish or destroy the disks' credibility when I reveal that story. Anyway, what do you have to lose by giving me the name of the surgeon, if you're so sure the disks are—what did you call them? —doctored fakes?"

"An accusation this heinous could destroy a career, even if it's proven to be fraudulent."

"Not if it's you who proves it's fraudulent. If the facts are on your side, a medical nobody like me stands no chance in a 'he said-she said' battle against someone of your reputation and international standing. Just wait for me to hang my credibility and reputation out in the court of public opinion and destroy both by proving I'm the fraud and charlatan you've already decided I am."

He smiled, but it didn't reach his eyes. "Your passion moves me. I will requisition the records from Qumraan."

"That would be very foolish. The last name 'al-Qumraan' identifies the recipient as a member of the royal family. The hospital would never yield the records. So, the only way to get the truth is through the surgeons on staff at the time, narrow it down to two or three suspects, then play one off the other to see who flips.

"Wait a minute. There may be another way. We don't need the whole chart; we only need the operative notes."

"But how do you get the op notes without the chart?"

The million-kilowatt smile reappeared, but his eyes were oddly opaque, showing nothing of the excitement in his voice. "From a vault in my house where the op notes and scan images of every liver transplant performed in Qumraan are stored. With full permission, I might add. They are the source material for all the papers I have written over the years. So, that's where we'll find the op notes of the 'al-Qumraan' transplant. We find who did that surgery, we find who harvested the boy's organs."

Alexis felt her excitement surge. "How long will that take?"

"They're catalogued, so maybe half an hour after I get home tonight. But I must warn you how dangerous this is. If the Qumraani

206

royals suspect what we're doing, our lives won't be worth a brass farthing. Or a plugged nickel to a Yank like you."

She found it amusing that he assumed she was a 'Yank' because she was Jonathan's daughter. Not that it mattered. She let it go.

He continued. "There's a particularly vicious Qumraani underworld in London linked to the royal family that wouldn't hesitate to kill on their behalf."

"Really?" she replied nonchalantly. "We'll just have to be extra careful, then."

"You can't be flippant about this. Our lives could be in jeopardy."

His sudden transformation from belligerent non-believer to Nervous Nellie irritated Alexis. She decided to end the conversation.

She got to her feet, saying, "I'll keep it in mind," and held out her hand. "May I have the disks, please?"

"Can I hold on to them to compare with what's in my files?"

She shook her head. "I'm sorry, Mr. Kureishi, but I can't leave them with you. I owe that to the person who got them. Once you locate your records, I'll bring them to you to compare with the scans in your vault." She paused, then added lightly, "To convince you I'm neither a charlatan nor a gullible fool."

It wasn't intended to be a barb, but she saw his expression harden for an instant. Then that same dazzling smile appeared, and he handed them back with a surprisingly affable protest. "Come, come, Dr. Wolff! No need to rub it in. You've convinced me."

She didn't smile back. "I'm not rubbing it in. I expect to be called much worse when I go public."

"That's the spirit. And please call me, Saleem. A cloak-and-dagger relationship surely merits first-names."

"Agreed. I'm Alexis."

"Great. Now, all I need is your room number and the hotel where you're staying. I'll call you around six-thirty this evening to discuss strategy."

She scribbled down the information he wanted and handed it over. "There's nothing to discuss. The strategy is simple. You find him. I unmask him."

"Fair enough" Kureishi replied. "Until tonight, when your crusade hopefully comes to its end."

He added, almost as an afterthought, "Successfully, of course."

Chapter 6

urderous rage.

Kureishi felt it sear him when the door closed.

Alexis Wolff hadn't just rattled the biggest, most deadly skeleton in his closet. She had awakened something that would slay him.

The backstory was immaterial. The disks were genuine, blue-chip authentic. But who was this journalist who resurrected the skeleton from its grave? Mirza had assured him that the skeleton was buried so deep it would never be found, let alone resurrected. As for that vaunted "early warning system" he boasted was in place? Mirza would have to be told that it was an abject failure.

Telling him could wait, though. First, he had to get rid of Alexis Wolff and those damned disks. If only she'd let him have them, he could've concocted some excuse for why they were ruined. Too bad she didn't fall for it.

At least, the gullible bitch fell for the story he concocted on the spur of the moment, pretending to suddenly remember he had the op notes in his house. It was very plausible, but the eagerness with which she swallowed it lock, stock, and barrel was quite laughable.

He was quite sure she would have come panting into his arms, like a bitch in heat, if he wanted. He had toyed with the idea when he first saw her, imagining those longs legs wrapped around him. But she had to go and rattle that skeleton. Now, instead of finding the door to heaven in Saleem Kureishi's bed, she would find Hell.

Alexis Wolff would die tonight. Brutally and painfully.

Chapter 7

K ureishi sounded hysterical when he called at 5:30PM.

"Alexis! We're in trouble. They're on to you. And they know I'm involved. Who else knows about the disks? Who did you tell about coming to see me in London?"

He sounded so terrified, that she told him the truth, just not the whole truth. "My father and brother know what's on these disks, certainly no one in London. So, who's on to me?"

"I was on my way home when I got a call on my mobile from some guy with a Middle-Eastern accent, warning me you were poking your nose into something that would get you killed. And I would, too, if I helped you. It scared me enough to pull off the road to call you from a payphone. I warned you the Qumraani mafia are deadly. I'm taking no chances. I've turned off my mobile and GPS so they can't track me."

"How come they found out so quickly?"

"I may have tipped them off. I tried logging in to the hospital database to access Ganga Prasad's chart with my credentials, but I was blocked and my access instantly terminated. We can't go through with it now."

She kicked herself for not thinking he might try that. Too late now.

"Nonsense! We can't stop now," she said emphatically. "The sooner we go public, the sooner you and I will be safe."

He took his time to reply, but he sounded less fearful. "OK. But, if you want me to go through with it, I insist we do it my way to keep both of us safe."

"What do you mean?"

"Leave your hotel right away, talking to nobody. Walk to Leicester Square and take the Tube to Morden, the southern terminus of the Northern Line. Exit left and wait at the street corner. My man, Yousuf, will pick you up there and drive you to my home in Epsom."

"Don't you think that's a bit much, Saleem?"

His voice rose to a hysterical shriek. "A bit much? I'll tell you what's a bit much. A fanatical quest to crucify some surgeon you don't even know, who did something decades ago, to some orphan you never met, in a country you never visited. That, Alexis, is what's a bit much. You'll leave after you get what you want. I'll be left to face the music. All I'm asking is that you don't get me killed. If that's a bit much, we end it here."

She saw his point. "I'm sorry, Saleem. We'll do it your way."

He seemed mollified. "Okay. Yousuf will come in his car, not mine. His phone will be off, so no one can track him. You must switch off yours, too. Do it now, please?"

This wasn't paranoia, it was borderline delusional! But she turned off her mobile to humor him. "It's done."

Then something struck her. "How will I know I'm getting into the right car?" she asked.

"Good point! Let's agree on a code-word."

"Okay. Pick one."

"How about you ask who he's waiting for, and he answers 'Ganga Prasad'."

Did she detect a hint of amusement in his voice? She wasn't sure, but it was in such poor taste that she responded angrily, "No! He answers 'Hippocrates'. That's what this is about."

"Perfect! Nobody could guess that. Yousuf will meet you...shall we say around seven-thirty? And remember to bring the disks."

She assured him she would and hung up.

Chapter 8

By the time she left the hotel, Alexis had bought into Kureishi's paranoia. The Batras' deaths proved that the Qumraani royals' reach was both formidable and deadly. So, she followed Kureishi's instructions to the letter.

She found a dark-skinned man waiting at the street corner outside Morden station.

"Who are you waiting for?" she asked warily.

He replied in a heavy Punjabi accent, "Hippo-cray-tiss" and she breathed a sigh of relief.

"I'm Alexis Wolff," she said by way of introduction and got another one-word response, "Yousuf." Then he escorted her to a Ford with tinted windows parked on a nearby street. She got in the front passenger seat and they drove away.

She tried striking up a conversation, but his monosyllabic answers were off-putting. So, she passed the time tracing their route on a 'London A-Z' book sitting on the dashboard, with maps of every street in the metropolis. It wasn't long before she realized Yousuf was sticking to secondary roads and neighborhood streets, avoiding all intersections he had marked with a red circle.

She asked why, and he answered, "Suckyortee cumayrah."

Security cameras! She knew London's thoroughfares were monitored, but this was beyond paranoia! Surely the Qumraani mafia couldn't be *that* powerful?

Twenty-five minutes later, they arrived at a secluded country home. Although modest by English country-house standards, it was replete with angled abutments and gargoyles that conveyed a brooding Gothic intensity in the evening light.

Yousuf ushered her into what must have been a large banquet or receiving hall in a distant past, but was now home to a formidable collection of medieval weaponry. From the walls, a variety of crossbows, maces, crested shields, broadswords, and battle axes glowered down on sets of medieval armor from across the world, with even a samurai warrior dress thrown in.

The ambience was one of gloomy menace, amplified by heavy draperies that excluded natural light, and low-level electric lighting from ancient wall sconces where gas jets once burned. At the far end of the room was the sole bright spot: a fireplace with two plush armchairs on either side of a lovely Kashmiri rug, radiating a cheerful coziness completely at odds with the rest of the room.

The sense of a room within the room was heightened by a massive stone mantel jutting out above the fireplace at shoulder height.

In stark contrast to the rest of the room, the wall above the mantel was bare, befitting the pièce de résistance of the collection. Resting horizontally on the mantel in solitary splendor was a magnificent *tachi*, the older form of Japanese samurai sword.

She walked up to the fireplace as if the tachi called to her and stared at it, mesmerized.

215

Sheathed in a beautiful *saya* (scabbard) decorated with intricate gold inlay shaped like a coiled dragon, it was, without doubt, a priceless antique, worth more than the rest of the collection put together. But its formidable monetary worth didn't come close to its cultural value in Japan. That was incalculable.

A large brass plaque on the mantel read:

"To my friend Saleem.

For Life

For Qumraan

For now, and forever

From Sayf

The Sword of Qumraan"

The choice of syntax was curious. Did "My friend, Saleem…For Life…For Qumraan," mean something more than "friend for life"? Or was it just unfamiliarity with English idiom? Either way, it was a gift worthy of a prince. Or even a monarch! 'Sayf' meant 'sword' in Arabic, and Crown Prince Sayf al-Qumraan was shortly to be crowned the next Emir.

Unable to resist the temptation, Alexis lifted the sheathed tachi with her left hand and wrapped her right hand around the hilt, feeling her nerves tingle at the perfect fit of her fingers in the grooves. She started to draw it from the saya, and the tingle turned electric. The blade slid along the saya with effortless ease as if on greased rollers, proving its maker was a supreme master of his craft!

The glittering blade was barely a third of the way out when she was suddenly overtaken by a premonition of great evil. A wave of nausea swept over her, and she snatched her hand from the hilt as if it was red hot. The partly drawn blade remained snugly held, sliding neither in nor out of the saya, befitting the exceptional craftsmanship of its maker.

Taking a deep breath to steady her nerve, she held the partly drawn blade up to the light, gripping the scabbard with both hands, and sighted along its length, first on one side then the other. The pattern hammered into the polished steel at the temper line, or *hamon*, was as unique to each swordsmith as the brush strokes of a painter. And this one was so distinctively unique that it might as well be a signature. It undulated in a pattern of peaks and valleys called *gunome midare*. And those undulations on both sides were *exact mirror images of each other!*

She knew then, without a shadow of doubt, that she held a sword made by the legendary swordsmith, Muramasa Sengo. He was renowned for making some of the sharpest and most deadly tachis in history. A Muramasa tachi, it was said, could slice a silk thread floating down on it. And this one looked like it would slice skin at the lightest touch.

Legend had it that Muramasa was a disturbed and violent individual; a psychopath possessed by great evil, who imbued his swords with his personality. She recalled scraps of ninja lore telling of the demonic nature of Muramasa blades. That they were possessed of a blood lust that prevented a tachi made by Muramasa from returning to its scabbard without tasting blood. That a warrior who drew it was compelled to either kill or commit suicide.

There were almost no Muramasa tachis in existence, because the famous shogun, Tokugawa Ieyasu, decreed that all tachis bearing his signature on the fish-shaped tang (the part of the blade buried inside the handle) be destroyed as personifications of evil. How this one escaped destruction was irrelevant. The distinctive hamon left no doubt that it was a genuine Muramasa tachi. So, that wave of nausea had to be her ninja instinct warning her that the tachi's diabolical nature was alive—!

217

Her rational mind reasserted itself, reeling in that foolishness before it spiraled out of control. What made her nauseous wasn't some fabled blood lust. It was irrational fear triggered by superstition.

Her mind was once again grounded in reason, but she still took care not to touch the hilt of the tachi. Instead, she gripped the saya with both hands and pushed the hilt up against the undersurface of the mantel to re-sheath it, before replacing it in its stand.

She stepped back from the fireplace and stared at it, unable to shake the memory of its cold, lethal beauty.

Chapter 9

A lexis heard a footfall and turned around.

She saw Kureishi come bounding into the room with an air of near-manic excitement and her ninja instinct came instantly alert, screaming of mortal peril.

He stopped three feet from her, rocking back and forth, as if poised on a hair-trigger. Without any preamble, he thrust out his hand and demanded, "The disks. Give me the disks."

Her combat instinct took over then, and she relaxed. Her unwitting choice of slacks and canvas slip-on sneakers was perfect for whatever might be coming.

"I have them," she replied, casually tapping her bag as she eased it off her shoulder with a shrug and let it slide down to rest on the ground. "What's got you so excited?"

Her mellow response seemed to surprise Kureishi. She saw him start, then his face dissolved into an effusive smile and he gestured to the armchair behind her. "Sit down and let me tell you a story."

She waited for him to take the other armchair before sitting down herself. He lounged back, his thighs spread and one leg draped over the chair arm in the classic pose of aggressive male insolence.

Her eyes were drawn to the shoe on his dangling foot—long and tapered, with a pronounced toecap and the edge of a metal plate visible in the sole. Seeing it, he laughed, with more than a hint of menace and straightened his knee. "You like my shoes? That's good. because I'm going to tell you a story and you can choose whether they should figure in the ending."

She knew, then, that the truth was about to be revealed. What came after that—the 'ending' he referred to—would have to take care of itself when the time came.

As Kureishi's story unfolded, the fury she felt when she first saw the scans came flooding back. Except it was ice-cold. And she was in complete control.

It was the story was of an amoral and ambitious surgeon who forsook all ethics to gain fame and fortune.

How he seized the chance to save the life of an aristocrat by harvesting organs from a servant beaten to death by the Crown Prince.

How he and Mirza Mullick took the next step, recruiting 'donors' who could be bribed or coerced or killed to save aristocrats far more worthy of life than the worthless nobodies whose organs were their only possessions of worth.

How that evolved to abducting an orphan—a penniless nobody who made his only worthwhile contribution to society by giving life to a prince.

How Kureishi monetized the Crown Prince's undying gratitude to set himself up for life, earning untold wealth, international recognition, and universal acclaim.

220

Kureishi ended with a sorrowful shake of his head, saying, "I'm sure you understand that I cannot let anyone jeopardize all the good I've done. Certainly not a renegade journalist who stole protected health information, or a sanctimonious busybody with a God complex and twisted sense of ethics. Give me the disks."

She stared at him, speechless, her eyes aflame with fury.

Angered by her silence, he snapped, "Why are you so obsessed with the death of a worthless palace servant. He was alive only because I chose to keep him alive so the liver remnant could be preserved until I took that, too. And that day was close. The half I transplanted years ago is failing, because of the recipient's regrettable affinity for alcohol. His death doesn't matter because we have an insurance policy. All will be well unless those disks become public. So, I'm going to ask you one last time to hand over the disks."

"And if I don't?"

"If you give them to me, your death will be quick and painless. If you force me to take them, it will be very painful and quite messy. I will systematically break every bone in your body, from your ankles to your collarbones, making sure you hear and feel each bone breaking. Then I will break your neck."

"You won't get away with killing me. You can hide surgical murder, not homicide."

He threw his head back and laughed. "Homicide? Whose? Where? And who's to know? There's no record of your coming here. My call to you was from a payphone with my GPS and mobile turned off. Your mobile is off, and Yousuf avoided every security camera on the way over. There's no trace of your coming here."

"You're forgetting something that *can* be traced. My body. Whether you bury it in your grounds or somewhere else, it'll be found sooner or later."

"Sorry to disappoint. You'll be buried, alright, but not where you'll ever be found. You see, I don't work on Fridays, so tomorrow I will be where I always am on Fridays. On my yacht, out at sea. The port officials in Brighton know me well and will think nothing when I board tomorrow with an extra cabin trunk. Inside it will be your body, surgically cut into manageable pieces. You will be buried at sea and the fishes will make sure your body is never found."

He bared his teeth in a predatory grin. "You see, I've thought of everything."

She pretended to be afraid. "You're mad if you think you'll get away with it. My father knows I'm here. He'll uncover the truth and expose you!"

"Oh, but he won't. All his money can't recreate the only proof there is. Without the disks, there is nothing. After I destroy them, I will call Qumraan to have the records erased. No body, no disks, no records. And no case. If the police question me, I'll say you came to see me in the office with a cock-and-bull story about something that happened long after I left Qumraan. I had no idea what you were talking about, but I warned you that the Qumraani mafia would kill you if you made such a slanderous allegation. You refused to heed my warning and paid the price."

He paused, waiting for her reaction. When she stayed silent, he said sharply, "Enough of this! If you don't hand them over, I will be forced to take them, and you will die in agony."

He slung back his leg to stand up, but she was on her feet before him. "You won't kill me. You're a coward who murders his anesthetized victims with a scalpel in a nice, clean OR. You don't have it in you to murder me in cold blood with your bare hands."

He threw his head back and laughed. "You can't be more wrong. You're looking at a sixth-degree black belt in karate and master in

Thai kickboxing. I've bested men far stronger, bigger, and skilled in hand-to-hand combat than ten pampered rich girls like you."

So! The arrogant bastard thinks I'm a helpless female who's no match for him. His overconfidence might just offset his advantages in strength, size, and reach. Let's reinforce that...

She shrank back fearfully, saying in a trembling voice, "Defeating men in a fight isn't the same as murdering with your bare-hands."

He responded with a derisive snort, saying, "I see you don't believe I can kill with my bare hands. Have you heard of the charmingly-named gang of 'Packy Vigilantes' who've figured prominently in recent tabloid headlines? Its cast of colorful characters includes the 'Bearded Mullah' and 'Black Widow'."

He bowed theatrically without taking his eyes off her. "You're looking at them."

Alexis stared at him in utter disbelief.

He laughed delightedly at her stunned reaction. "Who can blame you for not believing it? Even the police are convinced it's a gang. I could show you the Mullah's beard, and the Black Widow's wig, floppy hat, and raincoat in my closet upstairs. But I'd rather show you something even more convincing. The soul of both personas."

He reached into the small of his back and pulled out a sheathed janbiyah from his waistband. "Behold!" he said with a dramatic flourish, "The Dagger of Allah."

She felt her gut clench. The balance of combat had just been irrevocably altered.

Not because the dagger was a weapon. Because the fanatical reverence in his eyes showed it held a mystical significance from which he drew preternatural strength.

223

It was revealed in his next words. "This was a gift from the late, great Osama bin Laden for performing the kidney transplant that saved his life. Without me there would have been no 9/11."

She saw bitter hatred in his face as he went on. "I saved a life of unparalleled greatness only for the damned Americans to destroy it. But his vision lives on in countless others like me. To honor him, I became the Dagger of Allah. The slayer of infidels. Like you."

When she still said nothing, he snarled, "I have tried being nice, but you continue to spurn my offer of mercy. Your death will not be quick or painless. But I did say you could choose how the story ends, and I am nothing if not a man of my word. How do you want to die? By my hands?" He brandished the dagger, then used it to point to his shoes, "Or my feet?"

Seeing her eyes gaze follow the pointing dagger, he said decisively, "The feet it is!"

Then there was no time for thought. Kureishi dropped into a half-crouch, left hand on the floor, and spun around, his right leg extended in a sweeping horizontal kick aimed at her ankles.

Had the ashi-barai kick connected, the steel plate in the sole would have shattered her ankles, crippling her.

It didn't. Because her sakki anticipated his move.

The instant he launched his kick, she jumped up and back, leaving her shoes on the floor, so his foot blew through, unimpeded, sending him spinning around further than he intended.

She registered his breathtaking mastery of the kick as she came down, her calves brushing the edge of the armchair. Unarmed she stood no chance against him…

The instant the thought came, her ninja instinct took over. She leapt up and back again, but much higher, landing in a half squat on the seat of the armchair. Using the chair as a springboard, she exploded into a twisting vertical leap that propelled her above the stone mantel.

She landed on the mantel facing the wall, her back to him, going down to her haunches to absorb the shock of impact. Her left hand closed around the sheathed tachi and she jack-knifed erect, pushing off the wall into a soaring backwards layout that took her arcing high over Kureishi,

She somersaulted at the top of the arc, her heels flipping over her head to bring him back into view. He was at the fireplace, facing the mantel, with his head twisted over his shoulder, tracking her trajectory, slack jawed from shock.

She came out of her somersault, absorbing the impact of her landing by sinking into a full squat. She snapped upright instantly, holding the sheathed tachi at her left hip, convex edge forward.

She saw Kureishi whirl around as she came erect and freeze for a split second at the sight of the tachi in her left hand. Then he lunged forward, almost stumbling in his haste to get to her, dagger upraised, his face stark with terror.

In that moment of hesitation, her right hand blurred to the hilt of the tachi.

Alexis had practiced the *battojutsu*—the art of drawing the sword—countless times during her ninja training, never thinking she might need it in a life-or-death battle. It came to her instinctively now, in her moment of need.

The blade of the tachi sprang free and she felt its energy pulse like a living thing as the draw flowed effortlessly into a backhanded stroke at waist height, cutting edge forwards.

Kureishi's momentum and her strike converged at the exact moment the blade entered his right flank. The incredible sharpness of the tachi did the rest. It sliced his belly open, as if sweeping through

225

water. All she felt was a faint grating as it slid across the vertebral column before emerging from Kureishi's left flank.

She twisted away from the explosive gush of blood from Kureishi's severed aorta, lifting the tachi over and behind her left shoulder in a seamless continuation of her draw-and-strike. The twist flowed into a pirouette, allowing Kureishi's half-dismembered body to career past her, lurching uncontrollably.

At that moment, Yousuf appeared at the door, a Webley revolver in his left hand, pointing down. He gawked uncomprehendingly at his master, barreling towards him, bloody entrails spilling from his belly. Then he saw her, and his gun hand started to come up. Alexis knew she'd be dead before she could reach him.

Before he could squeeze the trigger, though, Fate intervened.

Kureishi's semi-disarticulated torso cannoned into Yousuf's outstretched forearm as it came up, and they both went down in a heap, Yousuf landing on his back with his master's body on him. The gun went off as Alexis leapt forward, tachi upraised. Then Kureishi's body rolled off, and she saw the revolver wedged under Yousuf's ribcage. It had blown a hole as big as her fist through his chest.

She knew Yousuf was dead, but she checked anyway. She didn't bother with Kureishi. He lay on his back, eyes open, the last of his blood trickling out onto the carpet.

She rose to her feet and dropped the tachi with a shiver. Its baleful reputation might be legend, but there was something eerie in the way the blade sliced through Kureishi. Almost like it was eager...

She shook off the thought. This wasn't the time for malign fantasies. She faced a far more nightmarish reality. She was trapped in a remote country house with two dead men, one with his belly sliced open by the tachi, the other shot by his own gun. How in God's name was she going explain to the police what she was doing here and how they died without incriminating herself?

As she was mulling over her dilemma, her eyes fell on Kureishi's body, partly draped over Yousuf, and the solution hit her.

Kureishi must have powder burns on his hand from grabbing Yousuf's gun when it went off. All she needed to do was put his fingerprints on the gun and Yousuf's on the tachi to fabricate a scenario that didn't involve her in their deaths. Kureishi himself crowed that there was no record of her coming here. And he wasn't expected at work tomorrow, so he wouldn't be missed before Monday, by which time she'd be long gone.

She would leave the ornate dagger where Kureishi dropped it. Whether or not the police connected him to the Dagger of Allah—or Bearded Mullah or Black Widow—wasn't her concern. He was dead in all his lethal incarnations. Ganga Prasad was avenged.

It was enough.

So, why wasn't it…enough? She should be rejoicing, not enveloped by a black cloud of desolation, as if it was all for naught.

She felt Jason reaching out to her through the bond, but she shut him out, unwilling to interact until she sorted things out for herself.

Emptying her mind of all thought, she set up the bodies and weapons to create the scenario she wanted. Then she vacuumed the chair and rug for any strands of hair that came loose during the fight, removing the dust bag to take with her, and wiped the armchair and mantel clean.

She returned to London in Yousuf's car, dressed as Kureishi's "Black Widow", avoiding every security camera marked on his London A-Z. She abandoned the car at a London suburban railway station without a red circle and caught a train to Victoria Terminus, changing out of her disguise en route. She took the Tube from Victoria to Leicester Square and walked to her hotel, where she emptied the dust bag in a trash can in the lobby restroom. That left only the costume and the A-Z. She would discard those in India.

She informed Jonathan's air crew manager that she would be leaving early next morning, then put herself into a meditative trance to escape the dark cloud enveloping her.

At some point, she drifted from trance into sleep.

Day 7-10

THE SWORD OF RETRIBUTION

Chapter 1

Alexis sensed her mood growing steadily bleaker on the flight. If she didn't find and confront the source of her desolation, it might drag her down to that trapdoor she thought was sealed forever.

One thing she knew for sure was that it had nothing to do with either the Muramasa tachi or Kureishi's death.

Her reaction to drawing the blade was driven by superstition, not some fabled blood lust! As for killing Kureishi, not only did she have *zero* remorse, she felt lucky to be alive. His advantages in strength, size, and reach, his steel-capped shoes, and his breathtaking kickboxing skills should've made it a slam dunk. And Kureishi had only to call out to Yousuf when he saw her with the tachi, and Yousuf's gun would have done for her. Thankfully, his smug arrogance couldn't conceive of an unarmed "pampered American" woman besting him, "a sixth-degree black belt and master of Thai kickboxing".

So, if it wasn't the tachi or Kureishi, what made avenging Ganga Prasad so different from when she avenged Pammie Siddhu? If anything, the death of a little girl she knew and loved ought to have left her feeling far more bereft. So, why this bleak emptiness over the death of an orphan boy she never even met?

The answer hit her right then. It wasn't the legacy of their *deaths*. It was the legacy of their *lives* that made all the difference.

Pammie Siddhu's life was bursting with joy and love, and that memory filled the void in Alexis's heart. Ganga Prasad's life was filled with sorrow, hurt, and pain, so the void in her heart was as empty and desolate as the memory of his life.

Embarking on the path of vengeance without understanding that critical difference was a terrible mistake. Even worse, she insisted to Jonathan it was just like Pammie, blindly embracing his whimsical name for her. The Sword of Retribution!

Worst of all—a monumental blunder, in reality—she ignored her sensei's teachings.

One of those was "There is no honor or satisfaction in vengeance, only dishonor and regret!"

Another was, "Vengeance is like a *yari*—spear—with two sharp ends. One stabs the victim, giving brief satisfaction. The other wounds the warrior, leaving lasting regret."

The third was so profound that she never grasped its deep mystical significance until now. "A warrior seeking retribution takes a life. A warrior seeking redemption saves a life."

She understood now why avenging Ganga Prasad felt so different from avenging Pammie Siddhu. It wasn't because Kureishi's culpability was materially different from Kalidas's. Nor was it because saving the faceless millions scheduled to die in Bloodbath was any more redemptive than saving Kureishi's future potential victims.

It was because she found redemption by saving Mohan and Seetha from Kalidas when she exacted retribution for Pammie. But there was no equivalent of Mohan or Seetha to save from Kureishi when she exacted retribution for Ganga Prasad.

If her only hope of redemption lay in saving another Ganga Prasad, it was essentially hopeless. Forget finding someone who suffered even half the misery Ganga Prasad endured. With Kureishi dead, there was no one left to save.

Maybe time would lighten her burden of hopelessness. It was her only hope…

Chapter 2

J ason was on tenterhooks while he waited for Alexis at the airport. His anxiety had been at fever pitch from the moment he was jolted from sleep in the early hours of the morning by a short pulse of extreme stress in the psychic bond.

It lasted only a minute, but it was what came after that left Jason shaken to his core. It wasn't the catatonic 'shutdown' from years earlier. Or the dreadful 'silence' Alexis sensed when he was knocked out.

A 'darkness' was as close as he could come to describing it. Like a shade drawn to shut out light, as if she was shutting him out deliberately. Try as he might, he couldn't penetrate it. For the first time ever!

He saw her emerge from the Arrivals Hall and his gut clenched, sensing the 'darkness' still hanging over her. She didn't smile when she greeted him, but at least her eyes were tranquil, so her psychic defenses were still intact. It was something to hold on to.

He put his arm around her and asked matter-of-factly, "How did it go with Kureishi?"

"Fine," she replied, her voice flat and emotionless.

Another first! She was warning him not to probe further.

They drove to Ravi's house without exchanging a word, until they pulled into the driveway. Only then did he break the silence, saying gently, "I know you're tired, Red, but Mohan discovered something while you were gone that's a real game-changer. Just hear him out after you shower and change, then you can rest. Okay?"

"I've had my shower on the plane. Let's do it now."

He saw a spark of interest in her eyes, and it gave him hope. It was the first sign of light in the darkness enveloping her.

Maybe Mohan's news would lift her darkness. It was something to cling to.

Chapter 3

The instant Alexis walked into Ravi's living room she sensed the excitement in the air. It was palpable. Even Malini was smiling. Mohan's discovery had to be pretty incredible to manage that!

Sadly, it wouldn't change what happened in London. Or lift the oppressive darkness in her soul. Still, she owed it to everyone not to let her mood dampen theirs. So, she would keep what happened to herself. She wasn't ready to bare her soul just yet, even to Jason.

He started things off. "You know we're with you, Red, in your quest to avenge Ganga Prasad. Death for death: Abbas's death for abducting him and the surgeon's professional death for harvesting his organs. Right?"

There it was. The opening to confess she killed Kureishi and admit the folly of her single-minded pursuit of retribution. But she couldn't take it. Not until she reconciled with the dreadful reality that redemption was out of reach. She just nodded.

Jason continued. "What if there was something better than retribution for his death?"

"What the hell are you talking about?" She couldn't stop her anger at herself from spilling out.

"Redemption for his life."

She gaped at him in disbelief. It was almost as if he read her thoughts on the plane. But it couldn't be. They didn't have *that* kind of twin connection! He must be referring to redemption of the religious kind. But the nerve it touched was brutally raw.

"Jason Wolff," she snapped at him. "You know better than anyone that I don't give a damn about redemption in some mythical afterlife. I care only about the here and now."

Jason ignored her angry use of his full name, saying gently, "This isn't mythical or in the after-life, Red. The redemption I'm talking about *is* in the here and now. A chance to rescue the next Ganga Prasad before he or she is murdered."

She stared at Jason as if he had gone mad.

Jason read her thoughts this time. "No, Red, I'm not crazy. Just hear what Mohan has to say and decide for yourself."

Mohan took his cue. "Alexis, remember when I found Ganga Prasad's name in the database of the lab that did HLA tests for IASC, you asked me if I found anyone else?"

She nodded. "Yes. You said you couldn't without their names."

"That's because I'm a certified idiot. Yesterday, my idiot brain finally figured it out. It wasn't about the other *names*. It was about the other *matches!*"

Alexis was mystified. "What difference does that make?"

"It makes *all* the difference, Alexis! What if Ganga Prasad's wasn't the only perfect match? If there was another, wouldn't that person be in danger now that Ganga Prasad is dead? What if the recipient needs a new liver? Transplants can go bad, right?"

237

Alexis felt her senses reel. All she could manage was a mechanical, "Any transplant, no matter how well-matched, can be rejected, unless it's an identical twin."

"I thought so!" Mohan said excitedly. "So, I searched again, looking this time for an exact match to *Ganga Prasad*. And I got a hit. You won't believe who it is."

Still shaken by Jason's 'redemption' bombshell, Alexis could only muster one word. "Who?"

Seetha took up the thread. "Alexis, do you remember me saying that IASC came to the Hostel for Destitute Women in Kolkata to get people to sign up for jobs in the Gulf?"

Alexis could only nod. Her mouth was too dry to articulate.

"A friend of mine from the Hostel, Ayesha Siddiqui, is the other exact match."

"So what? Alexis replied, feeling deflated. "With Abbas dead, she's not in danger."

"But she is, Alexis," Seetha cried. "She called me some time ago to say she got a job as a palace attendant in Qumraan. The Foreign Ministry database shows she left for Qumraan two weeks ago."

"My God!" Alexis burst out, recalling her conversation with Kureishi. "She's the insurance policy! They need her because the transplanted liver is failing." She cast a quick glance at Jason and added, "Don't ask me how I know. I'll explain later."

Hope exploded, erasing the darkness in her heart like sunshine bursting into a dark room. She couldn't save Ganga Prasad. But she would save this girl, Ayesha Siddiqui.

She was on a mission now. A mission of redemption. Not for Ganga Prasad.

This was for her.

Chapter 4

Three days later, Alexis left Delhi with Jonathan, Seetha, and Jason in the early morning hours, aboard the Lone Wolf corporate jet, bound for Qumraan.

The plane made a stop at the Lone Wolf refinery, ostensibly to refuel, but in reality to allow Jason to deplane at the refinery, which was his jump-off point. He was the linchpin in the plan to rescue Ayesha Siddiqui, but its success depended on the other three members of the party laying the groundwork in Qumraan.

Jonathan's job was to drag out negotiations for the sale of LWOQ until it was time for Ayesha to disappear.

Seetha's role was to convince her friend that her life was in danger if she stayed in Qumraan and get her to agree to the rescue plan.

Initially, Alexis's participation was supposed to be purely permissive, allowing Seetha, the critical 'Ayesha contact', to be included in the party as her 'personal assistant'.

There was one gaping hole in Jason's plan: they didn't have a plausible excuse for contacting Ayesha. Seetha couldn't ask to meet a lowly palace attendant without raising an alarm.

With no obvious way to fix that hole, Jason's plan was stalled in limbo. Then, out of the blue, the Qumraanis fixed it for them.

It happened when Jonathan was discussing expedited approval of their online visa applications with Bilal Zaid, the palace manager. When he discovered Alexis was a physician, he became inexplicably excited. The reason became clear an hour later when Crown Prince Sayf al-Qumraan himself called. "Mr. Wolff, I hear your daughter is a physician. I wonder if she can do me a personal favor, in exchange for any fee she cares to name."

"You have a fully-staffed tertiary care hospital in Qumraan. What favor can she do for you that they cannot?" Jonathan asked warily.

"Something that only she can do. A new hire, a female just arrived from India, cannot start work in the harem without an internal exam to declare her free of transmissible diseases. Our laws forbid women from exposing themselves to any man other than their husbands, and the only lady doctor on our staff resigned three weeks ago. Finding a replacement could take weeks, even months, because the company that hires our staff is experiencing an unexpected business crisis. So, Dr Wolff would do us a huge favor if she could kindly perform the woman's internal exam and clear her to work."

It was the break they needed so desperately. With access assured, the next hurdle was getting Seetha to attend the exam, without any Qumraanis present. Overcoming it turned out to be ludicrously easy, thanks to Mohan. He discovered that all three female nurses in the clinic had also resigned when the lady doctor did. It wasn't clear why, but it left no qualified females to assist Alexis with the exam. When Alexis said Seetha would assist her, Zaid was only too ready to agree.

Alexis was elated. Not just because it gave them unfettered access to Ayesha, but also because of the karmic justice that enabled it. A single act—the murder of Ganga Prasad—started a cascade of inextricably linked events: the Batra brothers' actions, the bus bombing, Jason's trek through Uttarakhand, the foiled attempt to kidnap Malini, the second attempt ending in Abbas's death, aka IASC's 'unexpected business crisis', which gave them the unfettered access they needed to rescue Ayesha.

The cycle of karma would be closed by Ayesha's rescue, denying Ganga Prasad's killers the liver they needed *because they murdered him!*

Could there be a more delicious example of karmic justice?

She would put an exclamation point on it by donating her five-thousand-dollar fee to the Gandhi Orphanage *in Ganga Prasad's name!*

As satisfying as that was to contemplate, she couldn't get too far ahead of herself. There was a long way to go before she could add that exclamation point—a way that involved a long and difficult journey into Qumraan for Jason.

Chapter 5

J ason watched the plane disappear into the early morning darkness, taking Jonathan, Seetha, and Alexis to Qumraan.

They would lay the groundwork for Ayesha's rescue. His job was to get to Qumraan unseen and execute it.

The plan hinged on a decision by Jonathan years ago to locate the LWOQ refinery here, midway between the coast and the Qumraani oil fields. The location was ideal for transporting crude to the refinery and refined petroleum to the coast for export. It was also ideal for a 'booster' station to pump water to Qumraan from the Lone Wolf desalination plant on the coast. The original plan called for a two hundred-mile water pipeline across the desert, buried fifty feet below the surface to minimize an anticipated 60-70% loss from evaporation.

During site preparation, however, ground surveys discovered a subterranean channel fifty meters below the surface. Geological experts identified it as an 'artesian aquifer' through which an underground river coursed during the "wet Sahara era" ten thousand years ago. Long since dry, it ran down an incline all the way to a vast underground cavern four hundred meters below the palace in Qumraan.

242

Jonathan recognized the aquifer as an unconventional but far cheaper alternative to a buried pipeline, with a natural downgrade that made a booster station redundant. As a result, water piped from the desalination plant poured into the aquifer at the refinery to flow downgrade to the cavern, which served as a massive holding tank under the palace. From there, heavy-duty pumps lifted the water to a purification plant on the surface. A shaft with a still-functioning elevator platform used to convey heavy equipment during construction connected the cavern to the surface.

When construction ended, the Emir ordered the elevator landing be hidden in the wall of a giant warehouse to prevent anyone from messing with the hi-tech pump machinery. Twenty years later, no Qumraani even remembered it existed. Lone Wolf engineers performed all repairs and maintenance, accessing the cavern through the aquifer, riding a two-man Lone Wolf amphibious vehicle, or LWA-2. It took two engineers spelling each other about eight hours for the outbound trip from the refinery, riding downgrade on a water cushion. The return journey, travelling upgrade without a water cushion, took fourteen.

The aquifer and elevator would be Jason's gateway into Qumraan and Ayesha's getaway route out. With no one to spell him, Jason would need one-hour breaks every four hours to rest, recover, and rehydrate. He anticipated eleven hours for the outbound trip and an even more grueling twenty to return. Jonathan had briefed Mitch Hanson, the Refinery Manager, to make sure Jason had everything he needed.

Jason expected to reach Qumraan around 7PM tonight. If all went well, he would return with Ayesha late tomorrow night, to be picked up from the refinery by the Lone Wolf jet on its way back from Qumraan early the following morning.

Ravi had procured a passport in the name of 'Zahira Ali', Alexis's 'attendant', with an Indian Immigration exit stamp showing she left

243

India with Jonathan's party. And Mitch, who had the authority to grant entry permits to visitors to the refinery, would affix appropriately dated Qumraani immigration stamps to satisfy even the most officious Immigration clerk that Ayesha left and returned with everyone else.

Chapter 6

A delegation of high-level palace officials was waiting at the airport to escort Alexis, Seetha, and Jonathan in chauffeured limousines to the guest accommodations where they would be staying.

The drive allowed Alexis to absorb every detail in the landscape and security setup, to confirm they conformed to the blueprints.

The cars were meticulously searched by armed guards before being allowed to pass through the access gate at the southern end of the palace grounds—the reason smuggling Ayesha out in a car was not an option.

Inside the gate was a cluster of barracks where the guards were housed, after which the road burst into the open. Alexis saw the warehouse, the focal point of Jason's plan, looming in the distance. Its dimensions in the blueprints couldn't do justice to its monstrous proportions, dwarfing the water tower and purification plant and the heavy equipment shed flanking it on either side.

It dominated the view as they sped north along the perimeter road until they went past it, bringing the clinic building where she was scheduled to see Ayesha into view. A large housing complex for palace servants extended half a mile beyond that. All of it conformed to the blueprints.

Then, a ramshackle shack-like structure appeared out of nowhere in the middle of the barren landscape. Set apart from the servants' housing and surrounded by a high fence, it was jarringly rickety compared to all the buildings built by Lone Wolf, and it didn't figure in the blueprints. It was clearly an add-on.

Beyond the shack was a vast, rock-strewn expanse of dry-packed earth, barren as any Martian landscape, except for the rare cactus. The monotonous terrain was interrupted at the geometric center of the compound by the palace, a sprawling complex enclosed by an electrified fence. After that came another mile-long stretch of barren dirt until they arrived at the guest accommodations at the north gate.

The hospital where Ganga Prasad died and Kureishi committed his atrocities lay just fifteen miles north of the gate in the town of Qumraan. Alexis felt her stomach churn briefly, but crushed the reaction with a stern rebuke to focus on what lay ahead, not in the past.

The guest bungalow where they were housed had three connected private suites, which Alexis scanned for bugs. There were none, but that still left them vulnerable to high-tech laser eavesdropping of the kind used by Kalidas's goons. Therefore, any sensitive discussions would be held in Jonathan's wheelchair-accessible closet.

Bilal Zaid, the Palace Manager, arrived after lunch to inform Alexis that the exam was scheduled for 4PM. A limo would pick her up at 3:40PM to take her to the clinic where the patient would be waiting. He made a point of mentioning that a supervisor would be there "to make sure the girl behaved during the appointment."

Alexis was having none of it. She pushed back immediately against the sly attempt to monitor the exam, asking sharply, "Is she medically trained?" She knew the answer.

"No, Madam."

"Then she is not permitted to attend the appointment. My assistant and I can handle the girl."

He had no choice but to agree. He handed Alexis a form to document her exam, with a list of tests that included vaginal swabs, and left.

Chapter 7

Outside the clinic was a grandiose sign proclaiming 'Asad al-Qumraan Outpatient Medical & Surgical Care Center'.

Alexis found it quite amusing. Jonathan said that no surgical care had ever been provided there during its twenty-year existence. Consequently, its operating table, anesthetic gas machines, walk-in freezer, and full panoply of surgical instruments were unused, gathering dust. Jonathan predicted that no doctor would perform any surgery there, when there was a full-service hospital just twenty minutes away, calling it "a monumentally profligate waste of time and money". He was overruled by the Crown Prince.

Inside the clinic was indisputable proof that Jonathan's prescience was spot on. The waiting area for the "Surgical Clinic", "Procedure Room", and "Operating Suite" to the left of the central staircase was abandoned and empty, without a single chair. On the right, by contrast, the waiting area for the "Medical Clinic", "Doctors' Offices", and "Dispensary" was packed with chairs for patients.

They were met by the clinic manager, who apologized profusely for "a last-minute glitch in transportation". He assured Alexis that the patient would arrive in ten minutes and escorted them to an office labelled 'Lady Doctor'. He showed Alexis how to call him on the intercom when she was ready and left.

Alexis scanned the office and annex for bugs. Then, telling Seetha to wait behind the drawn curtain, she sat down at the desk and called for Ayesha.

Seconds later, she frowned, hearing someone approach, but the "clunk-pause-clunk" sounded nothing like footsteps. Then the door opened…and it was as if she was sand-bagged.

The girl in the doorway was on crutches. *With her right leg in a plaster cast!*

Alexis stared, speechless from shock, until the girl said hesitantly, "Doctor *Sahib*?"

The deferential honorific, "Sahib," was genderless when addressing a doctor. The lilting cadence conveyed an unmistakable question that snapped Alexis out of her paralysis.

She hurried over to help the girl to a chair, saying, "I'm so sorry for being rude." She then pulled up a chair for herself and, placing her hand on Ayesha's forearm, asked gently, "Ms. Siddiqui, do you know why you're here?"

"To be cleared to work in the palace," Ayesha replied. She coughed and cleared her throat before continuing. "But please call me Ayesha, Doctor Sahib."

"My name is Alexis Wolff. It's okay to call me Alexis, but if you aren't comfortable with that, you can call me Dr. Wolff."

Words came tumbling out of the girl. "Dr. Wolff! I couldn't believe it when they said you were coming to examine me. My best friend, Seetha Sinha, told me how you saved her and Mohan! I was hoping—!"

She broke off, putting her hand on her mouth in alarm and said, in a voice devoid of all emotion, "I'm sorry I interrupted you."

It was a hopeful sign, but Alexis let it pass without comment. She needed to earn the girl's trust before taking the next step. "The exam is pretty straightforward. A history, a physical including an internal exam, and samples for lab tests."

She opened the one-page file Zaid gave her. "Let's start with your medical history. It show you use an inhaler for a chronic cough from Allergic Bronchitis/Asthma. Anything else?"

Ayesha cleared her throat again. "No, Doctor Sahib."

Alexis pointed to her leg. "How did you injure your ankle?"

The girl looked up fearfully. Then her eyes shifted, and she said uneasily, "I was...I mean I tripped down some steps and twisted my ankle. It swelled up so badly I couldn't walk."

"Did you break it?"

Ayesha cleared her throat yet again. "No, Doctor. X-rays showed nothing broken, so they applied this cast and said to use crutches. They'll check it in four weeks."

Alexis was taken aback. Treating an ankle sprain with a plaster cast and crutches was archaic! Standard practice was a walking boot for mild sprains, and surgery if ligaments were torn.

Alexis didn't show her surprise, saying noncommittally, "I see. Let's go with a few questions before the examination."

She ran through Ayesha's asthma history, confirming it was seasonal (she only wheezed during the monsoons in India), and regional (she hadn't needed her inhaler in Qumraan), suggesting an environmental trigger. Her persistent cough and constant throat clearing indicated a post-nasal drip from chronic allergic sinusitis.

Alexis ended by adapting her usual enquiry to identify a patient in distress. "Ayesha, it's tough to leave home and friends for a foreign country, where you know nobody. Are you happy, or are you home-sick or sad and want to return? You have my word that what you say will be confidential. I can help you if you're unhappy."

Alexis had to strain to hear the girl's reply. "It doesn't matter if I'm unhappy, you can't help me. They have my passport, so I can't leave. The others say no one ever leaves."

"What 'others'?"

"Seven other orphans, with no family to care if we didn't return."

Alexis felt her gut clench. Seven more! Was there no limit to the depravity in Qumraan? "Surely those who can leave would have re-ported that some of you are prisoners?"

"The rest don't know we exist, let alone that we're prisoners. They have nice houses and work in the palace office, the kitchen, or the gardens during the day. We eat and sleep in a shed, work as cleaners and sweepers in the night, and are always accompanied by a supervisor to make sure no one comes near us. And we dare not open our mouths if anyone is close enough to hear."

"So, eight of you live together in a shed. Do you have separate rooms?" Alexis asked.

Ayesha laughed. "For filthy orphans? No way! The shed is parti-tioned, one part for the five girls, the other for the three boys."

Alexis saw an opening and took it. "You called yourself 'filthy orphan'. Is that how they treat you?"

Ayesha hesitated. "All of us share the same name. 'Filthy orphan'. That's what we say if anyone asks. If you're a Muslim, like me, your Palace ID shows your real name. But Hindus and Christians are given Muslim names and punished if anyone hears them say their own name. To make sure we never forget who we are, we have a ritual started by an orphan who is no longer here. Twice a day, before going to sleep and after waking up, we all recite our names and where we came from fifty times, like a mantra."

Alexis felt deep anguish. That was the mantra Ganga Prasad was reciting as he died. Pushing away her pain, she asked, "You said you are punished. How?"

Ayesha's reply was barely audible. "They beat us. Five lashes for you and the person whose name you use. So, ten for you if you say your own. Ten for disobeying. Twenty for speaking without permission. And if you dare to talk back, you're beaten until you repent."

"Tell me the truth. Is that how you injured your leg?"

"Yes. I talked back to my supervisor, and she hit me on my leg so hard that I fell down some steps, twisting my ankle. And she kicked me four times. I was lucky it wasn't worse."

"What do you mean, worse?"

"Just before I arrived, a boy who was here for years told the others that death was the only escape from this hell and he was going to embrace it. Not like a coward who commits suicide, but as a warrior who is executed for refusing to betray himself. He never returned from the palace that night.

"The next day, the Chief of Palace Personnel, Hakim Elahi, came to tell the others he beat the boy to death because he wouldn't stop shouting his real name and where he came from. He said he would beat them to death, too, if they dared to do anything similar. Not that we would dare. He was a warrior. None of us has the courage to embrace death like he did."

Alexis felt fury explode. This man, Hakim Elahi, was so sure he'd never face retribution for murdering Ganga Prasad that he bragged about it. She tamped down her rage, reminding herself she was here for redemption, not retribution.

"Was his name Ganga Prasad?" she asked Ayesha gently.

The girl's head snapped up in shock. "How did you know?"

"He's why I'm here," Alexis said. "And you're who I came for."

Seeing Ayesha speechless, Alexis continued. "I know you're shocked, Ayesha, but get ready for an even bigger shock. Someone else is here with me, and she—"

At that moment, Seetha came out from the annex. Ayesha emitted a muffled shriek when she saw her, and they embraced, tears mingling with laughter. They somehow managed to keep it down enough so no one outside would hear them.

While Seetha was helping Ayesha to hop over to the annex and undress, Alexis confronted the predicament created by Ayesha's injury. Jason could forget taking her out through the aquifer. She wouldn't last five minutes on the LWA-2. He'd have to find some other way to get her out.

That wasn't the only problem, though. If the orphans slept together, Jason couldn't get her out without the others clamoring to go with her. If he left them behind, the Qumraanis would find out Ayesha escaped and kill the other orphans to eliminate the only evidence supporting Ayesha's story when it became public.

A part of her mind continued to wrestle with the problem posed by the orphans' communal sleeping arrangements when she began Ayesha's examination. Ayesha needed to be separated from the other orphans for the rescue to work. But where...?

Just then, Ayesha cleared her throat and coughed again, and she had the answer. She let the idea germinate while she completed the exam and drew blood for lab tests. By the time she was done, she knew exactly how to separate Ayesha from the other orphans.

Alexis laid out her plan while Ayesha was dressing. Then, telling Ayesha and Seetha to stay quiet behind the drawn curtain in the annex, she summoned the clinic manager and handed him the specimen vials. "I've drawn blood tests and taken vaginal swabs as required to clear her of sexually transmitted diseases. The swab results won't be available before I leave, but any doctor can interpret those and clear her."

"I will pass that on, Doctor."

"Good. But there's a much bigger problem. I am concerned her cough might be TB."

The manager appeared horrified. Alexis was counting on his rudimentary knowledge of the disease. Tuberculosis was now uncommon in the Gulf, but it was an ancient scourge, and the superstitions and beliefs associated with it were probably still pervasive.

Alexis smiled reassuringly. "Don't worry. You can't get it from your short exposure to her. But she cannot sleep in the same room with anyone until TB is ruled out. She must be quarantined until the blood tests come back. Is there an isolation room in the clinic?"

"There is one upstairs, Madam," he replied. "For Chicken Pox and Scabies."

"Perfect."

"I'll have the room ready and arrange for meals to be delivered. Will she need monitoring by a nurse, or is her supervisor okay?"

"The supervisor is okay, but she can't sleep with her."

"I understand, Madam. How long will she need quarantine?"

"It depends on how long the TB test results take. The hospital pathology lab will know. Do you have their phone number?"

While he was writing it down, Alexis asked, "Who put the cast on the girl's ankle?"

"The doctor in Casualty."

"Don't you have an orthopedic surgeon?"

"Yes. But he's on leave in Pakistan."

The ER doctor must've punted the treatment decision until the orthopedic surgeon returned. So, there'd be no pushback if she removed it. "Is there a cast saw in the clinic?" Alexis asked.

"Yes, Madam. I'll get someone who can use one."

"Don't bother. I know how. But she'll need a walking boot. Do you have them here?"

"Yes, Madam. Do you know what size?"

"Small, I think, but get a Medium too, just in case."

He nodded and left.

It was almost 5PM. She had to tell Jason that Ayesha's ankle injury had upended their plans. But not when Ayesha might overhear and have her hopes crushed. Better wait until Jason called when he took his last break, around 6:30PM.

It would be up to him to find some other way to get Ayesha out, otherwise she might have to stay in the cavern until her ankle healed.

Chapter 8

The first seven hours of Jason's journey down the aquifer were stress free. Riding the LWA-2 down the aquifer on a cushion of water flowing downgrade wasn't particularly taxing once he got used to handling it.

Small comforts, like ventilation fans and lighting, and Remote Antenna Units for communication via optical fiber cable, made a big difference. Those luxuries were made possible by the limitless supply of solar energy on the surface.

Travel had become far more arduous in the last three hours. With the downgrade too steep for water-mode travel, he had to switch to land mode with the water shut off. Without a water cushion, steering the LWA-2 on the boulder-strewn surface was very strenuous.

He took his last break at 6PM, rehydrated, ate four energy bars, and did some stretching exercises. Then, he spent the next thirty minutes in a restorative trance, emerging reinvigorated, and called Alexis. And heard the devastating news of Ayesha's injury.

The rescue plan was in shambles. The journey downgrade wasn't easy, as fit as he was. Forget going upgrade on an injured ankle. Ayesha wouldn't survive the pounding for even five minutes. And Alexis's idea of leaving Ayesha in the cavern until her ankle healed was sheer madness. Ayesha would go mad! He advised aborting the rescue and rescheduling it for a later date.

Alexis wouldn't countenance it. To call off the rescue after igniting Ayesha's hope would shatter her spirit, she said. She insisted they find another way, even if it meant going overland.

Jason tried telling her it was impossible. Palace security, by all accounts, was foolproof.

Her retort was sharp and swift. She wouldn't accept "accounts", only *facts*. And only facts he himself verified.

To placate her, Jason had no choice but to promise to keep an open mind and search for loopholes in the security setup.

Going to Qumraan was a fool's errand. Of that he was sure.

Chapter 9

I t wasn't until Ayesha was finally alone in quarantine that it sank in that her time in Hell was coming to an end.

She actually pinched herself to make sure she wasn't dreaming. Or, more aptly, that her nightmare was ending!

She had only herself to blame for being in Hell in the first place. In her desperation to escape Purgatory—the Hostel for Destitute Girls—she never paused to think whether she might be going somewhere far worse. Seetha warned her that IASC's job offer sounded too good to be true if all it took was a five-minute interview, a cursory medical exam, and a blood test. The warning fell on deaf ears.

The salary was all that mattered to Ayesha. Twenty-four hundred dinars a year—thirteen thousand rupees a month! More than enough to realize a dream she thought was lost to her. Medical school.

Her grades were just short of what was needed for admission on merit, but she would have enough saved in four years to afford the hefty fees at one of the many accredited "capitation" medical schools that had sprung up all over India.

Six months later, she boarded a flight to Abu Dhabi, with her passport and a Qumraani work visa, eager to put six years of Purgatory behind her.

Six hours later she entered Hell.

She was dragged off the plane by armed guards when she arrived in Qumraan, and her passport and luggage were confiscated. When she protested, saying she was an approved employee of IASC, Hakim Elahi, the Chief Supervisor of Palace Personnel, slapped her viciously, threatening to have her flogged if she dared to speak.

Terrified, she shut up, clinging to a desperate hope that someone at IASC screwed up, and it would soon be sorted out. That hope vanished when she arrived at the ramshackle shed she would share with seven other orphans abducted and brought to Qumraan like she was. Just like her, they also refused to believe, at first, that their fate was sealed. Once they realized there was no hope of escape or rescue, they embraced hopeless passivity. The sooner she embraced it, they said, the better, because any show of resistance or defiance would earn a flogging at the hands of their supervisors. The worst was the female supervisor, a brutal woman who demanded they call her 'Begum', because she was their 'queen'.

Begum walked in right then and ordered Ayesha to fall on her knees and beg for forgiveness for defying "Sheikh Elahi". When Ayesha refused the woman hit her so hard on the shin with her walking stick that Ayesha fell awkwardly, twisting her ankle.

When she returned from the hospital that evening with her leg in a cast, she was still defiant, insisting to the others she wasn't kidnapped from an orphanage, like they were. She had a friend who'd get suspicious if she didn't hear from Ayesha and track her down.

They just shrugged, saying it was foolish to hope. Death was the only escape from Qumraan, they said. Then they told her the story of Ganga Prasad, an orphan abducted at age six, who had his organs taken from him to give life to Crown Prince's son. He suffered twelve years of endless beatings before finally deciding to embrace death as the only escape from a life of unremitting misery. The next day, Hakim Elahi boasted of killing him for insisting his name was Ganga Prasad, not Mohammed Wasim.

That extinguished the last glimmer of hope. Ayesha knew she would be kept alive like an animal for slaughter until her organs were needed. Then she would die and no one in the world could prevent it. Not even Seetha.

Despair mounted, dragging her down to a place of such darkness that, one morning, the thought of suicide crossed her mind for the first time. Just two hours later, when Begum came that morning, a miracle occurred.

She said, "Your life of leisure ends in two days, filthy orphan. A firangi doctor named Alexis Wolff is coming to Qumraan to clear you to work. Then I will make sure you make up for all the work you've avoided."

And hope was reborn!

It *had* to be the Alexis who Seetha and Mohan spoke about with such reverence and devotion. Even though it was stupid to pin her hopes on someone who probably didn't know she even existed, she clung to it, if only to keep despair at bay.

Not in her wildest dreams did she imagine Alexis Wolff was coming to *rescue* her.

Chapter 10

I t was 8PM when Jason reached the terminus of the aquifer.

His first act was to don noise-cancelling headphones to protect his ears from the reverberation of the pumps in the cavern.

Then, after a short rest, he switched on his LED headlamp and waited for his eyes to adjust to its nine thousand lumen beam, before taking stock of his surroundings.

In the rock wall on his left was a cleft some fifteen feet wide cloven in the rock by an earthquake in the remote past—what surveyors called a 'vertical bedding plane' forking off the aquifer at a sixty-degree angle. That temblor had also produced a rock fall that sealed off the aquifer some fifty yards ahead, forcing the underground river down the cleft to empty into a vast subterranean cavern to form an underground lake about a mile down the bedding plane. After the river ran dry, the lake disappeared over millennia, leaving the massive cavern that now served as a holding tank under the palace. The cleft continued past the cavern to a smaller cave, where a manmade shaft had been drilled, connecting it to the warehouse on the surface.

That shaft would be his gateway into Qumraan.

He made his way down the bedding plane to reach the cavern. Standing at the lip of the opening, he stared into an ink-black darkness so vast that his headlamp didn't penetrate it. He knew there was an opening somewhere off to the side in the far wall because the bedding plane clove through the cavern at an acute angle. And getting there wasn't a problem. When the rock split open, the upper half of the cavern wall to his left slid away, creating a twenty-foot wide ledge around the perimeter. Called an 'abutment', it formed a natural walkway from one opening to the other.

Jason followed the abutment to the other side and continued down the plane to his gateway into Qumraan: a smaller cave with a manmade shaft leading to the warehouse. A ten-foot-square elevator platform rested on the floor of the cave, and an electric service box was mounted on the wall, bearing a "Danger! High Voltage" sign. He threw the electric disconnect switch to power up the motor and pressed the 'START' button on the elevator's operating panel. The platform lurched and juddered, then settled into a smooth ascent into four hundred meters of impenetrable blackness.

Twenty minutes later, the platform's ascent slowed. He looked up and saw an expanding rectangle of light, as hinged metal floor plates rose up to accommodate the platform flush with the floor.

The room at the top of the shaft was a fifty-by-twenty-foot rectangle, with a bathroom alcove indenting one corner. Jason walked to a bank of screens on the far wall displaying camera feeds from inside and outside the deserted warehouse.

He clicked on the icon on the computer monitor labeled 'Warehouse Entrance', and a ten-foot section of wall retracted and slid open. He entered the warehouse and saw immediately why Mitch was so sure that nothing would ever be placed against that wall.

It was covered by a mural depicting a rampaging lion in the pose of the Asad al Qumraan, attacking hordes of Crusaders, shown as tiny figures in white robes with red crosses. The backdrop was a walled city (presumably Jerusalem), with towers and minarets placed strategically to camouflage the opening.

Jason detected Jonathan's hand behind that stroke of genius. Access would never be impeded, because no Qumraani would dare cover any part of that magnificent mural with storage cabinets or equipment. And the room itself remained undetected, because a twenty-foot discrepancy in a five hundred-foot-long structure wasn't evident to the eye. And, like the warehouse, it was soundproofed, so it was undetectable by ear, either.

A dais had been placed some distance from the wall for tomorrow's presentation. The Asad al-Qumraan stood beside the dais, clamped to the base plate of a titanium case Jonathan brought for the purpose. After the ceremony, the case would be lowered over the statue and screwed to the plate, and Jonathan would place tamper-proof seals on every edge, corner, and screw-head. The case would then be inserted into a padded wooden crate sitting on the other side of the dais, using a forklift parked in the warehouse for the purpose. Jonathan would seal the crate, too, and lock the warehouse with a one-time security code so no one tampered with it before transport to the airport early the next morning.

Jason walked through the warehouse hoping for inspiration to strike. He reached the workshop at the far end where he found tools of every description for carpentry and construction, and shelves stacked with lumber, packing materials, and hardware of all sizes and types…but nothing that remotely resembled a solution to the dilemma of Ayesha's escape. The solution, if there was one, must lie outside the warehouse.

Jason walked back to the dais, reviewing what he learned from Jonathan about palace security. He would keep his promise to Alexis to look for loopholes in the setup, even though he was convinced it was a fool's errand. As he approached the dais, deep in thought, his shoulder brushed against the crate...and he stopped dead in his tracks to stare at the crate.

And there it was. The inspiration he was waiting for had been sitting next to the dais all the time, waiting for *him* to bump right into it!

He examined the crate very carefully, paying special attention to the hinges on the door. Then he went back to the workshop to get the tools he needed.

It was now 9PM. Eight hours before daybreak. Time enough to transform inspiration into a solution that would truly delight Alexis.

Ayesha wasn't going to escape through some loophole in security. She would literally fly the coop!

Day 11

DOUBLE-EDGED SWORD

Chapter 1

J ason watched the guests being ushered out on the monitors in the elevator room. The presentation ceremony was at an end, and only Jonathan, Alexis, Mirza Mullick, and a work crew remained in the warehouse.

Jonathan sealed the titanium case containing the Asad al-Qumraan and supervised its insertion into the crate by forklift, which he secured with tamper-proof locks. Then everyone exited the warehouse, and Jason switched to the outside camera feed.

It showed Mullick handing Jonathan a tablet to program the warehouse door lock so no one could tamper with the crate in the warehouse. It was intended 'for one-time use only', according to Mullick, who expected it to default to the Qumraanis *master code* after Jonathan disarmed the lock early tomorrow morning.

Except it wouldn't default. Jonathan had programmed the lock with the Lone Wolf *super code*, which overrode all others. Jason would do the same to the clinic door, so the Qumraanis would have to break down the door to discover Ayesha was gone.

Jason waited until the limousines departed before opening the sliding panel and set to work on re-opening on the crate.

He didn't tamper with Jonathan's locks or seals. Last night, he had reversed the screws holding the hinges to make them accessible from outside, covering the screw heads with wood putty to make them invisible. After removing the hinges, he used the forklift to extract the titanium case containing the Asad and drove it onto the elevator platform. He took it down the shaft and drove the forklift to a recess in the walkway midway between the openings of the bedding plane. The Asad, hermetically sealed in its rust-proof titanium case, would be safe there until retrieved.

Jason returned to the warehouse and parked the forklift where he found it. Then he turned his attention to the empty crate. Over the next two hours, he braced the inside of the crate with two vertical struts and two crossbeams and drilled several dozen breathing holes that were small enough to escape detection.

Next, he collected the tools he needed to re-affix the hinges from inside and to break out and put them in a duffel bag, using bubble wrap to prevent clanking. He secured the bag inside the crate after adding flashlights, two dozen energy bars, and drinking water. The crate was now a perfectly functional escape pod.

He then wiped down everything he touched and swept the floor clean. It was 7PM when he was done. It left him an hour to shower and rest before leaving to get Ayesha.

Everything was going according to plan. They were now in the home stretch.

Chapter 2

Mirza Mullick was fuming with rage. Jonathan Wolff had ignored him throughout dinner.

Who the hell do you think you are, he thought viciously, *you cripple with your withered legs and grotesquely misshapen body,? How dare you act like I don't exist, like I'm one of those filthy orphans! I'm not as rich as you, but I'm rich enough to transfer 367 million dollars from my account to yours with one keystroke, making me a forty-nine percent stakeholder in the Qumraan Petroleum Corporation. What's more, I can at least piss and shit normally, which makes me more of a man than you can ever hope to be.*

As for that bitch-witch you call your daughter? How dare she look at me with those evil green eyes, like she wants to turn me into ashes! If I had my way, she'd be burnt at the stake as a witch. Fuck her!

Oh wait! You don't know what that means, you pathetic excuse for a man.

He let his thoughts wander into a happy daydream, imagining Khuda ki Talwar melting the flesh off the witch's bones. Then Sayf's voice brought him crashing back to earth. "Will you have problems with Customs when you land in New York, Mr. Wolff?"

"No, Your Highness," Wolff replied. "Once TSA verifies the seals are intact, Customs will clear the crate for delivery to the Metropolitan Museum of Art, where curators will open it and certify it as a genuine antique."

"Are you exempt from Customs inspection?"

"Oh no, Highness! Personal luggage is not exempt. Nor are most of the artifacts I acquire for the Met. Large objects the Met certifies are too valuable to be handled or opened by anyone but an expert are given pre-clearance if sealed by me personally."

"Still," said Sayf, "it must be nice to have the trust of two such difficult agencies. Not many countries allow such exemptions."

"You're quite right, Highness. Indian Customs take a more suspicious view of anything brought to their shores. They, of course, will open the crate to examine it."

Sayf frowned. "Why? You're going to New York, not India."

"Yes and no, Highness. We're going to the U.S., but via Delhi."

"No!" Sayf snapped angrily. "You can't change flight plans that have been approved."

Wolff's smile didn't reach his eyes. "You are mistaken. There is no change in the flight plant we filed with Qumraani flight operations and was approved. It was always our intention to fly back to Delhi to drop Seetha off before heading to New York. But you are needlessly concerned. The Asad is as magnificent as it is priceless, and Indian Customs will clear it after one look."

Mirza felt a tightening of his throat. He leaned forward to whisper in Sayf's ear. But Sayf brushed him off, saying to Wolff, "Then you must leave it here for safekeeping. You can pick it up on your way to the United States."

"It will be an unneeded detour for us and an imposition on you."

"I insist, Mr. Wolff. Or I will revoke your flight authorization."

Mirza saw Wolff's face stiffen. There was steel in his reply. "I must ask you not to insist, Highness. A gift, once given, cannot be taken back. Telling me what to do with what is no longer yours violates both the Arab tradition of generosity and the spirit of my friendship with the late Emir."

"The Asad is still in Qumraan, Mr. Wolff. It can be taken back."

It was the perfect putdown. Seeing the cripple with no rejoinder, Mullick started to gloat. Then Wolff said very softly, "Was it not the Messenger of Allah who said, 'He who takes back his charity is like the dog that eats his vomit'?"

Mullick was stunned by Wolff's effrontery. To be called a dog—implicit in Wolff's words—was among the worst insults in Islam. Sayf *couldn't* let it pass. Except he seemed to be struggling to respond.

When he found his voice, Mirza was flabbergasted. "No need to take offense, Mr. Wolff," Sayf said hoarsely. "The Asad is yours to take where and when you want. I request only that you call me the minute you land in Delhi, before Customs examine it, and again after they clear it. That way, I will know when to start and stop worrying. Is that acceptable, Mr. Wolff?"

Mirza was appalled. If Indian Customs examined the Asad, they would find the Sword of God, and Qumraan would become an international pariah.

"Of course, Highness," Wolff said. "I understand your anxiety. The Asad is Qumraan's national treasure. I would leave it here but for your brother's deathbed wish."

Mirza saw his chance and seized it. Throwing caution to the winds, he pleaded, "Your Highness. Mr. Wolff just admitted that the Asad is *Qumraan's* national treasure. So, you have the right to protect it from being confiscated by a corrupt Indian official."

271

Sayf turned and Mirza almost crapped in his pants. No one else could see the murderous rage in Sayf's eyes. He knew he was a heartbeat from death. But Sayf's voice remained soft and mellow.

"Mirza! You forget yourself. Don't question my decision. The Arab tradition of charity is sacred. From what I hear, it isn't in India."

He turned back to Wolff. "If I recall, Mr. Wolff, in America you call someone who takes back a gift an 'Indian giver'. Have we just seen why?" He laughed. Mirza knew it was a cover for that murderous rage from a moment ago.

Wolff didn't laugh. "No, Highness. An 'Indian giver' isn't someone from India—"

Sayf cut in, clearly angry that his joke backfired. "It fits Mirza! Leave it at that."

When Wolff didn't respond, Sayf was forced to add, "The Asad will go with you tomorrow morning." He turned around to Mirza. "Is transport to the airport arranged?"

Mirza could barely articulate coherently. "Arranged, Your Highness...under Mr. Wolff's supervision...2AM."

"Excellent. And when do you take off, Mr. Wolff?"

"Around 4AM, Highness."

"Then I must bid you farewell now. I wish you a safe journey. Remember to call when you land in Delhi. *Before* Customs opens the crate. Do you know approximately what time you might call?"

"We need to make a brief stop at the refinery to refuel, so around 8:30AM, your time."

"Very good! We shall meet again, Insha'Allah."

"God willing, Your Highness. Or should I say, Your Majesty." He bowed from his wheelchair. "The next Asad al-Qumraan."

"Don't call me that, Mr. Wolff! My brother, may Allah bless his soul, is the Asad al-Qumraan. Until my coronation, I remain Sayf, the Sword of Qumraan."

"Qumraan is fortunate to have you as its next monarch."

Sayf's voice hardened. "Indeed. I will end economic imperialism in Qumraan. The sale of LWOQ is only the first step. I intend to take ownership of all our natural resources. Only then will Qumraan take its rightful place in the world."

Sayf stood up and held out his hand to Wolff. Mirza held his breath. Sayf was setting Wolff up for a crushing putdown. The proper response was to bow over the hand, not shake it, as an American would assume.

Wolff didn't take the bait. Instead, he tilted his head fractionally and touched Sayf's palm with the tips of his fingers, forcing Sayf to turn it into a handshake.

Several seconds passed while they locked gazes. Then Wolff said softly, "Yes, Highness, Qumraan will take its rightful place in the world when the *Qumraani people* take ownership of Qumraan's natural resources."

Mirza was dumbfounded. Wolff's words were beyond reproach, but his subtle emphasis made Sayf's own words boomerang on him.

Sayf walked away without replying, sending Mirza scuttling to open the door for him. When he turned to shut it, he saw Wolff's daughter looking at him. And he quailed in terror.

In those green eyes, he saw Malak al-Mawt, the Angel of Death, come to claim his soul.

Chapter 3

Mullick scurried after the Prince's entourage, struggling to control his terror before it loosened his bowels.

The vision of Malak al-Mawt was a terrifying premonition of what he had coming. He might be Sayf's confidante and lover, but he wouldn't be spared for questioning his decision. Men had died for far less when Sayf's fury ignited. Some for just being there. Like that servant Sayf beat to death, all those years ago.

Sayf grabbed a riding crop when they reached his quarters and laid into the servants, screaming profanities at Jonathan Wolff. They cowered, as blows rained down, while Mirza hid behind an armchair. After a while, Sayf collapsed in a chair, his fury spent, and dismissed the servants. Summoning Mirza to him, he said, "The next time you contradict me in public you will be beheaded. Understand?"

Mirza grabbed Sayf's feet and begged for his forgiveness.

"All right. But you must understand why I let that filthy cripple take the Asad to Delhi. He dared to call me, the Sword of Qumraan, a dog who eats his own vomit. His blasphemy deserves nothing less than incineration by the Sword of God. It will be my revenge."

Mirza addressed Sayf from his knees. "Your Highness, your wisdom and insight are as incredible as my mind is feeble. I cannot comprehend it, so may I be allowed one question?"

Sayf laughed. "Mirza! Stop this pretense. I was enraged because you defied me in public. In private, you are free to tell me what you think. And what happened to 'Sayf'?"

Seeing he was back in Sayf's graces, Mirza said, "Thank you, Sayf. I share your hatred of Wolff, and I would love to have the Sword of God melt the flesh off his bitch-witch daughter's bones. But satellite images will show it detonated on Wolff's plane, just arrived from Qumraan, and the Indians will blame us for it."

"You overestimate the Indians. They are incompetent idiots who can't think past the Pakistanis. And their technology is primitive. I want no argument about this. Death by the Sword of God is the only appropriate punishment for Wolff's blasphemy. What if he isn't in New York when it detonates? My decision is final. It will be Delhi. Enough of arguing. How about a game of chess?"

Mirza kept his mouth shut and set up the chess set.

Sayf's opinion of the Indians capabilities was totally wrong, but why argue? If Sayf did trigger Khuda ki Talwar tomorrow, he had to get out of Qumraan before the worldwide blowback hit.

He would lie low in Abu Dhabi and, once the dust settled, he would send out feelers that he had fissile material and access to an expert bomb maker. Someone—the Somali or Yemeni Taliban, ISIS in Africa, Al-Shabab, Boko Haram, Al Qaeda in the Islamic Maghreb...the list was endless!—would be willing to pay a king's ransom for it. Maybe not enough to offset his investment in Qumraani oil, but infinitely more valuable.

It would be his contribution to Islam's final victory.

Chapter 4

With Jason Wolff due to arrive within the hour, Ayesha's excitement was approaching fever pitch.

It had been escalating all day, but it now threatened to explode into fits of uncontrollable giggling each time she thought about Begum being punished for her escape.

The only damper was that Elahi would get off scot free.

She had hoped never to see him again. It wasn't to be. He came earlier today, wearing a malevolent grin, to tell her, "Pray you don't have TB, filthy orphan girl, otherwise you will pay me one lash for every day of your six-month vacation. That's one hundred and eighty-three lashes, plus ten percent interest for making me wait six months. It means *you* can look forward to two hundred and one lashes. And *I* will look forward to giving your pretty buttocks ten lashes every week for twenty weeks! Be sure to massage them daily to keep them tight and firm for me."

She was still quaking with fear an hour later when she related what happened to Alexis and Seetha at her 'follow-up appointment'.

Alexis heard her out in silence. Then she said softly, "Tell me what he said. *His exact words.*"

Ayesha recited them verbatim with her eyes closed. When she opened her eyes, she saw a strange light in Alexis's eyes and shuddered with superstitious dread, thinking, *I have seen the eyes of Death.*

Her terror vanished and she stopped shaking—only for her terror and shaking to return with redoubled force when it was time to go.

Alexis grabbed her by the shoulders then, saying fiercely, "Ayesha! Listen to me. As long as you are under my care you are out of Elahi's reach. He *cannot* hurt you now. His *threats* can't hurt you. And he can *never* hurt you after tonight. But guess who will hurt very badly? Elahi will when his bosses find out you escaped under his watch. A hundred times worse than anything he threatened to do to you."

Later, when she was alone in her room, Ayesha used those words all day as a talisman to ward off her terror. Now, with her escape all but assured, her mind broke the stranglehold of fear, and a whoop of delight rose from her chest. Before it could reach her lips, though, she remembered Begum asleep three doors away and crushed it.

Begum will get an epic thrashing when Elahi discovers I escaped from under her nose! Wouldn't it be great if he gives her the 201 lashes he wanted to give me?

Laughter threatened to explode, but she managed to muffle it into a series of snorts and gulps too muted for Begum to hear.

She gave herself a sharp rebuke to stop it from resurfacing. *Keep it together, you idiot. Getting excited is fine. Getting hysterical isn't.*

Then the insane image of her fat supervisor massaging her buttocks for Elahi to thrash popped unbidden into her head.

It triggered waves of uncontrollable giggling. She was helpless to stop it. She could only stifle them into squeaks, snorts, and gurgles.

Chapter 5

The Isolation Room was equipped with a hidden electronic listening device to allow sick patients to be monitored from the nursing station on the ground floor. With no female nurses currently on staff, and the filthy orphan girl not actually sick, the monitor's output was relayed to the main surveillance center on Hakim Elahi's order "to hear her in case of an emergency".

The guard manning the monitoring station was startled awake by Ayesha's first strangled whoop. The snorts, gurgles and squeaks that followed sounded weird, so he called his supervisor, Sergeant Asif.

When Asif arrived a few minutes later, the sounds convinced him that the girl was in trouble, so he called Elahi. "Your filthy orphan girl is having a breakdown," he said. "What do you want me to do?"

Elahi was in a fix. Taking the girl to the ER meant the ambulance used to transport her would have to be decontaminated. Not that he had to do it himself. The filthy orphans would do it, but there'd be hell to pay if one of *them* got TB! Much better if they got a doctor to come to her.

But who? The doctor on call wouldn't leave the ER unattended to come here. As for the palace physician-in-residence, even if he wasn't in his daily drunken stupor, he'd refuse to attend a filthy orphan. There was no one else available…

He stopped in mid-thought, realizing there was someone else. Alexis Wolff!

He recalled the witch staring at him at dinner, her green eyes cold as death, and remembered thinking, *Who the hell do you think you are? You don't scare me, She Devil!*

He would show her now exactly who the hell she was! He would force her to attend on a filthy orphan, whose sole purpose in life was to clean toilets in the harem, discard the concubines' menstrual waste, and wipe up their vomit when they got drunk.

It would serve her right for putting the girl in isolation. Let her deal with the fallout. And if she got TB from struggling with a lunatic, she'd deserve it!

Unfortunately, he didn't have the authority to make such a demand from a royal guest. So, Elahi called Bilal Zaid, the Palace Manager, saying, "The filthy orphan girl has gone mad in quarantine and needs a doctor. Since Dr. Wolff put her there, she should attend on her. If you okay it, I will send a car with attendants to bring her to the clinic and help handle the girl."

Zaid said he didn't have the authority to ask a guest to do that. Only the Crown Prince could, and to ask him now, after what happened at dinner, was to risk a flogging. Or worse.

Elahi suggested asking Mirza Mullick, the Prince's confidante, to get his approval. Zaid said he would and hung up.

He called back ten minutes later. "That was really smart, Hakim," Zaid said. "Mullick was with His Highness when I called. He got his approval to ask Dr. Wolff to attend on the orphan girl."

"Good," Elahi replied. "I will call her—"

"No! He told *me* to ask her. You will arrange transport to take her to the clinic, along with two attendants and a supervisor to assist with restraint."

Elahi felt thwarted He had been looking forward to putting the bitch-witch in her place. But all was not lost. Zaid's instructions left considerable room for creative interpretation.

'Transport' didn't have to mean 'limo'. And who said the 'attendants' and supervisor had to be 'medical personnel'? Or that 'restraint' had to be gentle?

As luck would have it, Sergeant Asif was the shift supervisor on duty tonight. Not only was forcible restraint his forte, he knew the right 'attendants' to bring with him and would disable the bug in the isolation room to leave no audio evidence of their fun.

Asif would find the prospect of restraining a filthy orphan girl particularly alluring. He had a particular affinity for parts of the female anatomy when inflicting pain—which suited Elahi quite nicely. Unlike Asif, he had no gender or anatomical preferences for inflicting pain, so the field of opportunity was wide open for them to share.

They better not lose control, though. He couldn't afford another death like Wasim's on his hands. Not that he wouldn't love an encore performance—the memory of how it unfolded brought a shiver of delight.

The filthy orphan shouting "I am Ganga Prasad from the Gandhi Orphanage in Bareilly!"

Khalil beating him with a riding crop when he refused to stop his ridiculous chant.

Elahi offering to take over when Khalil's energy flagged.

And take over he did! With three times Khalil's strength and the limitless stamina of someone who truly enjoys his work.

Wasim still wouldn't stop his chant. So, egged on by Khalil, Elahi discarded the crop in favor of a wooden club and hit Wasim so hard that he collapsed. Elahi shivered, remembering the sound and feel of crunching bone.

He managed to escape punishment because the imminent arrival of the girl made Wasim expendable. There would be no such reprieve if the girl suffered the same fate. So, he had to be careful. But that might be even more fun. He knew how to choke just hard enough to make her thrash around, fighting to breathe, to make look like she was resisting. It would justify even more 'forcible restraint'!

As for that green-eyed firangi witch, she couldn't do a thing once it got started. If she interfered, he'd have an excuse to hurt her, too.

Chapter 6

Alexis hung up the phone, numb from shock. The news of Ayesha's breakdown was shattering.

Not because it put Ayesha's rescue in terrible peril, but because she, Alexis, was responsible for it.

She was so caught up in the excitement of Ayesha's rescue that she disregarded the flashing lights and blaring sirens telling her this was coming. The most egregious of those was brushing off Ayesha's claustrophobic fear of being locked in a crate—"my coffin"—as overwrought. That, too, in the context of multiple prior stressors, each by itself capable of breaking most people. Devastating childhood loss. A brutal and dehumanizing two-week ordeal in Qumraan. Extreme mood swings in the last forty-eight hours, from despair to exhilaration. And the coup de grace in the last twenty-four: the sensory and social deprivation of quarantine.

A tranquilizer would have prevented a breakdown, but for her willful ignorance of the warning signs. Now, Jason would have to—!

Her train of thought screeched to a halt.

Jason!

He was on his way to get Ayesha! It would be disastrous if he found her having a psychotic breakdown. In a panic, she snatched up her wristwatch communicator and beeped Jason.

It was 8PM.

Jason inserted the earpiece of the wristwatch communicator in his ear and headed for the warehouse door. He was dressed in all black, from the balaclava covering his head and face to his sneakers. He was carrying a silenced Mauser pistol in a shoulder holster, and his Bowie knife was strapped to his hip.

He was reaching for the door handle when the communicator started to vibrate, and he knew something had gone disastrously wrong.

He lifted his wrist to his mouth and said calmly, "Red?"

"Red?"

One calm word from Jason was all it took. Alexis's panic subsided.

In short, rapid-fire sentences, she told Jason what happened. "Ayesha's having a breakdown. They're sending a car to take me to the clinic, with two attendants in case Ayesha needs restraint. I've given strict orders for no one to go inside before I get there. I only wish I'd—"

Jason cut in sharply. "You're not responsible, Red. Just tell me what to do."

She regained focus. "Go to the office labeled 'Lady Doctor' and wait in the annex behind the curtain. I'll make the attendants wait outside when I come to get Xanax and Ativan for Ayesha. We can talk then."

"Okay Red. Is there a plan, or are we winging it?"

"It depends on Ayesha's condition. If it's a panic attack, I'll give her a mild sedative and leave, taking the attendants with me, so you can get her out later. But if she's in a full-blown breakdown and needs restraint, she'll need Xanax or Haldol and I'll have to stay with her. That'll mean disabling and sedating the attendants, leaving them to be found in the morning. They'll tell the Qumraanis who's responsible, so any plans Jonathan has in Qumraan are done and dusted."

"Forget plans, Jonathan himself is done and dusted with Qumraan. The deed of sale's signed, and he's made out like a bandit, so what's not for him to like?"

"I know. But I don't like that it's ending like this."

"He won't care. So, get your head straight and focus on what's coming up. Are you ready to move?"

His words were bracing—exactly the tonic she needed. "I will be in five minutes. I have to bring Jonathan and Seetha up to speed."

"Okay. Keep your channel open, so I can hear what's going on."

"Sure."

She donned black slacks, shirt, and sneakers, grabbed her shoulder bag and stethoscope, and knocked on the communicating door to Seetha's suite. When it opened, she was surprised to see Seetha, fully dressed in a black outfit, and Jonathan behind her.

Before she could ask, he said, "I heard the phone and knew something was wrong, so I told Seetha to be ready. Anything you need from me?"

She kissed him on the forehead, saying softly, "I feel so spoiled. You and Jason know exactly what to say even before I have to ask."

They went into the walk-in closet in his suite, where she quickly related what had happened and told them her plan. Seeing the worry lines in Jonathan's face, she said reassuringly, "It's going to turn out okay. Ayesha's still coming with us."

"We may have to delay departure," Jonathan said. "I'll take care of it once it's clear for how long."

"And I'm coming to help you with Ayesha," Seetha added.

"Yes, you are." Seetha's presence would be priceless if Ayesha was having a breakdown.

Alexis spoke into her communicator. "Jay! You there?"

"Yes, Red," Jason whispered back. "I'm in the annex in the Lady Doctor's office. I've relocked the front door with the old code for now, so whoever's coming with you won't know any different."

"Okay, Jay. Good thought."

She heard a vehicle pull up outside and honk. Giving Jonathan a quick hug, she said, "Wish us luck."

She heard him call out, "With all my heart," as she raced out of the room with Seetha on her heels. She went down the stairs three at a time, giving the attendant a quick nod as she went through the front door…and came to a dead stop, alarm bells ringing in her head.

Standing at the curb was an open-top Jeep, not the limo she was expecting. And two armed guards in desert camouflage, not medical attendants, one lounging behind the wheel, and the other, a sergeant, leaning insolently against the passenger-side door.

Alexis walked up to the sergeant and said sharply, "I asked for two attendants and a car, not guards with automatic rifles in a Jeep."

The sergeant maintained his insolent pose, answering in passable English, "No attendant is there, only guards. Only Jeep for guards."

It sounded plausible, but something felt very wrong. The sergeant's attitude screamed blatant disrespect. But this wasn't the time to stand on ceremony. Not with Ayesha in crisis.

Gesturing to Seetha to get in the Jeep, Alexis started to go to the other side when she saw the sergeant snap upright to bar Seetha's way. Stabbing his gun at Seetha, he snarled, "Not her. Only you."

"She is my assistant," Alexis snapped back. "I need her help."

The guard's gun barrel did not shift. "Pick up for you. Not her."

Seeing him raise his hand to push Seetha away by the chest, Alexis yanked her back, saying sharply, "Don't touch her!".

Turning to Seetha, she said gently, "Go back inside. I'll be fine."

Seetha left without arguing.

Alexis got into the back of the Jeep and, as they drove off, she heard Jason murmur, "Not good, Red. They're spoiling for a fight."

She responded by clearing her throat once to signal agreement in their secret childhood code. Twice in quick succession was "No." A cough meant "Maybe."

"You said two guards with rifles. Automatics?" Jason asked.

She signaled "Yes".

"Side arms?"

"Yes" again.

"Okay. A vehicle just pulled up outside. Let's hope it's the attendants, not more guards. Gimme a total when you get here."

She made one last throat clear, and he fell silent.

Chapter 7

lexis saw the fat, pot-bellied man in a kaftan waiting outside the clinic with an armed guard and felt an electric tingle go up her spine. Fate had just cast the die.

Hakim Elahi, self-confessed murderer of Ganga Prasad! A man she thought was out of the reach of her justice had come to her!

Alexis jumped out of the Jeep as it rolled to halt, leaving the sergeant and driver to scramble after her, and walked briskly to Elahi. In a voice as cold as the stillness inside her, she said to him, "I expected to be met by someone with the brains and competence to help manage a hysterical girl."

She paused, then added, with her lip curling in contempt, "Instead, I see three brainless goons and a glorified clerk who wouldn't know competence if it kicked him in his butt."

"Red!" Jason whispered urgently "Stand down!"

Elahi recoiled as if struck, then snarled, "I am Hakim Elahi, Chief Supervisor of Palace Personnel. Take great care how you talk to me. The Prince won't tolerate guests who dare to insult his senior staff."

"I care nothing about how I talk to an ignorant thug who doesn't care about hurting the girl."

"If I'm ignorant and don't care, what about you? You broke her mind with your clueless diagnosis of TB and insistence on quarantining her. What is it you Americans like to say? You broke it, you fix it." He laughed with cruel delight.

Alexis's guilt resurfaced. Before it could take hold, Elahi erased it.

Glancing at his watch, he said, "You have six hours to fix her mind before you leave. Then I will decide whether her mind stays fixed. We need her body, not her mind, so no one will care if I break it. And if you tell His Highness, Sergeant Asif and the guards will swear I didn't say it. Who do you think he'll believe?"

Alexis felt her fury erupt. Elahi saw it in her eyes and flinched involuntarily. Then he rediscovered his bravado, knowing he had three armed guards with him, and hustled her to the clinic door by the arm.

She offered no resistance, noting the weakness of his grip. Inside, she easily wrested her arm away, saying sharply, "The keys to the drug cabinet. I will need medications to calm the girl."

He handed her a set of keys. "Get what you need while I go wake the supervisor. The guards will wait here for you."

"Don't go to the girl until I'm ready."

"I won't. I want you to be there when I restrain her, to watch and know you can't do a thing."

Alexis's fury subsided into ice-cold stillness.

Fate may have cast the die. Elahi just determined its shape.

Chapter 8

Ayesha heard Elahi's voice and almost fainted.

If Elahi was here, it must be because he knew she was escaping and had come to inflict terrible punishment.

No way Jason was coming now. She would never escape Hell.

Tears began streaming down her face. No sobs. No wails. Just the silence of hopelessness.

Her liver was all they wanted. Her body was merely a vessel to keep it healthy until "harvest time." Just like Ganga Prasad. They could hurt her body as much as they felt like, so long as her liver survived. It was their only reason to keep her alive...

The thought came and she jumped to her feet.

The tears still flowed, but now hope blazed, stiffening her resolve like the tempering of steel. It wasn't the hope of freedom. That dream lay in ashes. It was the hope of freedom *from enslavement.*

She would deny them their 'harvest'. Not just for herself. For Ganga Prasad, too.

It took years of waiting under a sentence of death, like an animal for slaughter, before he realized death was his only escape. His example was the reason it took her just three weeks to realize it. She would embrace death now.

Death for her. And for the prince.

She started rummaging around in the drawers, looking for something she remembered seeing earlier today .

Chapter 9

A lexis locked the door and walked to the curtained annex, whispering, "Jay! You there?"

He came out from behind the curtain, looking grim. "What's got into you, Red? This is tough enough without you provoking them. Now they're on their guard."

"No chance of that. By acting too big for my boots, I've reinforced the stereotype of an arrogant firangi woman who doesn't realize she's in Qumraan and is helpless and at their mercy. The way Elahi manhandled me proves they think I'm no threat."

"Elahi seemed to press a particularly nasty button. What gives?"

"Ayesha said he bragged about killing Ganga Prasad. And he's looking forward to hurting Ayesha. My guess is that Asif and the guards are cut from the same cloth. So, no pussyfooting around. We play for keeps. If they can't raise the alarm, it buys time for Ayesha's story to go public. Might just be enough to save the other orphans.."

Jason nodded. "Okay. So, what's our play?"

"You take the guards, but Elahi is mine. The woman too."

Jason might have qualms about killing an unarmed woman in cold blood. She didn't. Not when the woman hit Ayesha so brutally.

She saw Jason nod and continued. "I'll go upstairs with the guards. You follow and wait until I figure out what to do with Ayesha. If she needs an injection to calm her, they'll have to put down their rifles to restrain her. That's when we take them out. They won't know what hit them."

He pointed to several syringes sitting on a surgical tray. "I drew up Haldol and Xanax for Ayesha. And Ativan for the attendants, which we don't need now."

She touched his cheek. "You and Jonathan spoil me.

"Let me spoil you some more. Here's something I found in the surgery that you might like."

He held out a solid steel cylinder with a slight sinuous double bend, like a long and very flat 's' about eight inches long and thick as her thumb. She recognized it from her gynecologic training.

"What would I want with a Hegar dilator?" she asked, mystified.

"Quit thinking like a physician, Red. Think like a ninja."

She looked again…and gasped. "A *vajra*."

He grinned, and she hugged him tight, amazed by his inventive genius. Where she saw a humdrum surgical implement, he had seen a vajra, a weapon used in ancient India to deliver disabling pressure-point and bone strikes during hand-to-hand combat.

She had no words to say. All she could do was touch his cheek again. Then she became all business.

She slipped the syringes and makeshift vajra into her bag and walked out, heading for the staircase. The guards fell in behind her.

Chapter 10

J ason waited until Alexis and the guards were out of sight before following them, silenced Mauser in hand.

He was halfway up the stairs when he heard Elahi issue a peremptory command in Arabic and an unintelligible reply from a woman. Then he heard Alexis shout, "Ayesha! This is Dr. Wolff. I'm here to help you."

There was a tremulous cry from Ayesha, followed by the jingle of keys, and another shout from Alexis, "No! Gimme the keys. She is my patient. I will open the door, not you." She was clearly letting Ayesha know that she was coming in, not a bunch of violent goons.

Jason ascended the last few steps on all fours to peer around the stanchion...and his heart sank.

Alexis was ten feet from him. On her far side were Elahi and a hijab-wearing woman, who must be Begum, Ayesha's supervisor. Between him and Alexis, on the near side were two guards, with their backs to him. And they were covering the sergeant!

"Red! I have only two," Jason whispered urgently.

"No worries!" Alexis shouted. "I have three…guards with me, Ayesha, but only I will come in. Okay?"

Jason recognized Alexis's momentary hesitation as a clever ruse and relaxed.

Alexis went on. "Put on your mask and stand back from the door. No one but I will come in, but the door must stay open. Do you understand?"

"I understand, Dr. Wolff."

"Are you okay? They told me you were having a breakdown."

"M-m-me? A b-b-breakdown?" Ayesha stammered. "They lied. I'm *not* having a breakdown. And you're here, so…"

Ayesha's voice broke.

Jason saw Alexis slip her right hand inside her shoulder bag and glance over her shoulder at the sergeant crowding her from behind. Then she opened the door and stepped across the threshold.

He heard her hiss, "NOW!" and snapped erect…

Chapter 11

Alexis stepped across the threshold with her right hand inside her bag, gripping her makeshift vajra, with half of it protruding from the back of her clenched fist.

Feeling the sergeant crowding her from behind, she hissed, "NOW!" and delivered a vicious backward strike to his solar plexus with her vajra.

She heard an explosive exhalation of air, punctuated by twin pops from Jason's silenced Mauser, and dropped to her haunches as the sergeant lurched forward. As his torso folded over her, she grabbed his flailing left arm in the crook of her left elbow and jackknifed erect with an explosive grunt. She drove her right shoulder into the man's groin, lifting his feet off the floor and upending him.

The sergeant hovered head-down in the air for a split second, then Alexis dropped to her haunches again. Gravity did the rest— accelerated by a violent assist from her left hand. He smashed face first into the stone floor, breaking his neck. He was dead on impact.

She was still on her haunches when Begum leapt forward with a scream, pulling a janbiyah dagger out from her robe. Gripping it by the hilt with both hands, she raised the dagger to her forehead, aiming to strike down at Alexis.

Staying on her haunches, Alexis pivoted on the balls of her feet and swept a backhand strike at Begum's ankle with the makeshift vajra. She felt the distinctive crunch of shattering bone and Begum's ankle gave way. She pitched forward, her scream turning into a high-pitched shriek of agony.

Alexis leapt up and twisted out of the way of Begum's headlong fall, bringing the hallway into view. To her left was Elahi, bent over to reach for the sergeant's rifle, and to the right she could see Jason racing towards her, Bowie drawn and ready to throw.

In her state of molten fury, she wouldn't countenance anyone else taking Elahi out. Not even Jason. Elahi was hers and hers alone.

She brought the makeshift vajra down to strike Elahi's right temple with such violence that her feet came off the floor. There was a sharp crack of splintering bone, and Elahi flew sideways like a rag doll. He keeled over onto his back, eyes wide open, with blood spurting from his nose and ears, legs jerking spasmodically. She didn't bother to check on him. He was dead before he hit the floor.

Begum lay face down, with bright red blood spreading under her lifeless body. The janbiyah had buried itself in the root of her neck, severing the carotid artery when she fell. She, like Elahi, was dead before she hit the floor. The sergeant, unlike the other two, died *when* he hit the floor—his head lolled, as if anchored jelly, when Jason touched him.

A high-pitched wail, like a kitten mewling in agony, made her whirl around. Ayesha was standing at the far end of the room, her clenched fists crushing her mask to her face.

With blood streaming from her right fist!

Alexis stood rooted to the spot for a split-second. Then she leapt forward, hurdling over Jason and the bodies sprawled in the doorway to get to Ayesha. She pulled away the mask and embraced Ayesha tightly, saying again and again in a soft, caressing voice, as if comforting a terrified toddler, "I'm here Ayesha. No one can hurt you now. You're safe."

Ayesha remained rigid and wide-eyed, her pupils dilated like pools of black liquid, emitting that keening wail. Alexis's voice sliced through it. "Jay! Ativan!"

As Jason reached into her shoulder bag for a syringe, Ayesha pushed away and started beating Alexis on the chest with clenched fists, babbling, "Where were you? You left me to die! Why didn't he come? He was going to hurt me! I was going to kill myself!"

Alexis absorbed the blows without flinching, saying in the same caressing tone, "I know, Ayesha. And I'm so, so sorry you went through this. But I would never leave you to die. I'm here now and I won't let anyone hurt you."

Gradually, the blows slowed and softened. When they finally stopped, Alexis gently forced Ayesha's clenched fist open...and gasped. Embedded deep in the base of her thumb was an old and rusty double-edged safety razor blade.

Ayesha spoke between sobs, "I thought...you weren't coming...I was going...to kill myself. I forgot...it was in...my hand..."

Then, the dam burst, and she began to cry. "Oh m-m-my g-god! I-I hit you. P-please f-forgive m-me."

"You did nothing that needs forgiving," Alexis replied. "I need *you* to forgive *me* for subjecting you to this. I deserve to be whipped."

Alexis put one arm around Ayesha and coaxed the girl to sit on the floor with her head resting on her shoulder. Supporting the girl's injured hand with her own, she looked at Jason and gestured with a tilt of the head, first at Ayesha's palm, then at the door.

She didn't have to spell it out to Jason. He gave a quick nod and left, closing the door behind him after heaving the sergeant's body out into the corridor.

Chapter 12

J ason headed for the Procedure Room where he got the Hegar dilator Alexis wielded as a makeshift vajra to such lethal effect.

It was stocked with everything Alexis needed—gauze, sutures, saline, syringes, sterile gloves, local anesthetic, and tetanus vaccine. While he was gathering the items, his thoughts drifted to the eerie symmetry in Ayesha's and Malini's reactions to their 'liberation'.

On the surface, the similarity was consistent with the parallels in their ordeals—abduction, an imminent threat to life, witnessing violent death, and a last-second reprieve when all seemed lost.

Those parallels were deceptive, though, hiding a much more profound difference in the trauma inflicted by their twin ordeals. Ayesha's reprieve ended her trauma. Malini's ordeal was ongoing. The trauma of a brutal gang rape was inconceivable, by itself. Compound that with witnessing the cold-blooded execution of two loved ones and Malini might be in a place of agony no hell could match.

Even with therapy and support, Malini faced a long and perilous road to sanctuary from those traumas. At least the first step on that road had been taken: Malini and Saluja were now in California.

The road ahead wasn't nearly as arduous for Ayesha. She would find sanctuary with the very first step. The healing would begin with her escape from Qumraan.

When he returned to the Isolation Room, Jason found Ayesha sitting on the floor next to Alexis, her hand resting on a small stool.

While Alexis was scrubbing her hands at the sink, Jason soaked a wad of sterile gauze in saline and cleaned Ayesha's palm and forearm. Noticing him for the first time, Ayesha asked, "Are you Jason?"

"Yes, I am," he replied with a smile.

Without warning, she said indignantly, "You left Alexis alone to fight all of them by herself."

He gaped at her, flabbergasted, not knowing what to say. Fortunately, Alexis bailed him out. "Jason didn't leave me to fight by myself, Ayesha. If he hadn't taken out two guards, we'd be dead."

Ayesha was mortified. "Oh! I'm so sorry. I didn't know—"

Jason cut her off. "Nothing special," he said blandly, tapping the shoulder holster, "It's a good thing I had a gun. If I tried to take out someone twice my weight by throwing them over my shoulder, like she did, I'd get a hernia. Then, what good would I be? I'm supposed to take care of you, not the other way around."

Ayesha burst into a fit of giggles, which was exactly his goal. A victim-savior relationship was the last thing he needed while they were in that crate, and humor was its best antidote.

When the giggles subsided, she said shyly, "If you're with me in that coffin, I won't be afraid."

"It *isn't* a coffin, Ayesha," he replied firmly. "It's a custom-made escape pod. And I'll be there to remind you you're safe."

Saying he'd be there to *remind* her she was safe, not *keep* her safe was a subtle but critical distinction.

It registered. She responded with a smile, "And I'm glad you'll be there to *remind* me not to be afraid."

Alexis returned and sat down by Ayesha just as Jason finished cleaning Ayesha's palm. While she was donning sterile gloves, he peeled open a sterile pack containing a prefilled syringe of lidocaine local anesthetic. She took the syringe, saying gently to Ayesha, "I'm now going to numb the wound before I extract the blade. Ready?"

Ayesha nodded calmly, showing no signs of anxiety.

Alexis began delicately injecting lidocaine into the skin around the blade embedded in her palm.

Chapter 13

Ayesha couldn't remember the last time she was this happy.

The pain and terror of the past two weeks had vanished. A long period of healing—for her mind, more than her hand— lay ahead and there would be scars. But the healing had begun because she had found the most potent healing balm of all: a deep well-spring of inner happiness she never knew existed.

Its wasn't because of her impending freedom—as happy as that prospect was! It was because Alexis and Jason Wolff had restored something she thought was lost forever: her trust and faith in humanity. That two people she never met in her life cared enough to come to this hellhole just to rescue her!

What little she knew about Alexis and Jason was from Seetha, and that was next to nothing. She was weirdly reticent about them, saying only that they were twins and very close. And that their combat skills were other-worldly.

Everything Seetha said was true. Except that what she *didn't* say spoke louder than anything she said! Although, in fairness to Seetha, it was impossible to convey what and who they truly were in words. Like using a ray of light to describe the sun!

The key to who they were was something in their relationship...something that made her heart ache because it was lost to her forever.

Not just love, or camaraderie, or kinship, all of which she sensed in abundance. It went much deeper. So much deeper, in fact, that she just couldn't find the right word for it. A 'connection', maybe? That was as close as she could come to it, but even that was so far away as to be in another universe!

Whatever it was, it was integral to who they were. Not as individuals, but as a unit. And it transcended physical, emotional, or blood ties.

Some of it might be that weird twin thing—two bodies with a shared soul and all that. She read somewhere that it came from spending nine of the most critical months of life in the exact same environment, when their bodies, brains and souls were forming. Like the forging of a coin with two sides...

No! Not a coin. That was way too mundane.

More like a sword. A *double-edged* sword. Each edge as sharp and lethal as the other.

You would hardly believe it if you saw them right now.

Alexis Wolff, crouched over her injured hand, assessing the extent of the damage caused by the blade. Her edge was lethal enough to cut down three of Ayesha's tormentors in one blinding instant. Yet, she cared enough to envelope Ayesha in a cocoon of affection that dulled the pain of the past.

And Jason Wolff, kneeling next to his sister, watching her work. She hadn't seen his edge, but it had to be just as lethal. Forget about taking out two guards armed with automatic rifles. "Nothing special," he said. What *was* special, though, was how, according to Seetha, he stood resolute in the face of death in Myanmar, continuing to fight even as his life ebbed away. A man with that edge cared enough to wrap her in a cocoon of humor that erased her fear.

Suddenly, the thought of being trapped in that crate didn't seem so frightening.

Jason would be with her. She felt safe.

Chapter 14

J ason had work to do, but he couldn't leave until he was sure Alexis didn't need his help.

She had anesthetized the wound and was meticulously walking Ayesha through a series of gentle thumb movements. When she was done, she looked up, clearly relieved. "The nerves seem intact, and the muscles of the thumb haven't been sliced through and through. So, this isn't something that only a hand surgeon can fix, or I can screw up too badly. I've got this, Jay. You can go."

Ayesha looked up fearfully. "Does he have to go?"

Jason said gently, "No need to be scared, Ayesha. A few loose ends to tie up, that's all. What happened here wasn't part of the plan, you know."

Ayesha shivered, "What happened here is why I'm scared. Elahi wouldn't have come here unless he knew I was escaping."

"Not so, Ayesha," Alexis replied firmly. "Elahi hadn't the faintest idea you were escaping. He genuinely thought you were having a breakdown. I have no idea why he thought that, but it doesn't matter. He's dead and you're escaping tonight. Keep telling yourself that."

"I know he's dead, but I can't stop feeling terrified. I'm not strong like Seetha. I'm a real scaredy cat."

"Don't say that!" Jason said forcefully. "Anyone who survives what you went through is anything *but* a scaredy cat. You are sensible, resourceful, and, most of all, brave."

"Oh, no! I'm not brave. I'm a coward. I was going to kill myself, not fight them."

Jason was taken aback. What she called cowardice was, in his book, courage of the highest order. To deny her tormentors victory she fought back with the most precious weapon she possessed—her life! There was no greater sacrifice a human could make.

He didn't know how to say that without trivializing it. Thankfully, Alexis did.

Her voice was soft, but there was no mistaking its intensity. "*Bukyo.* The creed of the samurai warrior. To die a good death with honor intact."

"That's it!" Jason said excitedly. "Death with honor." He turned to Ayesha. "You were willing to die to defeat your enemy, Ayesha. That makes you anything but a coward. It makes you a samurai."

"You really think so?" Ayesha asked shyly.

"Yes, I do, I am honored to know you, *Ayesha-san.*" He bowed, hands on knees.

"I'm the one who is honored," Ayesha said softly. "If I am a samurai, I must live up to it. I won't be afraid in the escape pod, so you won't have to *remind* me I'm safe.."

Jason was amazed. Ayesha had used his own words to prove she had regained her composure. He said as much.

"You amaze me, Ayesha-san. I guess you don't need me with you in the escape pod anymore, but I hope you'll still let me share it with you. I don't want to be left behind in Qumraan."

Ayesha's response was predictable. She burst into a fit of giggles. Satisfied that she had regained her equilibrium, he nodded to Alexis and left, closing the door behind him.

While Alexis was evaluating Ayesha's injury, he had worked out the three loose ends he needed to tie up. One, he had to make the Qumraanis believe Elahi and company were 'missing', not dead. Two, he needed to hide the jeeps out of sight of the transport team when it came at 2AM. Three, Alexis had to get back to the guest bungalow without the attendant realizing her escort was dead.

He started by removing the sergeant's uniform, cap, sidearm, and rifle. Then he carried all five bodies down to the walk-in freezer, and locked it with the master code, after which he mopped the corridor to remove any traces of blood that could undermine the 'missing' narrative. With the search taking precedence over Ayesha's disappearance, the freezer was the last place the Qumraanis would look if they thought Elahi and company were alive. That could keep the other orphans alive long enough for Ayesha to go public.

All that remained now was to drive Alexis back to the bungalow in the jeep that brought her here, wearing the sergeant's uniform. He would wave to the attendant from afar before driving away to establish that the sergeant was alive when he dropped Alexis off and absolve her of involvement in his 'disappearance'.

His last task would be to hide both jeeps in the equipment shed next to the warehouse.

Chapter 15

A lexis gave Ayesha a tetanus shot and sat back with relief.

Repairing a hand wound was a delicate and tricky task that called for a skilled hand surgeon at the best of times. Her task wasn't to repair it. It was to close it to stop bleeding and prevent infection. She had done that. A course of oral antibiotics from the drug cabinet downstairs would stop any infection from taking hold until Ayesha saw a hand surgeon in Delhi, who would correct her handiwork, if necessary.

She told Ayesha as much and stood up. Just then, the communicator buzzed, and she heard Jason say in her ear, "Red! You there?"

"Yes, Jay—"

Ayesha gasped. "Are you talking to him? How?"

Realizing she had unwittingly 'outed' the wireless communicator, Alexis showed Ayesha her earpiece. "With that."

"Did he hear me say anything bad or embarrassing about him?"

"No, Ayesha. He left while I was tending to your hand, and you hardly spoke after that. Anyway, there's nothing you can say that's close to what he's heard from me. Many, many times. So, he's immune to being embarrassed. Plus, he's too dumb to be embarrassed."

"Gee, Red, thanks for the dumb endorsement," Jason said.

"No need to thank me, Jay. Always happy to endorse my brother's exceptional attributes for the world to hear."

Ayesha's laugh was loud enough for Jason to hear. "Fantastic, Red. Looks like Ayesha's on the mend, and it isn't just her hand."

"Agreed. We're in the home stretch, in more ways than one. Why did you buzz me, though?"

She listened is silence, as he laid out his ingenious plan to hide the bodies in the freezer, drop her off masquerading as the sergeant, and park the jeeps in the equipment shed. When he was done, she couldn't contain her astonishment.

"My God, Jay!" she exclaimed. "I don't know how you do it, but you've figured out everything!"

"Not everything, Red. I haven't figured out what to do with Ayesha when I take you back. She can't go with us, and we can't leave her in the clinic after what just went down there. That leaves the warehouse. How's she going to handle her 'coffin' being right there?"

Alexis said, "Leave it to me!" and turned to Ayesha.

"You know I have to go back to the bungalow, right, Ayesha?"

"Of course," Ayesha replied, "But how will you go there? Is Jason taking you?"

"Yes, he is. Would you be okay with staying in the warehouse until he gets back? It'll be about half an hour, but you'll be safe there."

"Of course," Ayesha replied. "The warehouse will be perfect."

"I'm proud of you for being so brave. Jason was worried you'd be afraid to be alone."

Ayesha's response was shy and hesitant. "Is he happy I'm not afraid?"

Alexis couldn't pass up the chance to take another dig at Jason. "He heard you, Ayesha, and he'd better be happy, or else. He knows I heard too. Anyway, don't go getting a crush on my brother. You're too good for him. I should've saved that female supervisor for him."

Ayesha laughed even more loudly.

Jason said, "Ouch!" but he was laughing as he said it.

"We're set, Jay," she said. "Buzz me when you're ready and we'll meet you at the back door."

"Okay. In thirty."

Alexis got to her feet, her spirits soaring.

The Triangle of Terror was on the brink of destruction.

When Ayesha's story went public, Qumraan, its home, and Sayf al-Qumraan, its patron, would become international pariahs. Mirza Mullick, its banker in Abu Dhabi, would shortly be bankrupt. And Talwar-e-Rasool, its progenitor in India, was dead and buried.

Best of all, its victims had been avenged. Saleem Kureishi, the fulcrum of its evil, and Abbas, his enabler, were both in Hell. And Khalil al-Qumraan, the beneficiary of its malevolence, wouldn't be long in joining them. Best of all, Elahi, the one murderer she thought was beyond the reach of justice, was dead, thanks to her ploy to isolate Ayesha from the other orphans—

Her train of thought stopped dead in its tracks.

The other orphans! Elahi's death had surely sealed their fate. Once the Qumraanis realized Ayesha had escaped, they would kill the other orphans to eliminate the only tangible proof of Ayesha's story.

She bowed her head in sorrow.

Ayesha noticed her abrupt change of mood. "What's wrong?" she asked.

"The other orphans. I wish we could—"

Jason interrupted urgently. "Red! No! Survivor guilt is the last thing Ayesha needs."

Alexis gasped at her thoughtlessness. But Ayesha seemed unaffected. "Don't feel bad, Alexis. They aren't here,"

"What do you mean?"

"The Palace Manager sent them to the hospital for x-rays to check for TB, because they were exposed to me. One girl named Poonam always gets terrible diarrhea at the slightest change in routine. She made such a mess during her x-ray that the doctors thought she had a very contagious infection with a funny name. Sounded like 'know-your-virus'?"

"No-*ro*-virus?"

"That's it! They quarantined the orphans at the hospital, fearing it could spread to everyone at the palace, even the royals. They're miles away, so we couldn't take them with us even if we wanted to."

"How do you know that?"

"It was quite comical. First, they send the orphans for x-ray to check if they'd caught TB from me when I don't have TB. Then they send a nurse to see if I've caught Poonam's diarrhea when her diarrhea isn't contagious. And they force me to eat with plastic spoons and paper plates, and the attendants all wear gloves and gowns before entering my room, even though I don't have this virus diarrhea. I've been quarantined in quarantine!"

Alexis couldn't help smiling. "Their circular reasoning is pretty comical! But I still feel bad about leaving the others behind."

Ayesha's reply had steel in it. "It's on me to get them out. When I tell the world what they did to me and Ganga Prasad, the Qumraanis will have to release them."

Alexis clapped her hands. "Did you hear that, Jay?"

"I did, Red. This one has guts, like her best friend."

Alexis repeated to Ayesha what Jason said and she replied, "Tell him if he doesn't get me back to India in that crate, he'll have to get them out himself."

Jason guffawed. "My God! Have you been coaching her to bully me?"

Alexis laughed, then she got serious. "How are we with time?"

"We're still okay. It's ten-thirty now, so I have three-and-a-half hours to drop you off and get us settled in the escape pod before the transport team arrives. I just hid the first jeep and am headed back to the clinic. Have Ayesha ready to leave in fifteen minutes."

She looked at Ayesha. "Is there anything you want to take with you?"

Ayesha went to the closet and got her backpack. "This is all I take with me. I leave behind nothing but pain, sorrow, and fear, and Qumraan is welcome to keep those."

"Amen to that," Alexis said with feeling.

She was content for the first time since seeing Ganga Prasad's scans. Her sensei's words had come true. She had found redemption through Ayesha.

And she owed it all to Mohan for finding Ayesha.

Day 12

THE SWORD OF DAMOCLES

Chapter 1

It was nearing midnight when Mohan finished his fifty-page report. He sent it to the printer and sat back with a tired yawn.

He had been working virtually non-stop since Seetha left for Qumraan two days ago, grabbing what sleep he could on Ravi's camp cot at the office while Ravi was in Singapore on official business. He had beaten his 2:30AM deadline with two and a half hours to spare before Ravi's flight was due to land, knowing he'd come straight to the office from the airport, as was his usual habit.

Imagine Ravi's surprise when he found the report waiting on his desk and realized Mohan had cleared the backlog that accumulated while the Talwar-e-Rasool business was playing out.

It had come at a dangerous price. He had broken his promise to Seetha to "get plenty of sleep and not overwork" while she was away. If he showed up at the airport tomorrow looking sleep deprived, there'd be hell to pay. Thankfully, it was only midnight. He had a good ten hours to sleep before Jonathan's plane landed.

He went to drop his report on Ravi's desk, resolving to leave immediately afterwards.

His resolve stayed firm for all of twenty seconds. It vanished when he saw the manila envelope from the Passport Office on Ravi's desk. It had to be Mirza Mullick's passport application for Ganga Prasad which Ravi requisitioned, hoping it would show who conspired with Mullick to abduct Ganga Prasad.

The temptation to take a quick look was irresistible, so he opened the envelope, his excitement at fever pitch, and leafed through the contents.

It was a major letdown. The passport application contained nothing even remotely interesting, except for Mullick's net worth: a mind-boggling eight hundred million. In *dollars*, not rupees, according to financial records submitted by MAQ Associates, PLC, a prestigious accounting firm in Delhi.

Then something curious caught his attention. Two of the three testimonials attesting to Mullick's worthiness as an upstanding Non-resident Indian were from ex-college mates, both of whom were government clerks of modest means. The third, however, stuck out. It was from Mir Abdul Qasim the CEO of MAQ Associates, who identified himself as Mullick's 'childhood friend'.

The contrast was intriguing, so Mohan did an Internet search on Qasim. It turned out to be equally anti-climactic. Qasim had led a blameless life, growing up in Mumbai and graduating with honors as a Chartered Accountant, with a brief stint in government accounting, before founding MAQ Associates. The company was an accounting powerhouse, listing dozens of high-profile clients in India, the Gulf, and the Far East on its website.

He was scanning desultorily through the client list when a name jumped out at him. The Indo-Arab Services Corporation!

Then he saw Saltech and Raman Saluja also on the list and shot upright in the chair with a jolt.

Was it a coincidence? Or were Qasim's links to Saluja, IASC, and Mullick part of the mosaic in the Triangle of Terror?

He slumped back in his chair, knowing he was way out of his depth. This wasn't something he could figure out at even the best of times. Past midnight and sleep deprived? No way.

Better to head home and get the sleep he needed. Ravi would figure it out tomorrow.

Qasim wasn't going anywhere.

Chapter 2

Mirza Mullick couldn't fall asleep.

Something was bothering him, and he couldn't pin it down, try as he might. Like a pebble in the shoe that you couldn't get rid of no matter how hard you shook your shoe!

At 10:30PM, he finally gave up on sleep and sat up to figure it out before it drove him crazy. It meant working through everything that happened today until something triggered his memory.

The last event before he retired was the filthy orphan girl's breakdown. Sayf authorized the Wolff woman to attend on her, and the Palace Manager said he would make the arrangements. Nothing there to overlook.

Sayf's rage tantrum came before that. It was terrifying, but he emerged unscathed, so nothing there to overlook, either.

Preceding that was the fiasco at Wolff's farewell dinner, with Wolff's putdown triggering Sayf's rage. It exploded when Mirza pushed back against the Asad going to Delhi. He had to come to terms with Khuda ki Talwar detonating in Delhi, not New York, although it would come as a crushing disappointment to Mackie—

Mirza's heart almost stopped beating.

He had just found the pebble. He forgot to warn Mackie to get out of Delhi!

It was 10:40PM—ten past midnight in Delhi. Whether or not Mackie was awake didn't matter in what was the ultimate life-or-death emergency.

Mackie's emergency burn phone was intended precisely for this purpose—the reason it never left his side, even though it had never been used in two decades.

Mirza knew he had to be very careful about what he said. The Indians had a nasty habit of monitoring calls to and from the Middle East.

He dialed Mackie's burn phone for the first time ever.

Chapter 3

The parking garage was empty when Qasim left for home—not a surprise, seeing it was a quarter past midnight.

What was a surprise, though, was that he had stayed past midnight at his office for the first time ever. It had been getting closer to midnight with each passing day because he hated going home now —another first! Recent events had left him demoralized, so the office was now his refuge from the despair he felt in the spartan isolation of his home.

One bright light in all the doom and gloom was the upcoming debut of Khuda ki Talwar. It would leave Qumraan for New York tomorrow, hidden in the Asad's belly—

His emergency phone rang for the first time ever—a third 'first' so shocking that he nearly swerved off the road. Luckily, there was almost no traffic, so he managed to stop before he hit the shoulder.

He fumbled in his pocket for the burn phone reserved for life-or-death emergencies. It was programmed to accept calls from only two people. Abbas, who was dead, and Mirza, who would only call if something terrible had happened to the Sword of God.

He spoke in Urdu, "Mirza? Has something bad happened?"

"No, my friend. Things are great. The gift will be delivered to-morrow."

Qasim's relief was immense. "Allah be praised! The Lion and the Sword—"

Mirza cut in sharply. "Gifts mustn't be described!"

"I am really sorry for that. Blame it on your incredible news. It set off fireworks in my heart like it's the Fourth of July!"

"Not the Fourth of July, Mackie. Diwali. That's more appropriate for where it's being delivered."

It took a couple of seconds for that to sink in. Then Qasim pan-icked. "No!" he screamed. "How dare you change the routing of the gift without asking me! Am I an idiot whose opinion doesn't matter?"

"No so, Mackie. Trust me when I say I risked my life trying to change the courier's routing. It is impossible."

"No! No! No! You have to cancel it and schedule a later date for delivery to the original address."

"It's too late for that, my brother. But it isn't too late for Sheikh Abdul. He should leave Delhi early tomorrow. He doesn't need to be there to receive the gift."

"No! No! I—uh! —he cannot leave at such short notice."

"Yes, he can. A seat is prearranged on an early morning flight."

'Prearranged' meant the connection was through Muscat, not Abu Dhabi ('booked') or Dubai ('reserved'). Qasim protested, "You can't expect me to—uh—to force *him* to drop everything and leave."

"Why not? There's nothing holding him back."

"But what if—uh—the Sheikh doesn't want to leave?"

"Doesn't matter if he wants to or not. He *must* leave before the gift arrives."

"So that's it? Is this how it ends?"

"No! This is how it *begins*! This gift gives the Sheikh a fresh start on writing history with me."

"It looks like I have no choice," Qasim said, reluctantly. "I will make sure the Sheikh gets on the flight. I hope you remember what he looks like and will meet him at the airport."

"Of course, I do! I'll be there when he lands in Qumraan."

Qasim hung up and sat staring at the phone. His emergency burn phone had been a comforting lifeline, inseparable from him for years. But it was meant for one-time use only, leaving him no choice but to abandon his lifeline. He didn't think this moment would ever come. But neither did he imagine abandoning his life in India so abruptly.

He switched off the phone. For the first time ever! It was the fourth and most significant 'first' of them all. A symbolic gesture, to be sure, but a perfect way to close the book on his life in India.

In reality, though, that book was as good as closed, anyway. Abbas, his right hand, was dead. Talwar-e-Rasool, the heart and soul of his existence, was on the verge of extinction, with each day bringing fresh reports of TeROR cells being destroyed across India. So, if ever there was a time for Mirza's "fresh start" this was it.

Tomorrow, he would open a new book and history would be written when Khuda ki Talwar struck a death blow at the very heart of the Hindu Shaitan.

'Delhi', after all, was an Anglicized corruption of the city's original name in Hindi, which was '*Dilli*'.

Literally, 'the heart itself'!

Chapter 4

Mohan returned to his cubicle, determined to leave right after logging out and gathering his stuff.

His determination didn't survive past the first hurdle. When he went to log out from his computer, he saw a red icon flashing on his monitor. It was his tracking software warning him it just recorded a call by one of Abbas's contacts. He couldn't help opening the call log to 'take a quick peek and log off right away'.

Even that little hedge was blown away when he saw who it was. *Mullick. And he had just called someone right here in Delhi!*

Mohan felt a shiver of superstitious excitement. At the exact time he, Mohan, discovered Mullick had a childhood friend in Delhi, Mullick had called someone in Delhi. A coincidence? Or destiny. Only one way to find out.

With his heart pounding with excitement, he played the call back…only to be thoroughly deflated. All he heard was a nonsensical back-and-forth between Mullick and some guy called 'Mackie'.

They spent the whole time arguing about where some gift should be delivered, whether a fireworks celebration was worthy of July

Fourth or Diwali, and some Sheikh who either must or couldn't leave before it arrived.

He didn't know who the other guy was, but it wouldn't be a stretch if 'Mackie' was a nickname for 'MAQ' Associates' founder, Mir Abdul Qasim. The software's GPS tracker showed Mackie was headed towards Greater Kailash in South Delhi when the phone turned off. That was where Qasim lived—along with three million Delhiites!

It was all circumstantial to be sure, but it was more than what he had on this 'Sheikh', which was zero. But something about that absurd 'Sheikh' discussion worried Mohan...something he couldn't quite pinpoint...

He replayed the call, focusing this time on nuances in the conversation. And he found three hesitations by Mackie, suggesting he was covering an inadvertent slip-up.

"*I—uh—he* cannot leave at such short notice."

"You can't expect *me to—uh—*force *him* to drop everything and leave."

And "But what if—*uh—*the Sheikh refuses to leave?"

Each sounded as if 'Mackie' was backtracking from a slip-up that betrayed 'Mackie' was the Sheikh, due to leave Delhi on that 'prearranged' flight. But which flight? To where?

That was bizarre enough. What to make of this mysterious gift that Mackie referred to as the 'Lion and Sword' before Mullick cut him off? Why did the 'Sheikh' have to leave Delhi before it arrived? Mohan's gut clenched, remembering the terror in Mackie's voice when he insisted the delivery be canceled.

Could the 'gift' be code for something terrible about to happen? Like "26/11", Mumbai's multi-pronged terrorist attack? Or the Delhi 2005 and Mumbai 1993 serial bomb blasts?

Whatever it was, this 'gift' was hanging over Delhi like the sword in that Greek story Seetha made him read years ago. What was it called? Oh, yes! The Sword of Damocles.

Damocles was reprieved before the thread was cut, but Delhi wouldn't be so lucky unless Mohan did something about it. But what? And how was he to stop it? He hadn't the faintest idea *what* this 'gift/sword' was, or *who* was bringing it, or *when* it would fall.?

If only he could talk to someone. But Jason, Alexis and Seetha were fully occupied with Ayesha's rescue, and Ravi was incommunicado until his flight landed at 2:30AM. By then, 'Sheikh Abdul' might well have absconded to parts unknown. And the Sword of Damocles would fall on Delhi.

It was up to him to figure it out. But 'Abdul' was such a common Muslim name that there might be hundreds of 'Abduls' headed to the Middle East. Forget identifying which flight 'Sheikh Abdul' was on.

All he had was his suspicion that Qasim was the Sheikh. If it wasn't Qasim, there was nothing Mohan could do. But if it was, Mohan needed to establish it beyond doubt, identify him in his 'Sheikh Abdul' disguise, and tail him until Ravi could arrange his arrest.

He opened the Counterintelligence database and downloaded Qasim's passport photo, and details of his car registration, home address, and landline phone number, noting that it didn't have caller ID.

He left the office at a dead run.

Chapter 5

It took Qasim just thirty minutes to pack.

A lifetime distilled down to half an hour—that was all his life in India meant to him. And his possessions reduced to a suitcase with some changes of clothing, and a carry-on bag with his Quran and prayer mat.

There was nothing of value he was leaving behind, except his beloved car. Ten years old and still in pristine condition, it cost almost nothing to operate after being converted to run on liquefied petroleum gas (LPG). Nowadays, compressed natural gas (CNG) was considered safer and more fashionable. But LPG was cheaper, gave much better mileage, and was available at thousands of gas dealers across India. It would hurt to abandon it at the airport, but the consolation was that it was his sacrificial offering to Khuda ki Talwar.

His landline phone rang, interrupting his thoughts, and he frowned with irritation. Who could it be? No one knew the number, other than Abbas and...Mirza! He must be calling on the landline because the emergency phone was turned off.

Qasim grabbed the phone. "Mirza? What's happened?"

A voice that wasn't Mirza responded. "Hello? Is this Mr. Atul Shekhar?"

Qasim was taken aback. "No. You have the wrong number."

"No, no, no! This is the right number. You are the wrong person. Please tell Mr. Shekhar I must talk to him."

Qasim felt his anger rising. "There's no one here named Atul Shekhar. Check the number and dial again, you idiot!"

"Don't be rude. Be polite."

"Who the hell are you to tell me to be polite, you idiot!" Qasim shouted, enraged.

"I am Mukul Mishra, and I must ask you to be polite. You are very rude to call me 'idiot' twice. Instead, be nice and give my message to Mr. Shekhar."

"I don't care who you are!" Qasim screamed, almost apoplectic with rage. "You are the biggest idiot in the world!"

Qasim slammed the phone down. It took a few seconds for his anger to recede. Then he felt a vague sense of disquiet. A wrong number call after midnight for the first time ever? Right before he was due to leave India? Right before Khuda ki Talwar's tryst with destiny? Was it really a coincidence?

And the name, Atul Shekhar—it sounded so much like 'Sheikh Abdul'? Surely, the subtle differences *couldn't* be deliberate...

Could they?

Then he remembered the caller's name. Mukul Mishra! And his brain froze.

A first-ever wrong number call on this of all nights could be a co-incidence. So could the similarity between Atul Shekhar and Sheikh

Abdul. But it stretched the bounds of credulity that Mukul Mishra should also sound so like Mirza Mullick!

Just when his brain felt like exploding, he found something to calm his nerves. It *had* to be a coincidence. It didn't make sense otherwise. Why ask for 'Atul Shekhar' if they knew he was 'Sheikh Abdul'? And why claim to be Mukul Mishra if they knew about Mirza Mullick?

Was it bizarre? Yes. But sinister? Not unless he was *both* paranoid *and* delusional! But it was unsettling. The sooner he left the better.

To go where, though? The airport was out. Passengers were barred from entry until three hours before departure. So, he had to find somewhere to rest until 4:30AM. It couldn't be a hotel, because he'd have to register with ID as either Abdul Ayub or himself, which would be fatal if the police *were* looking for him.

That left just one option. A seedy, cash-only establishment where Regional Commanders of TeROR stayed when they came to meet Abbas. It wasn't a registered hotel, so ID wasn't needed, and it was just off his route to the airport.

He donned his 'Sheikh Abdul' disguise, debating whether to take the pistol Abbas gave him "for an emergency", only to think better of it. He was a man of peace and prayer, not action, who had never fired a gun in his life, let alone killed anyone. If there was an emergency, he was more likely to shoot himself than anyone else.

He picked up his luggage and left his home of twenty years without as much as a backward glance.

Chapter 6

Mohan was outside Qasim's apartment building, keeping a close eye on Qasim's Maruti Suzuki with its distinctive LPG decal in the parking lot.

Things were turning out quite well. Voice print analysis showed an exact match between Qasim on his crazy 'Atul Shekhar-Mukul Mishra' call and the voice of 'Mackie' on the 'Lion and Sword' call.

Mackie/Qasim would be making his run for the airport sometime tonight, disguised as 'Sheikh Abdul'. Mohan intended to stick to whoever got into Qasim's car like a leech until Ravi took him into custody. Then his job would be done. He would leave it to Ravi to figure out and intercept the mysterious 'gift' headed to Delhi.

He saw a man carrying a suitcase and shoulder bag emerge from the building. It was too dark to make him out but he got into Qasim's car and drove away.

Mohan waited ten seconds before following. Traffic was light, and the distinctive LPG decal was like a tracking beacon, allowing him to vary his tailing distance so he wouldn't be noticed.

A half-hour later, Qasim turned off the airport road into a seedy neighborhood, and Mohan breathed a sigh of relief. Qasim wasn't headed for the airport. He was going to hole up for the night, allowing Ravi to grab him without the drama of an airport arrest.

Maintaining his distance, Mohan followed Qasim into a neighborhood bazaar no different from so many others in the city. The shops were shuttered and dark, but a roadside food stall, called a *dhaaba,* was still doing brisk business. Dhaabas served some of the tastiest food in India, prepared in full view of the customer. Dining facilities were rudimentary, however, with rickety metal tables and folding chairs crammed into a small area.

Qasim's brake lights came on and Mohan saw him poke his head out to look across the road. Mohan responded by leaning brazenly on his horn, following Indian driving norms, knowing Qasim might get suspicious if he didn't. Sure enough, Qasim waved him around without looking, then turned through a gap in the median into an alley on the other side.

To avoid drawing Qasim's attention, Mohan drove to the next median break and made a U-turn before heading back. He parked a hundred yards beyond the alley near the dhaaba and walked back to peer into the alley. It was deserted, so he sidled down the wall to where the alley opened into a square cul de sac, thirty yards across. In the center, a single neon tube mounted on a metal pole cast a pool of dim light that did not penetrate the corners. In the near corner to his right, he made out the outline of Qasim's car.

A dilapidated 'U'-shaped building, three stories high surrounded the cul de sac on three sides. The limbs of the 'U' on either side stopped just short of the buildings lining the alley, leaving a narrow walkway leading off the square on either side. A battered hand-painted sign hung drunkenly askew above the building entrance across from him, with faded lettering proclaiming, 'Royal Hotel Best for Cheap Stay of Delhi'. Next to it was another that announced with similar agrammatical flair, 'Hotèl Guest Free Alone for Parking'.

Satisfied that Qasim was bedded down for the night, Mohan walked back to the dhaaba to get dinner. From there he could watch the mouth of the alley until Ravi mobilized the anti-terror squad to apprehend Qasim while he slept.

He checked the ETA of Ravi's flight and saw that it had landed fifteen minutes ago.

He sat down in his car and dialed Ravi's mobile phone.

Chapter 7

Qasim walked down the corridor of the Royal Hotel feeling quite content. So content, in fact, that he didn't even wrinkle his nose at the stink emanating from the communal bathroom.

The Royal Hotel's standards of hygiene and sanitation might be abysmal, but it was unmatched in the only standard that mattered to Qasim: Anonymity. That one attribute alone relegated the stink to an irrelevant inconvenience.

The overpowering odor of cigarette smoke in his room was another. It should have been unacceptable for a lifelong nonsmoker, but it was a welcome alternative to the obnoxious smell of urine in the hallway.

He set down his bags, feeling a rumble in his stomach. It reminded him he hadn't eaten dinner. One last dhaaba dinner would be a great way to close the book on his life in India.

He left his room, securing it with a heavy padlock he brought with him, knowing he couldn't trust the one the 'hotel' provided. As he crossed the cul de sac, he checked on his car, parked in the far corner, out of sight of any opportunistic thief passing by on the main street.

Satisfied it was safe, he headed to the dhaaba he had seen in the bazaar.

Chapter 8

Mohan told Ravi everything he found in the passport application and heard in the 'Mackie call', and how he tracked Qasim to the Royal Hotel.

Ravi heard him out, then said decisively, "Your instincts are incredible, Mohan. Whatever this gift is could well represent an imminent terrorist threat, and we must act quickly. I'm mobilizing the Black Cat Commando Squadron to round up the hotel guests and sort out which one is Qasim. They'll be in a black windowless van, with shoot-to-kill orders, so don't go anywhere near the hotel. Keep watch from the bazaar to make sure Qasim doesn't leave before they arrive, then get the hell out of there."

"Don't worry, Ravi. I'll run as fast as I can when they show up."

He got out of his car and went to the dhaaba to order dinner, paying in advance, as was customary. While he was waiting for it to be prepared, he glanced back at the alley, realizing he hadn't been watching it for almost twenty minutes. Not that it mattered. Qasim was bedded down for the night.

Mohan picked up his order when it was ready and maneuvered his way through the congested seating area to an unoccupied table. As he squeezed past the last seated patron in his path, a heavily bearded man stood up, bumping into Mohan and almost causing him to spill his food.

The man gave a surly grunt and walked off without even making eye contact let alone a pro forma apology.

Mohan shrugged and sat down to eat, keeping his eye on the alley. The man who bumped him was headed in that direction but Mohan ignored him. The scruffy, kudtha pajama-clad individual with a mullah-style beard bore no resemblance to the clean-shaven, nattily dressed executive in Qasim's photograph.

A minute later, he leapt up with a shock, his meal forgotten. *The man had just turned into the alley!*

Mohan started walking after him as fast as he could. He was halfway there when a black, windowless van crawled past and turned into the alley.

Abandoning all caution, Mohan began sprinting after the van.

Chapter 9

Qasim strolled back to the hotel feeling truly happy. Delicious food, safe sanctuary, and impending freedom. Could there be a better list of last-things-to-do before leaving Delhi?

As he entered the cul-de-sac, an uncontrollable desire to urinate wiped away the glow. Two cups of chai and three glasses of water to counter the spicy mutton curry would do that!

The demand was so urgent that he couldn't hold it until he got to the hotel. The dark walkway behind his parked car was both invitingly convenient and infinitely preferable to the stinking communal bathroom.

After some agonized coaxing, he got the hesitant stream going with several stop-and-starts. He recalled reading that precipitate urgency, hesitancy, and intermittent voiding indicated a prostate problem. He had been delaying having it seen, but it was time to fix that once he got to Abu Dhabi.

He re-tied his pajama drawstring and turned to step out of the walkway. At that moment, he saw a windowless black van roll silently into the cul de sac and coast to a stop. The doors burst open and a dozen heavily armed figures dressed in black leapt out and swarmed into the hotel.

Qasim stood frozen by fear for a few seconds. Then a primal flight response took over. Crouching down to stay out of sight, he scrambled into his car, cursing himself for parking head in, facing the wall. He started the engine and rammed the gearstick into reverse, stomping on the gas pedal as he released the clutch and twisting the steering wheel around without looking over his shoulder.

The car shot backwards like a jackrabbit escaping its burrow...and slammed into the light pole in the middle of the square.

The hollow metal pole was crushed flat at the point of impact, bending backwards into a 'V'. With the crushed metal unable to support its weight, the heavier upper segment started listing forward.

The car's rear hatch door flew open as the car's flimsy chassis wrapped itself around the pole, breaking the rear axle. The floor plates buckled, twisting the LPG tank bolted to the floorplates on its side. The metal LPG feeder line to the engine wasn't designed to withstand twisting shear stress. A hairline fracture appeared in the line, and a jet of suddenly depressurized gas blew out of the open hatch, forming a deadly cocoon around the car.

Oblivious to the smell of gas, a panicked Qasim rammed the gearshift into first and stomped again on the accelerator. The crippled car lurched forward and stalled, unable to overcome the inertial resistance of a buckled chassis and broken axle. Devoid of the car's support, the crushed metal pole listed further forward, stretching the wire supplying 220 volts of electricity to the Royal Hotel like a bowstring.

It held up the pole momentarily. Then the wire snapped, and the hotel lights went out.

The line recoiled like a whiplash and touched the metal pole, sending a shower of sparks into the expanding cocoon of vaporized LPG, which ignited. It exploded into a fireball that blew out the car's windows, sending fragments of red-hot metal and molten glass in every direction.

Mir Abdul Qasim, self-professed 'man of peace and prayer' and messianic architect of a fifteen-year reign of terror that claimed more than two thousand lives, perished in an inferno that vaporized his lungs from the inside as it incinerated his body from the outside.

His last lucid thought before the searing agony of live cremation swamped his brain was of his brainchild, Khuda ki Talwar. He tried to scream out its name, like a talisman to ward off evil, but the flesh of his lips and tongue melted before they could form the words.

Chapter 10

S ecurity officials boarded the Lone Wolf jet when it landed in Delhi.

They ordered everyone, pilots and flight attendants included, to stay on board and surrender their passports and cell phones. Then the plane, luggage, and their persons were searched systematically by hand, bomb-sniffing dogs and radiation scanners.

The reason for the search was a mystery. Jonathan's questions were met with stone-faced silence. Even some old-fashioned Indian 'name-dropping', invoking Ravi Iyer and the Prime Minister, had no impact.

Ayesha was initially terrified, fearing she would be sent back to Qumraan, but it quickly became clear the officers had no more interest in her than in Alexis, Jason, or Seetha.

They were finally allowed to disembark to the VIP Arrivals lounge at noon. That was when they learned that Delhi was under imminent threat of a major terrorist attack.

They cleared Customs and Immigration and exited the terminal to find Mohan outside, looking drawn and tired, with dark shadows under his eyes.

Seetha took one look at him and ripped into him. "You broke your promise to me not to work late! You haven't slept a wink."

"Seetha," Mohan spluttered, "You won't believe—"

Seetha cut him off. "You're right, Mohan. I won't ever believe your promises. If I can't trust you to keep them, don't expect me to believe your excuses."

As they drove off, Jonathan heard Mohan mutter to Jason in the front passenger seat next to him, "How can she be so mean? She won't even listen."

Jason whispered something in Mohan's ear that made him laugh. Jonathan turned to see if it made Seetha even angrier. To his surprise, Seetha and Alexis had their heads together, smiling like they were sharing an amusing secret. Jonathan was perplexed but knew better than to ask what was going on. This brother-sister thing was beyond his comprehension.

As they exited the airport, he felt his eyes throb in the glare of the mid-day sun and reached for his sunglasses. Instead, his searching hand found his cell phone…and he remembered his promise to Sayf al-Qumraan to call him the moment they landed.

He took out the phone, thinking ruefully, *He's going to be pissed that I'm two hours late in keeping my promise to call before Indian Customs examined the Asad. I guess I can say that Indian Customs had no problem with the Asad. It's the truth, just not the whole truth. He doesn't know it's still in Qumraan.*

He dialed the Crown Prince's private line.

Chapter 11

It was 11AM and Mullick was sick with worry.

It had been three hours since Mackie's plane landed in Muscat without word from him. His cell phone was dead.

To make matters worse, all hell was breaking loose in the palace.

The Palace Manager was frantic because Hakim Elahi had disappeared. Palace Security were in an uproar because three guards were missing, including Sergeant Asif, last seen dropping Alexis Wolff at her bungalow around 11PM. And the Clinic Supervisor was in a panic, asking Sayf's permission to break down the door, because the clinic door locks weren't responding to the master code, and Begum, the orphan girl's supervisor, wasn't answering her phone.

Mullick knew better than to ask Sayf now. He was almost apoplectic with rage, threatening to detonate Khuda ki Talwar at any moment, because Wolff's call was two hours late.

Mirza had managed to restrain him so far, arguing that taking Wolff's plane down above the Arabian Sea would waste Khuda ki Talwar's awesome terror potential. He couldn't hold him back much longer, though.

Mirza thought, *Why, in the name of Allah, won't the phone ring?*

It rang at that exact moment, and he felt an electric tingle go through him. When he saw 'Jonathan Wolff' on the caller ID display, the tingle became a superstitious shudder. It was an omen. Allah heard his plea!

He entered the programmed sequence of Cyrillic characters into Suleimanbayev's Kazakh satellite phone and waited with his thumb poised over the 'Send' key, his heart tripping like a jackhammer.

Sayf hit the speaker button and screamed, "Blasphemous liar! How dare you forget to call! Is this how you treat royalty, you filthy infidel?"

Jonathan Wolff's reply was like a slap in the face. "Royalty is treated as royalty behaves. Anyone who believes he is entitled to deliver crude insults isn't entitled to the courtesy given to true royalty."

Mullick saw Sayf's face turn purple with rage and knew the moment was here. He pressed 'Send'. There was one ring, a click, then a continuous tone. Khuda ki Talwar was activated, awaiting the four-digit detonation code. He entered the code, scarcely able to breathe, and nodded to Sayf, his thumb poised over the '#' button.

"American Dog!" Sayf shrieked. "You compared *my gift*, the Lion of Qumraan, to a dog's vomit. You called *me*, the Sword of Qumraan, a dog who eats his own vomit! Now you dare to question *my royalty*? For your triple blasphemy, you will burn in the fires of Hell for all eternity, infidel dog. See the Lion strike you down with the Sword of the One True God, Allah." He turned towards Mirza and shouted, "Allah-u-Akbar. Mirza?"

"God is great!" Mirza Mullick shouted back and pressed the '#' key.

Chapter 12

The detonation code was relayed by the geo-stationary Lone Wolf satellite to the transmission tower at the Lone Wolf refinery, down the fiber-optic cable in the aquifer to the remote antenna unit in the cavern.

The Sword of God's controller in the belly of the Asad al Qumraan received the code and its trigger transformer sent a high-voltage surge to the krytron trigger. The explosive charges arranged radially inside the beryllium shell of the plutonium 239 sphere fired in one synchronous explosion.

The hollow cavity in the sphere collapsed, transforming the plutonium into a dense ball that achieved instantaneous super-criticality. It took less than a thousandth of a second after the nuclear chain reaction was initiated for the implosion device to detonate.

The destructive energy released was equivalent to twenty kilotons of TNT, just like Fat Man, the atomic bomb dropped on Nagasaki. But the impact was dramatically different.

Fat Man detonated five hundred meters above Nagasaki, releasing its physical and thermal energy into the atmosphere, where it spread radially.

The Sword of God was confined in a cavern four hundred meters below the surface when it detonated. Its destructive impact was determined by the unique configuration of the cavern and the geochemistry of the surrounding rock.

A pressure wave reaching several million atmospheres smashed into the walls of the cavern, pulverizing the rock. The walls of the bedding plane—the twin clefts leading off the cavern—collapsed like valves, sealing off the cavern from the aquifer and elevator shaft and containing the radioactive fallout. It was the only mitigating effect.

Everything else amplified the destructive impact exponentially.

With the energy retained inside the cavern, pressure waves bounced back-and-forth from the walls, making the surrounding rock reverberate as if struck by a cosmic sledgehammer. With each successive reverberation, seismic waves expanded through the rock surrounding the cavern. The friable sedimentary rock in the cavern floor crumbled and compacted, displacing the surrounding rock outwards like a giant fist punched into a mountain of dough.

The simultaneous release of thermal energy raised the temperature inside the cavern to more than a million degrees Fahrenheit. It liquefied the superheated igneous rock above the roof, turning the deep strata a hundred meters above the cavern into molten lava. The lava acted like a thermal conductor, raising the surface temperature to a thousand degrees. Not sufficient to melt the rock near the surface, but forcing it to expand and fracture.

The combination of instantaneous thermal expansion, escalating seismic reverberation, and upward displacement caused the fracturing substratum to heave up in a dome-like mound, called a reverse crater (or 'retarc'), two miles in diameter. As the ground rose, the subsidence zone created by the compaction of rock under the cavern caused the whole mound to sink, creating a twenty-meter-high lip around the retarc.

The molten lava sank into the cavern, forming a saucer-like dimple in the center of the dome of the retarc. Fortunately, the superficial rock stratum held together, preventing the formation of a 'chimney' from the cavern to the surface, so the radioactive fallout was contained.

Massive amounts of methane gas released from the superheated volcanic substratum escaped through the fracturing rock. It ignited to form a fireball that obliterated everything in a three-mile radius around the retarc.

A hundred thousand gallons of water in the water tank were instantly vaporized. Massive clouds of super-heated steam blasted upwards and condensed in the sub-stratosphere, sending sheets of searing hot water smashing down into the subsidence zone, only to be instantly vaporized again. The repeating cycle finally ended when the ground temperature fell below two hundred degrees Fahrenheit.

Gradually, the dust, smoke and steam dissipated, revealing a hellscape with an artificial lake that sizzled and bubbled around the still-flaming mound.

Everything and everyone in the fireball's three-mile radius had been incinerated, leaving a desolate black wasteland. All that remained of the palace was a mound of smoking rubble.

Chapter 13

The phone went dead right after Sayf al-Qumraan shouted, "Allah-u-Akbar", giving Jonathan no chance to respond to the man's virulent diatribe.

The pit bull in him awakened. He tried redialing several times, but the call wouldn't go through. The wi-fi signal registered five bars, so the break in transmission made no sense. Unless the man disconnected his phone, realizing he crossed the line.

Jonathan looked around, saying to nobody in particular, "What the hell was that about?"

"It was Sayf al-Qumraan feeling the bite of Ole Jaws," Alexis said from the backseat.

Jonathan shook his head. "No, Alexis. It wasn't that. Sayf was raving like a maniac, gibbering about blasphemy, and burning in the fires of Hell for insulting him and demeaning his gift. Then, he said something about the Lion of Qumraan striking me down with the Sword of Allah—"

He was cut off in mid-sentence by a violent jolt as Mohan slammed the brakes and pulled the van over, screaming, "Oh, God! No, no, no! The gift he gave you. Is it a lion?"

"Yes, it is. Asad al-Qumraan means Lion of Qumraan—"

"Oh, my God!" Mohan exclaimed. "Oh God. No! And the sword. Did he say Sword of Allah or Sword of God?"

Jonathan corrected himself, "The Sword of the One True God, Allah."

"My God!" Mohan shrieked. "That's what they meant by the Lion and Sword. Did you bring it with you?"

"Relax, Mohan," Jason replied. "We didn't bring it with us. I hid it in the cavern beneath the palace, and used the crate to get Ayesha out. But why the panic?"

"Thank God!" Mohan said, adding sheepishly, "Oh God! I don't know how many times I just swore in God's name."

Jason laughed. "Six times, Mohan. But nobody's counting."

"Maybe God will excuse me because we're talking about Khuda ki Talwar. The Sword of God!"

There was pin-drop silence in the van. Everyone looked shocked.

Mohan continued. "I overheard Mirza Mullick on a call with a man named Mir Abdul Qasim—"

Jason cut in. "Saluja's accountant! Is he part of TeROR, too?"

"Not just a part, Jason. He's a card-carrying member of Alexis's Triangle of Terror. As Mullick's childhood friend, IASC's accountant, insider in Malini's kidnapping, and enabler of Ganga Prasad's adoption and abduction."

"It's my turn to say, Oh my God!" Jason replied.

"Oh God, indeed, Mohan" Jonathan added. "But why did you think of Khuda ki Talwar when I mentioned the Lion of Qumraan?"

"Mullick called Qasim, urging him to leave Delhi before a gift was delivered this morning. He didn't say what it was. But Qasim let slip something about 'Sher aur Talwar'—the Lion and the Sword—before Mullick cut him off. I put it together when you repeated what Sayf al-Qumraan said. The Lion of Qumraan is the 'Sher', and the 'Talwar' is the Sword of God. I—uh!—Ravi thinks it's a bomb or terrorist attack. That's why Delhi is under red alert!"

The silence that followed spoke volumes.

Alexis broke it, asking very softly, "Where is Qasim now?"

Mohan replied, just as softly, "Burning in Hell, I hope."

Chapter 14

S eetha had never seen anything like the Taj Mahal's Grand Presidential Suite. It occupied the entire penthouse floor of the hotel, complete with a board room, living room, dining room and three bedrooms, for Jonathan, Jason, and Alexis.

She and Mohan were in a two-bedroom Executive suite a floor below, with Ayesha asking to stay with Seetha rather than by herself. That small expression of insecurity was more than justified, given what she had been through. Ayesha's serenity in every other respect had been remarkable from the moment she stepped out of that crate.

No histrionics. Not a single tear shed in relief. Just a face glowing with happiness. Like it was now, while they waited in the Presidential Suite's board room for a full account of recent events.

Mohan started by describing how he "accidentally" stumbled on Mir Abdul Qasim's role as a key player in Alexis's Triangle of Terror, trailed Qasim through "pure dumb luck," and witnessed Qasim's incineration because he was "too stupid" to obey Ravi's warning.

Seetha wanted to scream at him, but it was pointless. Mohan wasn't pretending. He truly believed he was stupid and a coward.

Ravi, fortunately, was having none of it. He responded forcefully, saying, "Wrong! There was no accident, dumb luck, or stupidity involved. Delhi averted catastrophic disaster only because of Mohan's exceptional instincts, detective work, initiative, and courage."

Seetha saw Mohan squirming with discomfort, but Ravi didn't let up. "Mohan is the sole reason a truly evil man burns in Hell, instead of escaping to threaten the world. Qasim seems to have flown completely under the radar. His name never came up as a person who was radicalized after losing his family in the Godhra riots of 2002. He changed overnight from a hard-drinking, womanizing party animal to a devout and observant Muslim. And, in hindsight, a jihadist."

He paused, then continued, "Not just any jihadist, either. I believe he was TeROR's founder, not Abbas, because its reign of terror started well before Abbas left the Army. If Qasim had escaped, he would've surely restarted his terror campaign. A truly evil man can never terrorize the world, thanks to Mohan's courage and vigilance."

Mohan looked abashed. "It wasn't like that at all."

Seetha couldn't take it anymore. She yelled, "Shut up for God's sake, Mohan! Take a compliment for once in your life!"

Mohan shrank back in his chair, muttering "She's mad because I broke my promise."

Everyone laughed, even Seetha. "I'm not mad, Mohan. I'm proud, and I want you to be proud, too. So, thank you for breaking your promise. If you hadn't, who knows what might've happened?"

It was a feel-good moment. For just a moment. The mood took a hundred-and-eighty-degree turn when Alexis and Jason began to describe what happened in Qumraan. They gave plenty of detail, but when it came to the fight and its aftermath, Alexis compressed it into two sentences. "Jason shot the two guards, and I took down the others. Then I stitched Ayesha's wound, and Jason did the rest."

Jason's description of "the rest" was just as sparing. "I left the Lion of Qumraan in the cavern, locked myself and Ayesha in the crate, and broke out once the plane was airborne."

Jonathan completed the narrative by recounting what happened at the royal dinner. He then recited his mystifying phone conversation with Sayf al-Qumraan verbatim, until the phone inexplicably went dead a couple of minutes after noon.

Ravi asked sharply, "So, the call cut off right after he said 'Allah-u-Akbar, Mirza'. Right?"

"Yes," Jonathan replied.

"That tells us Mullick was there, which should make you happy, Alexis."

"Why?" Alexis asked, frowning.

"I believe it was a command to Mullick to detonate the Sword of God, not knowing the Asad al Qumraan was in the cavern under the palace," Ravi said. "That's why the call cut off."

Jason looked puzzled. "An explosion under four hundred meters of solid rock couldn't interrupt surface communications. Unless…" He broke off with a look of unspeakable horror.

"Yes, Jason. Seismic sensors across the world picked up the characteristic signature pattern of a nuclear detonation deep below the Qumraani palace grounds at 12:03PM, 10:33AM Gulf time, when the call ended. Satellite images showed an enormous fireball that consumed everything in a three-mile radius, attributable to the release of methane from the volcanic substratum. After the smoke cleared and the dust settled, the images showed a classic 'retarc', or reverse crater, from an underground nuclear detonation.

"The International Atomic Energy Agency has dispatched a team to investigate how much radioactivity was released in that fireball. If a chimney formed from the cavern to the surface anyone in a ten- or fifteen-mile radius is doomed."

Seetha sat benumbed, her hand on her mouth, as Ravi added very quietly, "If Jason hadn't left the Asad al-Qumraan in the cavern, Delhi would be a nuclear wasteland today. And millions would be dead."

"Th…The S-s-sword of Dam-m-mocles," Mohan stammered. "I-I imagined it hanging over Delhi last night. B-b-but I never imagined a nuclear weapon! Oh my God!"

"A *nuclear* Sword of Damocles, Mohan, to use President Kennedy's words during the Cuban Missile Crisis," Jason said.

"Make no mistake," Alexis said. "Everyone in Delhi, including everyone in this room, owes their lives to Ayesha's courage."

"But I did nothing, Alexis. I just sat terrified, like a dead weight, waiting for you and Jason to rescue me."

"No, Ayesha, you were anything *but* a dead weight. We are alive today because of your unflinching courage. Despite being warned how dangerous it was, you confronted your supervisor. That's how you injured your ankle. If you hadn't, Jason would've taken you out via the aquifer, and we would've brought the Lion of Qumraan to Delhi, with the Sword of God…"

Her voice tailed off, leaving everyone dumbstruck.

Jonathan broke the silence. "Ayesha, you have given me the most precious gift of all. My family. That's a debt I can never repay. If I could bring back your family, I would. Sadly, I cannot. But I can offer you a small consolation. Will you honor me by becoming part of my family, like Seetha and Mohan?"

Seetha saw Ayesha's hand fly to her mouth, and the tears she kept hidden for years spilled from her eyes. She got up and walked over to Jonathan, her face glowing with wonder and joy. Laying her hand on his forearm, she said hesitantly, "Mr. Wolff, I am—"

"If you're family, you have to stop being so formal, my dear."

Ayesha smiled. "So, what should I call you?"

"By my name. Jonathan. That's what Mohan and Seetha call me. And Jason and Alexis, too. So, if you want me to treat you like family, you'll have to learn to treat me like my family does." He paused, then added, "Without too much respect."

Everyone laughed.

Jonathan added, "As the senior member of the family, I welcome you into our hearts."

"I am honored…Jonathan."

"Thank you, Ayesha. But I have a favor to ask in return."

"Of course. Anything. Please ask."

"Ayesha, in my life I have achieved a lot, and experienced even more. And now I have so much more that fulfills my life. But there is one joy I have never experienced. Will you give that to me?"

"If I can, I will. What is it?"

Seetha saw Jonathan glance at her, and knew what he was about to say. During that fraught time in Qumraan, while Alexis was attending on Ayesha, he had stated his desire to pay for Ayesha's medical education. She warned him Ayesha would reject his charity, no matter how well-intentioned. By ignoring her warning, he was inviting that rejection. And he would be hurt. Badly.

Jonathan gave her a reassuring smile before turning to Ayesha and saying cryptically, "I want to dream."

Ayesha looked mystified. Like everyone else.

Jonathan pointed to Jason and Alexis. "These two are a lost cause. They came into my life too late for me to know they had any dreams. And those two—" he pointed to her and Mohan, "were living a nightmare when I met them. Which I shared, I might add, so forget about dreaming with them, either. My one and only chance to dream with my family now rests with you, Ayesha. Will you give me that chance, please?"

Ayesha looked even more befuddled. "I don't understand…What chance?"

"The chance to share in your dreams and your future."

"My future?" Ayesha asked.

"Yes. Seetha tells me your dream is to be a doctor. And I have never known what it means to dream. So, please let me help you become a doctor, so an old man can learn to dream."

Ayesha was standing next to Jonathan, with her hand on his forearm, when the light came on in her eyes, and she gasped. Then, she whispered, "How can I ever thank you?", and embraced Jonathan with such love that Seetha felt like crying. Like everyone else, apparently, seeing their faces.

Jonathan returned the embrace, saying gently, "You don't have to thank me, Ayesha. You have given me something I never dreamed of. That's all the reward I want."

Alexis said teasingly, "Want it or not, Jonathan, you've got much more than that. Remember the temple of Mammon? Didn't your sacred cow bring home a bundle there?"

Jonathan squirmed. "The temple was wiped out in Qumraan, and the sacred cow has left, taking the bundle with it."

"No, it hasn't. You cashed in the bundle before the temple was wiped out."

"You misunderstand me, Alexis. I wanted to keep it a surprise until we got back to New York, but now is as good a time as any, I suppose, to tell you where the cow has gone."

He took a deep breath. "After our talk in New York, I decided to donate all my personal profit from Qumraan to charity. The charity part stands, but instead of donating it, I intend to set up a charitable foundation to better the lot of orphans in India. Its charter will be to fund orphanages that adhere to standards that the foundation will set and monitor. And who has a better understanding of the lot of orphans than three orphans? Ayesha, Mohan and Seetha will set those standards."

Alexis looked absolutely mortified. "Oh my god, Jonathan! I feel like a heel for saying what I did."

"As you should, Red!" Jason exclaimed. "Not often do I get to see you squirm like this. You owe Jonathan an apology."

Jonathan waved Jason off dismissively. "I don't need an apology, my dear. But don't think you're getting off scot free, either. There's a price I intend to extract. I haven't yet come up with a name for the foundation, but whatever it is, it will be named for the five of you, Jason, Alexis, Mohan, Seetha, and Ayesha. You have no choice in the matter. It's my decision."

"It better not have my name," Alexis said.

"Or mine," Jason added.

Sensing that the feel-good moment was about to degenerate into an irresistible-force-meets-immovable-object stalemate, Seetha came up with an inspired compromise. "Five first names: Seetha-Alexis-Mohan-Ayesha-Jason. And Jonathan, you're part of the family, so you're not off the hook, either. Take the six first initials and you get SAMAJJ, which means 'Understanding' in Hindi. Isn't that what you said, Jonathan? That it's about understanding? 'Understanding the lot of orphans in India' makes for a great mission statement, too."

Alexis gasped, "That's sheer genius, Seetha."

Seetha saw Jason, Mohan, and Ayesha nodding with delight, and knew the bullet had been dodged.

Jonathan put an exclamation point on it, saying, "A tip of the hat to Seetha, the only one with the 'samajj' to head off a showdown between three alpha Wolffs."

Chapter 15

A lexis was humming under her breath when she entered the dining room, where she found Jonathan, Ravi, and Jason eating breakfast. Mohan, Seetha, and Ayesha walked in as she bent down to kiss Jonathan.

While they were filling their plates from the buffet, Ravi said, "Alexis, you know that transplant surgeon you went to see in London? Kureishi? He's dead. His man servant sliced his belly open with a sword, just as Kureishi shot him. Bizarre, isn't it?"

She had a momentary flash of unease, but Ravi's question was clearly rhetorical. He continued without waiting for her to answer. "There's something even more bizarre. It appears that he was the vigilante responsible for those murderous reprisals on skinheads. The tabloids have dubbed him 'The Dagger of Allah', because a dagger was found near his body, with those words inscribed in Arabic. Did you suspect he had such a dark secret when you met?"

"I had no idea when I met him," she answered truthfully.

Jonathan interjected, "What came of your meeting? Did he know the surgeon who harvested Ganga Prasad's organs?"

"He didn't know who it was when I showed him the scans." She stuck to the truth, just not the whole truth.

"So, what about the retribution you were hell-bent on getting for Ganga Prasad?"

"I am content with how things worked out. The nuclear explosion wiped out the last vestiges of that evil. Including the hospital where Kureishi—"

Ravi interrupted. "Not the hospital, Alexis. Satellite images show the fireball wiped out the palace and airport. It spared the town, fifteen miles to the north."

"The others! They're alive!" Ayesha cried out.

Alexis shook her head in anguish. "Nor for long, Ayesha. They won't survive the radioactive fallout."

"Who are these 'others'?" Ravi asked.

"Seven orphans like Ayesha and Ganga Prasad, who were kept like animals for slaughter. They were quarantined at the hospital on suspicion of a highly contagious form of viral diarrhea. They may have escaped the blast, but they'll be dead from the fallout in two weeks."

She turned to Jonathan. "Even if they're going to die, I want them to know they were freed from hell. Can we arrange for them to be go somewhere to get the best end-of-life care?"

Jonathan said without hesitating. "Once the IAEA clears the area, we'll evacuate them to the refinery and fly them anywhere you want in the world."

Alexis felt at peace. Even if the orphans were fated to die, Jonathan would make sure they got the best care in the world..

Not the outcome she wanted, but it would do.

EPILOGUE

Three hours into their flight back to the U.S., Alexis was having a quiet drink with Jason and Jonathan in the lounge.

She thought back on everything that happened after they returned from Qumraan, starting with the exhilarating news that the IAEA found no radioactive contamination. Ravi arranged for the seven orphans, between seven and fifteen years old, to be cleared to return to India, and Jonathan had them brought to the refinery and flown to Delhi in great secrecy. From there, they were whisked off to Saluja's home in Haryana, where they would stay for the foreseeable future.

In that last part was a small miracle. Jonathan had the idea to call Saluja in California to request temporary use of his considerable resources in India until the foundation was set up.

Saluja's response was beyond belief. He donated all four of his houses to SAMAJJ for use as residences for orphans: in Bangalore to the south, Pune in the west, and Darjeeling in the east, plus his estate home in Haryana.

Permanently!

He asked for only three things in return. First, that Jonathan make him a partner in SAMAJJ, in exchange for investing half-a-billion dollars from the upcoming sale of Saltech to his Indian partners. Second, that SAMAJJ be renamed 'SAMAJJ Charitable Mission', or SAMAJJ-CM, in a tacit tribute to Chetan and Malini. Third, that he be appointed "Managing Director" of SAMAJJ-CM, at a nominal salary of one rupee a month, because he needed something to do after selling Saltech. And—the best news of all—because the change of scenery had worked wonders for Malini. She had taken her first steps on the road to recovery from her nightmare and had started rebelling against Saluja's protective cocoon.

Jonathan agreed instantly. Saluja's experience navigating the hazards, pitfalls and traps of Indian bureaucracy was orders of magnitude higher than all five members of SAMAJJ combined. It couldn't have turned out better!

Once the first residents of the flagship enterprise of SAMAJJ-CM settled in their new home, Alexis was finally content to leave them in Seetha and Ayesha's charge.

Parting from them was painful. They had come to call her 'Alexis Ma'—Mother Alexis—over her vigorous protests. She tried getting them to call her like they did 'Seetha Behen' and 'Ayesha Behen'—meaning sister—but they wouldn't budge, much to Jason's delight. She got the last laugh, however. When the seven realized Jason was her brother, he became 'Jason Uncle'!

She left Delhi as happy and contented as she had ever been. Not only was JAMAS-CM tangible proof of her 'redemption', her sense of 'family' had expanded beyond Jason and Jonathan.

Jonathan seemed to read her mind, "I'm really happy for you, my dear. Thanks to Ayesha and the other orphans, you have the redemption you sought. In full measure, too, with the death of Kureishi."

Startled, she rounded on Jason, "You promised not to tell!"

Jason held up his hands in protest, "He wouldn't stop badgering me until I told him."

Jonathan said, mildly, "He only confirmed what I suspected. First, you return from London with that dark cloud over you and snap at Jason when he mentions redemption. Then Ravi tells me Kureishi died with his belly sliced open from a single strike by a tachi. Who but a trained ninja could do that?"

Alexis drew a deep breath, "So, it seems Ravi also knows I killed Kureishi. Who else? Seetha and Mohan, too?"

Jason answered, "I'm afraid so. Seetha wondered why you didn't cut his head off." Keeping a straight face, he added, "Mohan picked a more delicate part of Kureishi's anatomy."

"I hope at least Ayesha wasn't tainted by the rest of you ghouls?"

"Sorry, Red, she was with Seetha and Mohan, and her reaction was the most ghoulish of all. She wanted to know why you didn't also cut off the hands that operated on Ganga Prasad."

"Dear God! Did everyone rejoice in my killing Kureishi?"

Jonathan was quick to answer, "We rejoice in your redemption, my dear, not the killing."

"So, is that your new name for me? The Sword of Redemption?"

"If you want. Or even if you don't. I claim the right of a father to give a daughter any nickname he chooses."

He said it airily, without thinking. Then he gasped, realizing the import of what he just said, and she saw his face freeze in shock.

Then it was as if time stood still, and no one existed but her and Jonathan.

She wanted to say something. But she couldn't. Her throat and tongue seemed paralyzed. Not her heart though. It felt like it would burst. But her eyes must have told him what was in her heart, because he started to say, "Alexis, my dear, I didn't…", only to stop and swallow the catch in his suddenly shaky voice.

She found her voice, at last, after what seemed like an eternity, and it was as if she wanted to wrap the words around his heart, "A father has that right. So, call me what you want. No matter what you call me, I'll always be your daughter."

It was her heart speaking to his, and it seemed so natural and effortless that it took a few seconds to dawn on her that a barrier had just been shattered. For the first time ever, she had said the two words Jonathan had been longing to hear. "Your daughter".

Jonathan, of course, was wonderstruck.

He didn't have to say anything. His eyes, overflowing with joy, were saying everything she wanted to hear. Never had she known him to cry. Nor, she suspected, had anyone else. It was enough. Much more than enough.

Even Jason, the inveterate jokester, had been struck dumb. He knew what a seminal moment it was for her to acknowledge Jonathan as her father.

Not that he needed to say anything, either. The bond said it all. He was rejoicing.

She had put their awful past behind her.

Forever.

www.ingramcontent.com/pod-product-compliance
Lightning Source LLC
Chambersburg PA
CBHW070733180626
46818CB00007B/2821